SALLY JOHN

CROSSWAY BOOKS • WHEATON, ILLINOIS
A DIVISION OF GOOD NEWS PUBLISHERS

Also by Sally John
In the Shadow of Love
Surrender of the Heart

To Dream Again

Copyright © 2000 by Sally John

Published by Crossway Books
        a division of Good News Publishers
        1300 Crescent Street
        Wheaton, Illinois 60187

Cover design: Liita Forsyth

Cover illustration: Chris Cocozza

First printing, 2000

Printed in the United States of America

Library of Congress Cataloging-in-Publication Data
John, Sally D. 1951-
   To dream again / Sally John.
     p.   cm.
   ISBN 1-58134-186-5 (alk. paper)
    1. Drug traffic—Investigation—Fiction. 2. San Diego (Calif.)—
I. Title.
PS3560.O323 T6   2000
813'.54—dc21   00-008838
                                CIP

15	14	13	12	11	10	09	08	07	06	05	04	03	02	01	00
15	14	13	12	11	10	9	8	7	6	5	4	3	2	1	

To my children,
Elizabeth and Christopher

This one is for you, kiddos,
with gratitude for the memories of girls' basketball and
a green truck, and for filling my world with more delight
than I ever could have imagined

He heals the brokenhearted and binds up their wounds.

PSALM 147:3, NEW INTERNATIONAL VERSION

Prologue

TERROR FLOODED HER DREAM, then spilled out into the night.

Cat St. Clair bolted awake and jerked upright, flinging aside the tangled covers.

She quickly flipped on the bedside lamp, picked up the cordless phone, grasped the pillow, and clutched it to her side. It was a familiar routine, finished almost before her eyelids opened.

Her heart pounded. She gulped for air and pulled at the neck of the clingy nightshirt damp with perspiration. With a sweeping glance she inspected the now brightly lit corners of her bedroom. Through the open door a dim light assured her that the shadowy, hulking form had fled the apartment.

Again.

She punched all but the last digit of a phone number, then stopped.

He would only say, with just a hint of a sigh, "Catherine, this is becoming tiresome."

If he answered.

The last time, he hadn't answered. At 3:16 A.M. he hadn't answered his phone.

The time before that, someone else answered. At 2:30 in the morning a feminine voice had answered his telephone.

Cat shuddered and took a deep breath. The time before that, he said it was becoming tiresome.

She pushed the off button and laid the phone on the nightstand next to the clock radio. It was 3:53. Hugging the pillow with both arms, she scooted down and curled up under the covers, her face toward the open doorway. Slow, gentle tears meandered sideways down her cheeks.

Tiresome, yes, but less often also. That was a fact to hold onto, a fact that promised she would get through this.

Thankfully, she never remembered the nightmare's details, only a sense of having been pursued by a large, vague, dark form. She shuddered again.

Think about work! Think about work . . .

Yes, that would do it. She would plan her day at the motel.

The new employee was coming, a temp to fill in as second-shift maintenance supervisor. First on the agenda would be to introduce him to the staff, show him around, give him keys . . . No, first she should go in early and work on the budget. Then there was that ongoing tiff between some of the Housekeeping ladies. She'd better get them together and take care of it soon. What about the paint order?

She yawned and continued the mental checklist. Her eyelids soon grew heavy in the bright light.

One

DOMINICK STOPPED DEAD IN his tracks just inside the small office. His heartbeat ricocheted violently. It felt as if ice pulsated through him, then burst out into droplets of cold sweat.

The young woman sitting behind the desk was her.

No two ways about it.

The nameless stranger now rising to greet him was the one he had been searching for, the one he wanted so desperately to meet.

But not now. Not here.

She smiled at him. "Hi." The corners of her eyes crinkled.

He hesitated. Those eyes were what he remembered most vividly, and even at this distance he saw that his memory had not conjured the image. They were like sunlight dancing through honey.

She stretched her hand toward him across the desk. "You must be Dominick D'Angelo." She grinned. "Did I pronounce that correctly? Dee-ANN-je-lo?"

She didn't recognize him. The thumping panic in his chest ebbed, and he stepped forward. With a slight cough, he loosened his vocal cords. "Uhh, yes, that's it." Her handshake was firm. "Nice to meet you, Miss, uh . . ." He tilted his head to read the brass name plaque beneath his arm. ". . . Catherine St. Clair."

"Thank you. Please, have a seat—and call me Cat." She sat back down.

In spite of his still-tense nerves, Dominick automatically

slipped into his professional mode as he settled into one of the two armchairs facing her desk. *Name association.* "Cat. As in the curious one?"

She chuckled and shook her head. "I hope not. Actually, the nickname stuck because apparently I napped and purred away my preschool years. Easiest kid in Poway history."

"That's a community just up the freeway, right?"

"Right, about twenty minutes. I take it you're not from the area?"

"No."

"Well, welcome to San Diego, and welcome to your new job at Castillo de Cala."

He noted her perfect Spanish accent. *Cas-tee-yo day cah-lah.*

"Castle by the Cove." She spread her hands in an arc as if encompassing the whole property that lay beyond her office walls. "The most fun family vacation motel you'll find on Mission Bay. Will you excuse me for just a sec?" She swiveled in her chair to face a computer that sat atop a credenza behind her desk. "If I don't finish up a few figures here, I'll lose track."

"No problem." He took a silent deep breath, gave his shoulders an internal shake, and started cataloging.

There was a faint citrus-like scent in the air. Her perfume. Her hair was a dark brown with hints of a deep reddish hue. Chestnut. It fell to just below her collar in a casual, layered cut. She wore a short-sleeved, white silk blouse that set off her lightly tanned arms. An expensive-looking pale green jacket hung on the back of the leather chair. Gold watch, oversized face. One ring, right hand, dark red stone. Garnet? Focusing beyond her shoulder, he saw that what looked like a spreadsheet filled the computer screen as her fingers tapped across the keyboard.

He surveyed the office. Small—just long enough to accommodate two chairs inside the open door, just wide enough to walk around one side of the broad, oak desk. Walls papered in muted shades of beige stripes. Infusing that light citrus fragrance were whiffs of warm, sea-scented air that drifted through two open windows behind the computer. They framed a patch of blue sky and flat-leafed subtropical plants.

In the ceiling above the desk was a covered attic opening. He thought of the architectural design of the place. True to its name, the Castillo resembled a castle with its stone walls. It even had two imitation turrets. This office was in a corner of the lobby building, so one of the turrets must be right above them.

The desktop was neatly organized. The only personal items besides the name plaque were a fat, glazed pot that held pens, a pink camellia floating in a crystal bowl, and a green bottle of S. Pellegrino sparkling water.

Cat swiveled back around, her quick eyes catching his. "Well, did I give you enough time to get over the shock?"

His breath caught, and he forced a word past the heartbeat that had jumped into his throat. "Shock?"

Her chuckle was low, like the clear, confident alto voice. "I won't hold it against you. I see that look on a lot of faces. I go through this with everyone new to the staff. No one expects me to be the assistant manager because I'm not at least fifty years old and I'm not a man. All right, here goes."

Again his momentary panic subsided. She was still unaware of who he was. What must have been his startled expression only implied to her that he hadn't expected his new boss to be a young woman.

She folded her hands on the desktop, her direct eye contact holding his attention. "As assistant manager, I answer to Ron Hunter, the manager who hired you. He answers to the real bosses, the owners. If there's something you're not comfortable discussing with me, I don't mind if you talk to Ron. But I prefer that we communicate directly as much as possible, especially when we work together." She smiled. A dimple in her left cheek deepened. "Which we're scheduled to do Tuesdays through Saturdays, 3 to 11 P.M." She raised her eyebrows, waiting for a response.

He lifted a shoulder and felt a grin tug at his mouth. A genuine grin that he didn't hold back. "Well, what can I say to such a disarming invitation? I look forward to answering directly and only to you, Miss St. Clair."

There was a knock on the open door behind him. He turned to see a petite, longhaired blonde walk in, clapping her hands.

"Bravo! Can we keep him, Cat?"

Cat smiled. "I think so. He did answer well, didn't he? Dominick, this is Cissy Owens, front desk manager. Cissy, meet our new temporary maintenance jack-of-all-trades, second shift. And it's pronounced dee-ANN-je-lo."

"D'Angelo." The young woman kissed her fingertips in the gesture of a chef. "Umm, sounds like a pasta dish I'd order in a restaurant. A particularly delicious pasta dish. No offense."

"None taken." He stood and shook her hand. "Nice to meet you."

"Likewise." She squeezed his hand a moment longer than necessary and batted long black lashes over her green eyes. "Welcome aboard, Dominick D'Angelo. So, are you married, engaged, or otherwise involved with a significant other?"

"Cissy," Cat intervened, "you really beat around the bush too much. Try to get right to the point. Did you come in here for a reason?"

"Oh yeah, Trent called. He said he'll be here at 5:30."

Cat's eyes closed briefly. "Thanks."

Cissy nudged her elbow into his ribs. "Well?"

He winked down at her. "No, no, and no." *Fact. On all three counts. No wife, no fiancée, no one special. Uninvolved.*

"Really? Not even a semi-significant other?"

He shook his head. "Not even."

"So nice meeting you, Dominick." Cissy took a backward step toward the door. "So very, very nice."

Cat wadded up a piece of paper and whizzed it past his ear. "Go!"

"I'm gone!" Her spiked heels clicked as they hit the hallway's rustic stone tile.

Cat grinned. "As you can see, we're extremely professional here. Please, sit back down." Her eyes shifted again toward the door. "Tara!" She jumped up and hurried around her desk to embrace a little girl who had walked in. "How was Sea World?"

"It was awesome!"

A breathless woman arrived at the door. "I'm sorry, Miss St. Clair. She couldn't wait—"

"No, no, it's all right. If my door is open, you're always welcome to come inside."

The small girl tugged at her arm and held out a paper bag. "I got something for you."

Dominick settled back into his chair and watched Cat's interchange with what appeared to be motel guests. Her features were striking. Her mouth, now a circle of surprise, was wide, expressive beneath broad cheekbones. The teeth were shiny white, straight. Probably full of braces at one time.

She was as tall as he remembered, maybe five-nine or ten, the top of her head about level with his shoulder. The hair was different, though, of that he was sure. No bouncing ponytail. She looked feminine in the silk blouse and pale green, straight knee-length skirt and low pumps, but it wasn't a delicate femininity. There was a solidity about her. Healthy, athletic . . . like someone you'd find on a Wheaties box.

"Bye!" Cat waved a black and white stuffed animal as the visitors left, then shut the door and leaned against it, smiling. "I'm sorry. Where were we?"

Her eyes rested on his face, and for a split second his mind stalled again. He had once held a honey jar up to the sunlight, trying to recapture that color. *Dear God, I can't do this.* "Uhh, I was saying I'll be glad to answer to you even though you're female and under age fifty."

"That's all the further we got?" Sighing in an exaggerated manner, she walked back around the desk and sat down. "At least you're getting paid for this time. Why don't you tell me what you learned from the manager so I won't repeat things you already know?"

He thought back to yesterday's interview with Ron Hunter, the so-called official interview at the motel, not the earlier one at the agency. "I learned your regular second shift guy had surgery and might retire after he recovers. For now you need someone to fill in for him as a temp. My job is to follow the maintenance supervisor's schedule, take care of emergency repairs, close down the pool at 10:45, generally be available for whatever needs to be done."

"Exactly. Which is why we asked the temp service for a jack-of-all-trades."

"Ron said I had to keep up with the 'Jill-of-all-trades.'"

"Jill?" Cat's eyes widened. "What in the world is that? Ron's never called me that."

He smiled and lifted a shoulder. "My interpretation." *Turn on the charm, D'Angelo. She'll never recognize a charming man.* "Jill, also known as assistant manager, hostess," he counted off on his fingers, "activities director, baby-sitter, lifeguard, waitress, maid, shuttle van driver. Did I forget anything?" He glanced at the camellia on her desk and grinned. "Oh, yeah, gardener." He was on automatic pilot now. He could do this. He had to do this. It was his job.

A blush deepened her complexion, and she waved a hand in dismissal. "That's all just part of assistant managing. What I meant was, are you familiar with plumbing, wiring, hammers, paint brushes, pool chemicals? Shuttle van driving and the route to the zoo?"

"You got it." *Fact.*

"Good. And you kind of look like a security guard."

"I do?"

"Well, what I think one should look like." She squeezed her fists together and stuck out her elbows.

Oh . . . my build, Dominick thought. He chuckled, relaxing his face, trying to look pleasant and not like a security guard.

"So we can call you that too, if the need arises. The security people don't come in until we go home, but once in a while we have problems early in the evening. Anything else?"

He noticed that her hand stroked the stuffed whale now sitting on the desktop. "Shamu fan?"

She burst into laughter. "Not about me! Come on. I'll show you around so you can get started."

If she didn't implicitly trust Ron's thoroughness and judgment, Cat would have protested rather loudly the hiring of one Dominick D'Angelo.

The guy was scary-looking. Naive Cissy flippantly compared his name to a menu item, while Cat was hoping the Mob wasn't moving into her castle.

He strode beside her now as they followed the sidewalk through the courtyard between the two double-story, guest room buildings. On the positive side, he was the epitome of what you'd want walking with you down a dark alley late at night. Over six feet, probably by at least four inches. Trim waist. Arms and chest that filled out his short-sleeved, blue denim work shirt in such a way that there was no question of his strength. Deep, low voice.

Not that there were any dark alleys on the grounds or for that matter an abundance of troublemakers. For the most part the guests were pleasant young families on vacation.

She and Dominick reached the pool area at the end of the courtyard. "I'll show you where the chemicals are stored. The key is on your ring there, marked *pool*."

He pushed open the wrought-iron gate and stepped aside for her to walk through. "Sounds appropriate."

Cat led him along the end of the crowded pool, past the concrete bathhouse to a small shed. She thought of Cissy's immediate attraction to him. No doubt the young woman would say it was his rugged good looks. Cat, on the other hand, would call his looks a little rough around the edges and wondered if his 5 o'clock shadow was there most hours of the day like it was now at 3 o'clock. She also wondered if a brush would calm the thick black hair that grazed his collar. And what about his nose? The bridge of it was a little crooked. Now how had that happened?

His eyes were a clear gray. She had sensed only a sporadic

connection through them. It was as if they alternately froze over and then melted, like the ice at the indoor skating rink. His infrequent smile didn't seem to be related to the melting. All that combined with his size gave him the security guard look.

Oh, well. He seemed cooperative enough. He'd either get over the macho-guy-must-answer-to-female-boss syndrome or move on as temps often did. She wondered how he got along with Hispanics. "Dominick, do you speak Spanish?"

"*Por favor, gracias,* and *buenos dias.*" He shrugged.

"That'll work. Miguel understands English fairly well. He's on second-shift maintenance with you, part-time. And many of us are bilingual, so it's easy to find help if there's something you can't communicate."

They continued past the playground and miniature golf course toward a sports equipment shed. "When you close up the pool, it's a good idea to check to make sure the bicycles are locked up—this door here. Unless Kevin's working. He's very dependable."

"Is that the end of the property?" Dominick pointed behind the shed.

"Just beyond the basketball court, where that marina begins. The place is basically a rectangle. This is the southwest corner." They turned and headed back north along a sidewalk that paralleled a small beach area on the quiet cove. "This," she gestured toward the guest room building on their right, "is what I call the Castillo's west wing."

"I take it the other building across the courtyard is the east wing?"

"Of course." She smiled. "They're looking a little worn. That off-white color used to be white, and the turquoise trim is really hunter green."

"How many rooms are there?"

"Ninety. It's a small place and not a true resort. We don't have room service or gift shops or any luxurious amenities. And the restaurant's menu caters to kids, not gourmet types. It's a popular place though. Quite a number of local families visit reg-

ularly, just for a short getaway or for holidays. We always do special things on the big holidays. We're reasonably priced and near
all the touristy things, so we do get a steady flow of out-of-
towners."

"Another turret." He looked toward the restaurant in the
distance. "And you've got life-size armored knights and a stone
fireplace in the lobby. Where'd the castle motif come from?"

"Oh, the original developer had a daughter who loved the
Cinderella story and always asked what was it like after she married Prince Charming and moved into the castle. So he built her
one."

"Hmm. Creative."

She chuckled. "I made that up. We don't know where the
idea came from, probably a frustrated Hollywood producer-
turned-developer. But it works. We've been catering to families
for sixteen years now."

"You've been here that long?"

"Well, no, just six years. Three at the front desk and doing
those other Jill-of-all-trades things, part-time, while I took more
classes in business. My dad wasn't comfortable with just the
hotel management degree. He thinks the job market is too
unstable. So now I'm qualified to do all sorts of things I'm not
very interested in."

They reached the restaurant, two sides of which were table-
filled patios. "Cissy will show you inside later. We all get a dis-
count here. Let's go behind to the maintenance garage. Most of
what you'll need is in there. This is the north end of the
property."

"What's over there?" Dominick nodded to where the sidewalk continued beyond the garage, still paralleling the bay.

"Well, that pile of boulders is an unofficial boundary and a
busy place. See the kids climbing there now?" She smiled. "If the
playground equipment ever wears out, I don't think we'll need
to replace it. The property on the other side is a community center. They hold special cultural activities there. Much of the time

it's empty, which makes the Castillo seem bigger and more private."

She showed him around inside the storage garage, then locked it back up. "Now on the other side of that fence," she pointed through the small grove of eucalyptus trees toward a tall privacy fence, "is the kitchen door and the service drive. But I want to show you one more thing this way."

They headed back the way they had come, then circled around the patio side of the restaurant.

"Have you done maintenance work before?" she asked.

"Yes."

He sure didn't offer much extra information. She veered off the sidewalk onto a stone path. "This whole area is what we call the garden. It makes for a good shortcut."

In spite of the quiet stranger beside her, Cat took a moment to inhale the fragrant garden. Full of short and tall palm trees, flowering bushes and juniper, it was always a soothing place. They reached a narrow pond, spanned by a footbridge and full of enormous goldfish whose scales reflected glimmering sunlight as they slid through the water.

She stopped in the middle of the flat bridge. It was about four feet wide and twelve feet long, a couple of feet above the water. "Dominick, here's your first project. Can you fix this?" She wiggled the railing. "I think it's loose in these two places."

"No problem. I take it this is your castle's moat?"

Cat was surprised to see him smiling at her. "Well, yes. The closest we get to one anyway."

He nodded. "It works."

"I think so." She led him along a path that angled left and pointed to the right. "That way takes you onto the courtyard. This comes out near the lobby. Do you have any questions?"

"No."

They emerged from the garden and followed the sidewalk to the open lobby doors. "I think that's it. I have to get over to the dining room. Cissy will give you a walkie-talkie, and then you can get to work. If you need anything, she always knows where

I am. And she knows as much as I do; you can ask her anything. So welcome aboard, Dominick."

"Thank you, Miss St. Clair."

She stuck her hands on her hips and frowned.

"Uhh, I mean Cat."

"Are you from Chicago?"

"Yeah. Does it show?"

"Mm-hmm. Formality and flat a's."

"I'll work on it."

"You can keep the accent, but it's okay to lighten up a bit. After all, this is California." With a wave she headed down the sidewalk.

A moment later she peered over her shoulder to watch Dominick enter the lobby. She smiled to herself. Cissy latched onto him, just as she suspected she would. Her coworker could be bold and brassy, but she was also kindhearted and fun. Guests adored her. She was perfect as front desk clerk, the first person they saw as they entered the Castillo de Cala. No doubt under her direction, the new guy would soon be smiling more often.

~Two~

AFTER LEAVING DOMINICK in Cissy's capable hands, Cat strode toward the restaurant. She stepped through an opening in the low bushes that separated the patio dining area from the sidewalks and greeted a waitress who was arranging place settings at the empty square glass-topped tables. Inside the dining room she found Mandi setting tables. She was an efficient college girl working for a second summer as hostess.

"Mandi, did Kara show up?" Passing a supply cart, Cat grabbed a handful of napkin-wrapped silver and began setting a nearby table.

"She just called in sick, but we should be okay. There aren't many reservations."

Cat grinned at her as they worked side by side. "But the rooms are full."

"If I were a guest on this beautiful Wednesday in July, I'd be at Sea World, eating their food and waiting for the special summer night shows."

"Me too. I trust your judgment, but Andy said he'd like some extra hours, and he'll be home for a while this evening. You can call him if you need to."

"Okay. Hey, that new guy's a hunk."

"Mm." Cat set out salt and pepper shakers.

"Mm," Mandi mimicked. "What does that mean?"

She shrugged. "I think he'll do a good job."

"Oh, Cat," the young woman laughed, "how can you be so

businesslike and so likable at the same time? Admit it, he's a hunk."

"Hunk definitions vary. And he's too old for you."

"Now you sound like my mother."

"Good." Cat patted her shoulder. "Like I've said before, extra mothers keep you healthy. I have to go." She wove her way through the tables.

"Cat?" Mandi called.

She turned.

"Thanks."

"You're welcome. I always liked setting the tables."

"Well, that too, but I mean for being an extra mother."

She smiled and gave her a thumbs-up sign. "See you later."

Cat relished all the details of running a motel. Everything from counseling an employee like Mandi to setting a table to soothing an irate guest pumped adrenaline through her. Vying for reviews in national magazines and a spot on the Top Twenty list, keeping the average occupancy rate at 75 percent, creating ad campaigns, coordinating schedules—all the business details suited her competitive streak. And the other side—creating a suitable environment for guests and staff—seemed a natural continuation of the life she'd always known. As an athlete and one of five children in a close-knit family, she understood team relationships and hard work.

She made a quick swing through the kitchen, checking on dinner preparations, then stepped out the back door and through the employees' eating patio. Even nitty-gritty details like making sure the large garbage bins were shut and in place outside the patio's tall fence were enjoyable because she perceived it all as a part of the process of managing a motel.

Alongside the dumpsters was the service drive, the area she had pointed out to Dominick from the other side of the fence as they stood outside the maintenance garage. She made a mental note to double-check his memory tonight, make sure he remembered to lock that door.

A late afternoon breeze scurried the ever-present brittle

eucalyptus leaves across the concrete. Instead of retracing her steps through the restaurant, she turned right and followed the service drive to where it opened onto the main driveway and front lot. She hummed in her off-key way, jangling her bracelet-size ring of keys. She reached the corner of tall oleander bushes and headed right again, through the parking lot. Immediately she paused mid-stride. A silver, two-seater Mercedes was parked in a guest registration space near the lobby entrance.

Her humming halted abruptly, replaced by a low, strangled noise that was not quite a groan, not quite a sigh, not quite a curse, but somehow managed to express the emotions of all three.

It wasn't 5:30 yet.

Cat combed her fingers through her hair and moistened her lips. Should she go around to the employee entrance, duck into her office, freshen her lipstick, slip on her jacket, spray on a bit of cologne? No. The added touches would be unnoticed because of her tardiness. And it would be tardiness despite the fact that he was early.

Better to just go on in. If she'd worn the jacket, she'd have lipstick in her pocket. But it was too warm for the jacket. She tucked her blouse more neatly into the skirt, smoothed the waistband, took a deep breath, and strode across the lot.

It doesn't matter, Cat. It really doesn't matter.

Trenton William Carver, Jr. He was her definition of—well, not hunk exactly, but rather Prince Charming, even now. Six feet tall, just right for her five-ten. A slender frame made, it seemed, for the elegant draping of professional, understated suits, ties, and white shirts with French cuffs. Light brown hair brushed back from a handsome face with smooth angles. Baby-blue eyes. Intelligent, focused, corporate attorney eyes that warmed when he looked at her. An income that promised a North County home, small-castle size. Maybe a Palm Desert condo or a sailboat. Certainly time off for babies.

Not the dark alley type.

The lobby doors were propped open. Without pausing, Cat

entered and walked to the far end of the long registration counter. Sitting on the other side, Cissy looked up from the computer. She opened her mouth to speak, but Cat's face must have told her she didn't need to. So she subtly tilted her head toward the small accountant's office located behind her.

Cat swung around the counter, stepped into the office, shut the door, and dumped her keys on the desk. "Hi, Trent."

Seated at the desk, he glanced up from a paper in his hand. "Hello, Cat. Making rounds?"

"Mm-hmm."

"How are you?" He made eye contact now.

"Fine." She slipped into a chair across from him. Their conversations always started like this. Short, clipped sentences. Inwardly she fumed that her voice was breathy. Still, after all this time, after all that had happened, how could her heart skip a beat?

"Sleeping?"

"Mm, better." No need to mention last night.

"Good. Well, the inspection is just a little over two weeks away."

"I know."

"I thought we could do a trial run next Thursday."

"They're coming on a Monday. I thought we should do it a week from Monday."

"Cat, I don't want you working extra days."

Sundays and Mondays were her days off. "I don't mind. You know I don't mind."

"It's not necessary. Please don't bite your nails. Here's a revised list. The Group agrees that the front building painting can wait, but the bay side has to be done."

"It'll be done. Frank painted the south end before his surgery. The new guy started today, so—"

"New guy?"

"Dominick D'Angelo. He's a temp."

"I thought you were going to do without?"

Cat shook her head. "We tried for ten days. It's too disorganized. Miguel couldn't handle it. He's a honey, but he's sixty-eight years old. Anything else on the list?"

"Just some minor details."

"I'm sure I can read them." She cleared her throat, venting the sarcasm that coated her words, and tried again. "Trent, you could have mailed this. Or called. I'm fine. Really."

He stared back at her, as if unsure.

"My report was all right, wasn't it?" *This time. This time it was all right, I know it was.*

"It was well done, Cat. I'm proud of you." He stood, snapped shut his black leather attaché case, and handed her the paper.

Classic linen. Twenty-five percent cotton fiber. Jacobs, Pemberly, Carver and Carver's everyday memo stuff. "Thanks. We'll see you a week from Monday, then?"

Trent smiled and tugged at the white French cuffs beneath sleeves of subtle, charcoal gray stripes on black. It was never too warm for him to wear a suitcoat. "Thursday, Catherine. And don't worry about the painting." He squeezed her shoulder as he walked past. "Have a good evening."

"You too." Cat blinked rapidly, trying to read the paper in her hand, trying not to inhale the Obsession-laden scented air. The ache in her jaw suggested she loosen its clench, but it wouldn't budge. Not just yet.

Dominick stood at the check-in counter and shook Trenton Carver's hand. Only one word was needed to describe him—yuppie.

"Mr. Carver," Cissy explained, "represents The Bennington Group."

Carver smiled. "Nice to meet you. Cissy, I'll be back next Thursday for a mock inspection. You can spread the word. Good-bye." He strode out the door.

"Bye." Cissy leaned across the counter, watching him go.

"So who's The Bennington Group?" Dominick asked.

"Oh, they own the place." She glanced over her shoulder toward the accountant's office.

Cat was sitting in there, only one crossed leg in view, swinging. It occurred to him that it was a nicely shaped leg.

Cissy looked back at him. "They're in Phoenix. They own a lot of different things. When they bought the Castillo two years ago, Trent's law firm represented them."

"He's an attorney then?"

"Yeah. He did the sale, then there was a lot of legal stuff when The Group got out of the chain's franchise. Then there's all the INS paperwork."

"Immigration?"

She flipped her long blonde hair off a shoulder and leaned over to open a drawer. "We have immigrant employees. There's like a zillion documents to keep track of for employment eligibility. Cat knew more about it than Trent." She rummaged through the drawer. "Anyway, now he's kind of their liaison, I guess you'd say. Checks up on us now and then. Helps Cat with some things."

Dominick picked up the handwritten note he had been asking Cissy about earlier when Carver emerged. Now he noticed that Cat's leg had stopped swinging. "Well, thanks for deciphering this for me."

Cissy smiled at him as she pried the lid off a brown plastic prescription bottle. "Anytime. Barry's handwriting is a pain. Usually he'll be here when you come in. He had some appointment. Cat!"

She stood in the office doorway. Her eyes seemed unfocused as they swept across the empty lobby and passed over Dominick before finding Cissy at her side.

"Here." The younger woman lifted Cat's hand and poured something from the bottle into her palm. "Two?"

Cat dropped her chin in a sort of half nod. With hesitant steps she walked from behind the counter into the hall area and turned left toward her office.

"What was that all about?" Dominick asked. The assistant

manager's changed demeanor was too obvious for him not to mention it.

Cissy shook her head. "Oh." She ducked into the office and came out with Cat's large key ring just as the telephone rang. "Dominick, take these to her, please? Meet me at 6:30, behind the kitchen. Good evening," she said into the phone, her voice lilting. "Castillo de Cala."

Dominick could see Cat at the end of the hall outside her office door, wriggling the locked knob. She leaned her forehead against the door. Puzzled, he hurried toward her. "Cat . . ."

She peered at the keys through half-closed lids. "Thanks." She fumbled with them, her left hand still clutched around whatever Cissy had placed there. Her fingers trembled, and the key missed its slot.

He placed his hand over hers and unlocked the door.

"Thanks." Her voice was lower than usual.

He followed her inside. "Are you all right?"

"Headache. Ibuprofen." She held open her palm, then swallowed the white pills with a drink from a mineral water bottle. "Prescription strength. Cissy's my drug dealer." Massaging her temples, she sat and closed her eyes. "Hazards of the job. I'll be all right in a few minutes. Umm, we have to paint the bay side of the back building."

"That would be the west wing." He remembered Carver saying he'd be back on Thursday. "By next Thursday?"

She managed a small smile. "You're quick."

"I paint quick too."

"And I thought you'd have a hard time with a female manager."

"None whatsoever."

Cat's eyes opened then. "I'm sorry I misread you."

"No problem." That honey color, all shimmery liquid now, was doing something to his insides. He took a backwards step. "Do you want the door shut?"

"Yes, please. Dominick?"

He paused.

"No matter what Cissy tells you, Trent is a good man." She closed her eyes again. The fingers at her temples wiped at the tears that slipped through.

Quietly, he shut the door.

Cissy told him about many things. As he suspected, she was a wealth of information and, having a bubbly, flirtatious personality, was eager to share all she knew.

They sat on the kitchen patio at an aluminum picnic table. There were two such tables, both empty at the moment except for the two of them. A tall wooden fence separated the area from the service drive and the storage garage. He had eaten the night's special, hamburger and fries, taking his dinner break the same time as Cissy, as she had suggested. The sun was low; the fence threw long shadows. It was a typically mild July evening.

"Does Cat get uptight like that every time Carver shows up?"

Her green eyes widened. "This is nothing! You should have seen her four months ago. Migraines. We'd have to take her home. She even used an empty room a few times, but don't spread that around."

"Doesn't she do a good job?" He thought back to his conversation with Ron, the manager. He hadn't mentioned any problems in this area. He'd indicated the assistant manager was efficient. And what Dominick had seen so far confirmed that. She gave the impression that the motel was her home and other employees were more like family or team members. Guests were pampered in every sense of the word. It wasn't a snobbish performance, just an easy flow of friendly words, smiles, genuine attention to everyone. And despite her earlier tossing of a paper wad, there was a distinct air of professionalism about her. She was treated with respect, he felt, not simply because she was the boss but because of the way she conducted herself.

"Oh, Cat's naive but generally does a great job, which is really surprising considering her background."

"What's her background?"

Cissy leaned across the table and lowered her voice. "Silver spoon stuff."

Dominick pondered that for a moment. "You mean rich?"

"Filthy. Big house up in North Poway. Big family. Her dad owns a huge construction company. The house is on like seventy-five acres. Can you imagine what seventy-five acres is worth in southern California? Anyway, you get the picture. No concerns as a kid. Fairy-tale world. Which is why she's so naive. School was easy. Basketball was easy." She sipped her coffee.

"Basketball?"

"She played year-round—expensive camps and traveling leagues—then played at USD. Small, private college." She rubbed her fingertips together. "Why was I telling you this? Oh, yeah. Easy life. So when Carver dumps her, she falls to pieces."

"They dated?"

"They were *engaged*."

"What happened?"

"I don't know. They're both extremely closed-mouth about their private lives. What I know about her I mostly pick up here and there, just bits and pieces from her. We're not exactly what you'd call tight. No silver spoon in my background. Anyway, I discovered by accident they were dating—happened to see them at a restaurant about a year ago. Then last Christmas he gives her this humongous diamond. *That* she talked about. She was ecstatic, floating on air for about three days.

"Then her sister calls in, says Cat's sick. She's gone for ten days. When she comes back, her long hair's cut off. She looks sick; she's lost weight. Calls Carver five, six times a day. Gets these migraines, at least two a week for a while. Moves from her old apartment, which I know she was crazy about, into a different one in another neighborhood. Things start to fall apart around here, but Carver and Ron cover for her." Cissy shrugged. "I'm not one for coddling spoiled brats, but I admit, I did too. I figure she's better than somebody we don't know. Then one day, I think it was in February, she shows up without the ring. I

remember thinking Happy Valentine's Day to you too. Men."
She snorted.

It would have sounded like a soap opera, just street noise to
be ignored except . . . *Christmastime*. *Long hair*. Something
tugged at his thoughts. He filed it for later. "What happened?"

"I don't know for sure. She just said they weren't right for
each other. Rumor has it he was seeing someone else and forgot
to break it off before he gave Cat the diamond."

"Hmm."

"Men can be such—" She smiled and touched his forearm.
"Sorry. Present company excluded. Where are you from?"

"Chicago." *Fact.*

"How'd you get here?"

"My truck." *Fact.*

"Ha, ha."

"Got tired of snow, so I headed west. Ended up here about a
year and a half ago." *Fiction.* "It's a great place."

"Where do you live?"

"Mission Beach, just a little hole in the wall." *Fiction.* "How
about you?"

"Pacific Beach. We're neighbors!"

He smiled. "So are you engaged, married, or otherwise
involved with a significant other?"

"Thought you'd never ask. No, no, and no. Well, sorta no."

"Ahh. What do you do in your spare time?"

"Party. How about you?"

"Party." *Fiction.* He winked and stood up. "I'd better get back
to work. Don't want to get fired my first day."

"Cat won't notice what you do tonight. Here, I'll take your
tray for you." Cissy stuck her empty salad bowl on it. "Stop by
later and I'll introduce you to the night manager. She does the
accounting. And the security guy will be in just before 11. He'll
want to meet you."

"Okay. Thanks."

Dominick went out through the opening in the fence and
walked to the storage garage. He paused beside it and looked out

over the calm inlet. It was a warm night. A few families lingered on the small beach.

His mind replayed Cissy's chatter, sifted through it for pertinent details. Given the girl's personality, he reminded himself that much of what she said was more than likely a mixture of fact and fantasy. Her interpretation of Cat's life would be biased. Perhaps the "silver spoon" hadn't been there at all.

What haunted him, though, was the story that directly involved Cissy, the one that didn't leave room for interpretation.

Christmastime . . . six months ago . . . Cat St. Clair's life falling apart . . . long hair cut short . . . emotional upheaval, migraines. There has to be a connection, but does it have anything to do with—

Oh, dear God, what have I done?

—Three—

IT WAS NEVER TOO WARM for Trenton Carver to wear a suitcoat. He only perspired when he played tennis.

Thinking about that, Cat grinned to herself, dipped her right hand into a pail of water, and splashed a palmful onto the lump of wet clay that spun before her on the potter's wheel.

What really made him sweat was when she beat him at tennis.

She laughed out loud at her thoughts and then again just because it felt so good. It was like a vigorous mental broom sweeping at those sticky cobwebs that kept rebuilding themselves when she wasn't paying attention. They filled her mind with confusion, dread, and bitterness. A few good belly laughs would vacuum them up once and for all. *Oh, well. Maybe someday.*

She sat alone in the "pot shop," a long room at the back of an old rambling warehouse downtown. The row of potters' wheels sat mute along one wall. Only hers hummed as she bent over it, elbows braced against her knees. Shelves and worktables were everywhere else, flat surfaces that held an array of pottery in all shapes, all stages. Wet, dry, in-between. Some hidden under plastic. Gray, terra-cotta, bisque, greenware, glazed, unglazed. Bowls, platters, animals, casseroles, vases. In one corner were a dozen or so barrels, each containing a different shade of liquid glaze. A small room off to the side housed the kilns.

There were other rooms used for various art classes—paint-

ing, drawing, sculpting. At the front of the warehouse, art gal-
leries with large plateglass windows faced the street.

Cat's fingers nimbly shaped a bowl. With one hand against
the exterior, the other inside, she pressed evenly as it flew around
and around on the wheel. Gray droplets splattered everywhere.
Two hands, equal, working as one, creating something new from
a formless lump. Something beautiful, durable. Practical and
real, and yet a work of art.

That was it. She and Trent were two separate people, working in love on a relationship, one that was to have been durable
and real and practical. A beautiful creation. When one felt pressure, the other provided the support necessary to keep the thing
from caving in. When heat hotter than a kiln engulfed it, it
would only grow stronger. Because it had been properly prepared, it wouldn't explode.

Yeah, right.

She had followed the rules, played fair, worked hard, prepared properly—and what happened? *Kaboom!* Trent couldn't
handle one lousy nightmare.

Her foot let up on the pedal, slowing the wheel while she
surveyed her work. Oh, it would do. They were all getting lopsided pots these days. Annie and Elli said no one else had her
critical eye—the bowls, vases, and casseroles were wonderful.
She tapped the pedal again, setting the wheel in slow motion,
and her fingers gently fine-tuned the lip.

She really was all right, as she had told Trent last night. Two
months ago she would have squished the clay back into its original lump. Four months ago she didn't have the wherewithal to
enter the studio, let alone sit at the wheel. Time did heal
wounds. Thank God.

Thank God? A lot of good it had done to follow His rules.
If He had cared, the nightmare wouldn't have happened in the
first place and she'd be studying honeymoon brochures and
choosing delicate china patterns for when the in-laws visited.
Her family, of course, would use pottery, St. Clair pattern. She
would not be sitting alone in the middle of the pot shop spin-

ning out yet another bowl her sisters didn't need but said they
did. It was to have been a September wedding . . .

*Thank You, Jesus, for Your death and resurrection. I really do
understand and accept it, but I'll take charge from here.*

Mother said Cat was more in love with the idea of love than
with Trent. Cat disagreed but did admit to herself that she was
less angry with him for letting her down than she was with the
fact that life just didn't work out the way it was supposed to
when you followed the rules. Her heart probably skipped a beat
when he came by because of profound disappointment, not in
anguish that Trenton Carver had found someone else.

She really was fine with that development. It was only natural. She had glimpsed her once, sitting prettily in the Mercedes.
In Cat's imagination the girl was wealthy and knew which fork
to use without asking. She doubted the girl played tennis, but if
she did, she'd never allow herself to beat Trent. The only Bulls
she would know of were in Spain, and she'd break a nail just
picking up a basketball. She certainly wouldn't be the type to
enjoy a belly laugh.

Cat stopped the wheel and stretched her back, glancing at
the clock on the wall. Her hands and forearms were crusty gray,
covered with dried clay. She had time to glaze four other bowls
that were ready before going home to change for work.

Work. How she loved it! She loved making the guests feel
at home. She loved leading the other employees, encouraging
them to do their best. She would love to complete the entire
painting project, just to show Trent she really was fine. At any
rate they would pass inspection this time, unlike the last one.

That one was just three months after the incident, when the
nightmare still burned. Now, almost seven months after her
traumatic experience, she could handle an inspection. It seemed
the only thing she couldn't quite handle was Trent's friendship
visits disguised as business. The migraines and sleepless nights
were fading, but tension always filled her when she saw him, his
handsome face always reminding her of what she had lost.

Dominick studied the report. It didn't exactly read like Cissy's silver spoon version.

Catherine Michele St. Clair was thirty, born and raised in Poway. Parents were Betty, an elementary school teacher, and Stan, an ex-Navy man, a construction worker who had started his own company twenty years ago. A small company that paid its bills. Nothing to warrant a filthy-rich reputation. Two brothers, two sisters, Cat in the middle. Basketball guard in high school, all-state team; athletic/academic scholarship to SDSU— San Diego State University, a state school, not the private one Cissy had mentioned. Her income as assistant manager was average. Her credit rating was excellent; no unusual purchases or outstanding debts except for a school loan. Small savings; checking account was appropriate. Rent for an apartment in the Clairemont area was high, but probably average. No car payment. No arrests. Not even a speeding ticket.

Funny how these things said nothing about wholesome, healthy good looks suitable for a Wheaties box; outgoing; hums tunelessly; honey-colored eyes that unfocus when the ex shows up.

He flipped the paper over. He could have guessed—Cissy Owens was prone to exaggeration, her perspective tainted with envy.

He skimmed the other pages. Everyone looked clean. All the Hispanics were documented, legally employed. The food and laundry services were well-established. Nothing suspicious. Which meant everything and everyone was suspicious. The activity would more than likely involve the delivery trucks. He'd begin there.

Last night he had worked with Miguel. He liked the old man who spoke little English. This afternoon they were starting early in order to begin the painting project. In Spanish the man had told him he would cut off his right arm for *la gatita*. The kitten.

Cat.

He picked up the phone at his elbow and punched out Dr.

Adam Parker's private number. After seven rings his friend answered with a grunt.

"Sorry to wake you, bud."

Another grunt.

Dominick knew it was all right. Adam had told him more than once that he was always available, even after a twelve-hour shift of emergency room surgeries. No doubt last night had been one of those. "Missed you this morning. Waves were great."

"Hold on."

He heard creaking bedsprings, shuffling noises, then kitchen noises. Adam's wife Megan would have prepared the cof-feemaker. He imagined his friend now moving the carafe aside, holding his mug directly under the basket of grounds as the steaming, mud-colored water dripped into it. A few minutes ticked by, then he heard a clunk and a chair scraping.

Slurp. "Okay. What's up?"

"I found her."

Adam didn't reply.

He waited. He couldn't say the words, even now. His friend would know what he was referring to.

Adam sucked in a breath. "Oh, dear Lord."

"Exactly. I think it's something to pray about?"

"Of course. What happened?"

"She didn't recognize me." Dominick paused.

"But you told her?"

"I can't yet."

"I see." Adam sipped his coffee. "You're sure it's her?"

He thought of her eyes. "I'm sure."

"You have to tell her. You can't live with this."

Dominick rubbed his forehead. "I know, but there's a catch. This makes her a suspect."

"Again."

"Yeah. So maybe the first time . . ."

His friend sighed. "I don't know how you do this."

"I don't think *how*, just *why*. Tell Meg?" He always sensed that Adam's wife's prayers counted the most.

"Sure. How about Sunday brunch?"

"See you then. Thanks."

Cat hung her dress on the hook attached to the back of the door, locked it again, and stepped into the manager's office, right next to hers.

"Hey, Ron."

"Hey, Cat." He swiveled around in his desk chair to face her with a smile. "Early again, I see."

Although she was in fact early today, Ron's usual greeting didn't necessarily refer to the time. The teasing phrase had served to carry them through that brief period a few months ago when he often stayed late because she seldom arrived on time. It was his way of allowing her to make mistakes and not worry about jeopardizing her job. Cat would always be grateful to him.

She had admired him for years, trying to mimic his laid-back attitude that somehow kept the staff on their toes. He had survived eight years at the same motel, including the bumpy ride of ownership change. He was forty-something with thinning blond hair, an easy smile, a wife and two young children. "How was the soccer game, coach?" she asked him.

"We won, three zip." Ron eyed her T-shirt and shorts. "You must be going to shoot hoops. Those don't look like painting clothes."

"Painting?"

"Miguel and Dominick got here before 1. That makes four guys out there painting this afternoon."

"Wow. As Cissy would say, can we keep him? So, what do you think of Trent's revised list?"

"We could pass inspection today. Well, maybe tomorrow. We've taken care of everything except that painting job."

"I'm going to get the whole thing done, Ron. Front and back, east and west."

He raised his eyebrows. "Go for it, girl."

She grinned. "You don't think I can do it."

"On the contrary, I bet you can with Dominick. He seems like a worker. And Miguel . . ." He made a slashing motion with his left hand. "He'd cut off his right arm for you."

She laughed. "He's my honey."

"But no sixteen-hour days for you, Cat."

"Well, only one or two if—"

"No! N-o—no."

"Okay, okay. You didn't tell me much about Dominick. What other kinds of work has he done?"

He shrugged. "The temp service said his references are good. I get the impression he's lived all over, done all kinds of things."

"Ah, an unsettled drifter. Or maybe he's running from something. You don't think he's a convict, do you? He has that rough look about him. Have you noticed his nose? And his voice is sort of raspy. You know, like he's strained it." She headed toward the door. "Maybe from singing. That's it. He's a wild, hard-rock singer, tired of life in the fast lane."

"See you, Cat."

"Bye, Ron. Have a nice evening."

She strolled along the sidewalk between the buildings, greeting a groundskeeper who was mowing the grassy area near the patios beside the guest rooms. The area was empty for the most part. Being the middle of the afternoon, the majority of guests had either checked out, hadn't checked in yet, or were off sightseeing. She rounded the corner near the pool and waved to a few mothers with their children. At the equipment shed she entered the side door, then rummaged through the assortment of balls until she found the women's-size basketball.

She figured the teenager in charge of the booth must be outside working on the bicycles, but then through the large open window she spotted him halfway along the west wing, beyond Dominick and Miguel, with a paintbrush in hand. As she walked that direction, she heard singing and chuckled. *He is a rock singer.* Then the words reached her ears, one voice in Spanish and one in English: "Jesus loves me this I know, for the Bible tells me so." *Well, probably not rock.*

When the verse ended, she called out, "*Qué tal*, Miguel, Dominick!"

"*Qué tal, señorita!*" Miguel, standing near a patio door, waved his brush at her.

Dominick called down from the top of a ladder, "*Qué tal, gatita!*"

She laughed. "You're being tutored!"

"Yep. I mean, *sí*. What do you think?"

What she thought as she watched him climb down was that his muscles were for real. He wore a white T-shirt with the sleeves cut off. And she noticed she could see the back of his neck. His unruly hair was tucked up underneath a navy blue cap perched backwards. As she suspected, yesterday's 3 o'clock jaw shadow was a 2 o'clock one today. "I can't believe how much you've finished already."

He stood beside her and looked up at the second-floor balcony above the first-floor patio. He and Miguel were painting hunter green around the doors. The stucco walls had already been painted white. "First shift had some extra time, so they sprayed the white. I think they got about three-fourths done."

"Maybe we really can do it."

"Finish this side by next week? No problem."

She glanced at him out of the corner of her eye. "I was thinking the entire building by two weeks from next Monday."

"Hmm."

"What do you think?"

"Oh, a week from Saturday."

Cat took a deep breath and spun the basketball between her hands, avoiding his eyes. "What about the east wing too? Double overtime."

"Hmm. Actually, money's overrated in my opinion."

She tossed the ball and caught it. "Okay. How about, umm, a season pass to the Chargers?"

"I'm not a big football fan."

"Padres?"

"Nah."

She looked up at him and, raising her voice in mock exasperation, asked, "Well, what would it take?"

He narrowed his eyes at her. "A new longboard."

She hugged the ball to herself, calculating. New surfboards cost hundreds and hundreds of dollars. Maybe she could pay half, finagle Ron into budgeting extra—

"Cat, I'm just kidding."

"But I think I can—"

"He's not worth it."

"What?"

"Nothing. How about dinner? If we finish in time, you take us. For Italian. We'll stuff Miguel with pasta, put some meat on his bones." He wiped his hand on his jeans. "Deal?"

She shook his hand. "Deal. What if you don't finish in time?"

Quickly he made a slashing motion with the side of his left hand against his right arm.

Cat burst into laughter.

"It's the least I can do." He climbed back up the ladder. "I suppose you want Charger tickets?"

"Lakers."

"The right arm would be easier."

"Okay, dinner. Some gourmet fish stuff, though."

He gave her a thumbs-up sign. "You got it, *mi gatita*."

Cat headed toward the basketball court located behind the equipment booth. Dominick wasn't only quick at painting. He had picked up on the fact that preparing for the inspection was a personal challenge for her, an opportunity to prove herself to Trent, so important that she would even consider buying a surfboard to meet it. She wondered what Cissy had told him about Trent. Probably her usual number, an exaggeration. "He's not worth it" was somewhat of a strong reaction.

Dominick D'Angelo certainly was turning out to be an interesting addition to the staff.

~ Four ~

CAT SHOVED THE BLACK plastic trash bag with her foot over the kitchen doorstep, clicked off the lights, then pulled the door shut, turning the handle to make sure the lock was secure. With both hands she grasped the bag's handle and hoisted it over her shoulder. She made her way quickly across the darkened patio and through the fence opening into the service drive. A few moments ago the Friday night bread delivery man had driven off.

It wasn't part of her job description to greet the bread man. He had his own key and was capable of doing his job alone. Neither was her nightly stroll through the empty restaurant and kitchen at 10:15 part of her duties, tidying up what only someone with a subtle eye for detail would notice. Her family called her a perfectionist for a reason. But then again this garbage wasn't exactly subtle. The staff had to have tripped over it in order to walk out the door.

"Umpf." She pushed the bag through the opening in the huge, metal bin. A waste disposal service would pick up the motel's trash tomorrow morning. If they came as early as they sometimes did, the breakfast crew wouldn't have been able to get this bag out in time.

She walked through the other fence opening at the end of the drive, then meandered through fragrant juniper bushes and eucalyptus trees, heading toward the sidewalk that paralleled the small beach and inlet. Moonlight glittered off the water's surface. It was a nice, clear night, a change from the usual mistiness.

Cat never minded doing the extras, though she should probably talk to the staff about this. It was against regulations to leave
the trash in the kitchen, and this wasn't the first time it had happened. Had it always been on a Friday? It seemed to her that the
bin was near to overflowing those other times, just like now.

There was a rustling noise to her right. Something moved
quickly toward her—

Sheer terror shot through her, bolting her feet to the ground,
choking the scream in her throat.

"Cat." A large shadow stepped beside her.

"Oh!" she cried out loudly, her hands flying to her mouth.
She recognized Dominick, but the jolt of fear was impossible to
contain. She gulped for air and screamed, "Don't—don't ever do
that! Oh! . . . I mean . . ."

He touched her arm. "I'm sorry."

She couldn't catch her breath. Her chest felt as if it would
burst. Tree trunks swirled before her.

"Cat, sit down." He steered her a short distance along the
sidewalk to a wooden bench, then sat beside her, speaking gently in his low, almost whispery voice. "I'm sorry. I didn't mean to
scare you. Try taking deep breaths. I thought you had seen me.
I was inside the garage—I'd just turned off the light and locked
the door."

"Don't—"

"Deep breaths. That's it."

"Don't ever," she rasped, "*ever* do anything like that again."

"I won't. I promise. How about if I wear bells on my shoes?"

Her giggle sounded like a choking noise.

"That's better. Hey, I've got a new Jill-of-all-trades name for
you. Jill the midnight trash collector."

Through the shadows thrown by the dim pole lamps, she
could make out his grin. "It's—it's not midnight."

"Close enough. Seriously, is it safe for you to be wandering
around on the edge of the property so late? This beach is public,
right? And the sidewalk is open—anyone can use it."

"There's never been a problem." Maybe she should start carrying her Mace with her, even here at the castle. She became aware of her right hand clutching his shirt at the shoulder. "Sorry." She let go, smoothing the wrinkled fabric. "Sorry I yelled at you too."

"No problem. Are you all right now?"

Well, no, she wasn't, but that was a long story. It would explain her overreaction to this, but . . . she seldom talked of it and besides, she didn't really know this guy. She cleared her throat. "Uhh, yeah, I'm all right. I always feel so at home here, so safe. You know that feeling, like when you were a kid and you'd sit in the backyard counting stars?"

"My backyard was an alley in the big city. Not many stars."

"Ah ha!" Cat recalled her early impression of him. "Was it a dark alley?"

"What?"

"I knew there was a dark alley in your life. You just have this look about you, that security guard look. When we first met I thought you were the type I'd want walking *with* me down a dark alley." She chuckled. "I didn't think about what'd it'd be like to have you walking *toward* me."

"I'm sorry." As he looked at her, half his face was in darkness, the other half bathed in moonlight.

"I know. Don't worry about it. I'm all right now. My heartbeat's almost back to normal."

"Will you forgive me?"

She bit back an urge to make light of the question. His serious tone combined with that particular choice of words struck her as incongruent with her image of him—the independent, uninvolved, drifter sort. He sounded like a Christian! "Dominick, there isn't much to forgive, but of course I do. Have you been to the pool yet?"

"I'm headed there now. I can walk you back to the lobby first."

"Normally I cruise around the property—"

"Because it's like your backyard."

"Yes. So I'm going your direction." They stood and followed

the walk between the beach and the restaurant's patio. "I don't want to run into you again from the other direction."

"Now you can't keep bringing that up if you forgive me."

"I couldn't resist."

"Mm-hmm. Do you normally take out the trash too?"

She shrugged. "Well, when I find some left in the kitchen, I do. I often roam around, just tidying up here and there."

"There's another one. Jill the tidier-upper."

"Ha, ha. Okay, here's one for you. Jack the dark alley walker."

"Hmm. Is that good or bad? For scaring or protecting?"

She glanced at the profile of his strong angular nose and chin. His arm above hers appeared massive in the lamplight. It could go either way. He could easily intimidate. "Whatever's necessary. You grew up in the city then? Not a suburb?"

"Right."

She wondered how to get him to elaborate. "With no back-yards. So where did you feel safe?"

He was silent for a moment. "That's a good question. I'll have to think about it. What was your backyard like?"

Cat smiled. "Oh, it's wonderful."

"Present tense?"

"Yeah, it's still there. You can't see the neighbors, and it's deserty, with sage and manzanita and rocks and lizards and hills. Scrubby trees." She felt an odd sensation, like a longing to show it to Dominick, the big-city dweller. "There's a dry creek bed— it's been dry forever, I think—and my dad built this little flat footbridge across it."

"Do you live there?"

"No, my parents do. My dad grew up on the place. His parents had avocado groves, but most of the trees are gone now, and most of the property has been sold. It's the original house though. Mother and Dad added on to it when our family kept growing."

"You have a lot of brothers and sisters?"

"Two of each."

"Where are you in the lineup?"

"Right smack in the middle. There are about two years between each of us. Anne is the oldest, then Ben, me, Doug, and Elizabeth. A, b, c, d, e. Dad wanted Frank and Gloria, but Mother said no way. Now they've got nine grandkids."

"Frank and Gloria?"

"Felicia and Grant are in the bunch, but that's where it ends." She chuckled and glanced over at the newly painted west wing as they passed. "This looks very nice, by the way, already. Oh, good evening!" she called out to a couple sitting on the balcony outside their second-story room.

"Hello!" They waved back to her.

"See, Dominick," she turned to him, "there's always someone around. It's just like a big family here. Nothing to be afraid of." *Nothing to be afraid of.* She repeated the words to herself, clinging to their promise.

"Except Jack the dark alley walker," he murmured.

"Well, yes, I will have to watch out for him," she teased. They rounded the corner by the sports equipment shed. Kevin, the teenager working tonight, stood outside leaning against the doorway, watching two groups still on the miniature golf course. "Hey, Kevin."

"Hey, Cat. Hey, Dominick."

They chatted for a moment, then continued on, past the low wooden fence that surrounded the small course and the colorful, gimmicky figures at each hole. There were tiny dragons, knights, moats, castles, an ivory tower with a princess in the window. Just beyond that they reached the chain-link fence that surrounded the pool area. Dominick pushed the gate open and let her go ahead of him.

While he went into the bathhouse to turn off the lights and lock the doors, Cat settled into a lounge chair. It felt good to sit still. Dampness hung thick in the night's cool air. She pulled her cardigan more tightly around her neck and wrapped her dress more snugly around her knees.

She watched two children climb from the other end of the heated pool. Their parents swathed them in large towels. She often took a vicarious pleasure from eavesdropping on families like this one. There was such a comfort in the thought of their being on vacation, swimming late at night, laughing about the cool breeze and goose bumps, making plans for tomorrow, leaving behind the ordinary. Oh, there were times, of course, when she recognized that the threshold of too much togetherness had been crossed, when the kids whined and parents snapped.

Dominick walked around the pool, lining up the deck chairs against the fence. She thought she really hadn't learned much about him. Except for that moment of genuine concern in his voice when he asked for her forgiveness, he was rather stoic. He could easily pass for their security guard, in both the demeanor and the muscle departments. His face was usually closed—no emotions showing there, like what the Secret Service guys always looked like in photographs with the President.

Not like her. Everything showed on her face; she couldn't help it. Happy, sad, mad, whatever. Her eyebrows always moved, her voice fluctuated, her mouth was too wide to not be expressing something at any given moment.

The family walked by her and said good night.

Cat leaned back in the chair and looked up at the stars, dimmed by the moonlight and the city's illuminations. Then again, Dominick did have friendly moments. He flirted easily with Cissy. He seemed to enjoy painting with Miguel. And there was that teasing bet. Or was it teasing? Would he really expect dinner? Oh, probably not. Even if he didn't finish the job, she would see that he got extra on his paycheck, just for the effort. Enough maybe for a new longboard.

"Dominick . . ." She looked at him as he approached. "Do you surf?"

"No. I just thought a board would look good in my place, propped up in a corner."

He could be a smart aleck too. "Ha, ha. Where do you go?"

"Usually near the Crystal Pier. Pacific Beach. Bright and early."

The hotel phone, on the outer wall of the bathhouse, rang,

and he went to answer it. A moment later he returned. "Cissy needs to see you before she goes."

"On my way." Cat stood. "Amazing. She always knows where I am."

"I can walk with you."

"No." For a second, gazing down the empty, dimly lit courtyard between the two buildings, foliage blocking her view of the lobby in the distance, she hesitated. "No, but thanks anyway. See you tomorrow."

"Good night, Cat."

Just like my backyard. Just like my backyard. Crossing her arms to hold the cardigan shut, she hurried along the sidewalk, humming, pushing at the fear lingering on the edges of her mind. It hadn't been there much lately, had it? And never while she was at her castle. If Dominick hadn't surprised her, it never would have slipped into her consciousness here, would it?

She bent to pick up an empty soda can.

Jill the tidier-upper. Jill the trash collector.

Trash. It suddenly occurred to her that the trash containers weren't visible from the maintenance garage—the fence was in the way. If Dominick were in the garage, he couldn't have seen her shoving the trash bag into the bin.

Oh, she'd probably missed something in the conversation. She sighed. That had been happening a lot in recent months.

Cat heard the commotion from her office late Saturday afternoon. She hurried out to the lobby to see what was going on.

Cissy met her as she rounded the corner. Behind her were a man and woman, obviously distraught. "Cat, we're missing a little boy."

"Did you alert everyone?" Most of the staff had walkie-talkies.

Cissy turned back toward the check-in counter. "Maintenance, Housekeeping, and Kevin know. I'm calling the kitchen now. This is Mr. and Mrs. Lansky, the parents."

"Let's sit over here." She led the couple to a group of chairs in the corner. She saw the fear on their young faces and tried not to reflect it, although she felt as if she'd been punched in the stomach. "By now everyone is surrounding the property and is out looking for your son. What's his name, and when did you last see him?"

The father answered, "Brendan. He's six, and about an hour ago he was gone."

"From?" Cat prompted. She noticed now that Mrs. Lansky was pregnant and was wringing her hands.

"The room," he said. "I was out on the balcony, my wife was napping. Brendan was watching television. I went inside and he was gone."

She glanced at her watch. "So he probably just wandered out the door?"

"I guess. We've checked all his favorite places."

"It's a big place, lots of nooks and crannies. You couldn't be everywhere at once. I'm sure the staff will find him. They *can* be everywhere at once. He is your child, right? Both of yours?"

They looked at her in surprise.

"I just want to make sure there's no parent who wants custody."

"Oh, no," Mr. Lansky replied. "He's ours. He's got my big ears and his mom's red hair."

Cat smiled to herself. He should be easy to spot. "Good. Does he do this often? Go exploring by himself?"

"Not really. But he is an independent little guy."

Cissy joined them and handed her a walkie-talkie. "Well, dinner's been put on hold. All the cooks and waiters are out looking too. I sent the busboys both directions along the beach walk."

"Does Dominick know?"

Cissy smiled briefly. "He was my first thought too. Must be the muscles."

"Secret Service look."

"Yeah. I'm going out to the side parking lot. Jan's covering the phone for me." She left.

Mrs. Lansky sniffled, and her husband stood. "I can't sit."

"Of course not." Cat handed him the walkie-talkie. "Take this with you." He strode out the door. "Mrs. Lansky, is there something Brendan wanted to do that he hasn't done yet? Or something he wanted to do again?"

"Oh, everything. He loves this place. I get so tired these days in the afternoon, and Dan had work to do. We're on vacation, but he has to do his computer stuff! I told him to take Brendan on the bikes, but he said it would have to be later. He couldn't get a bike by himself, could he?"

"No, I don't think Kevin would give one to a little boy by himself. And they're locked up."

"He hates television, but his dad told him to watch for a while."

"So do you think Brendan was maybe a little upset?"

"Definitely." His mother shook her head. "He's a good-natured boy, but his feelings would be hurt that his dad told him to leave him alone while he worked."

"It makes sense then that he would just take off by himself." Cat felt a sense of relief. "I'm sure we'll find him soon. I think I'll go look around. Do you want to wait here? Cissy will be right back, and when someone finds him, they'll call her."

Mrs. Lansky nodded.

Cat found another walkie-talkie behind the counter and walked out a side door onto the patio behind the Housekeeping entrance.

Dear Lord—okay, I'm calling a truce. Will You do this one? Not for me, but for this family? Don't let Brendan be hurt. Please take care of him, and help us find him.

Foxhole prayer.

Jesus said I could ask You this stuff.

Was there something else she wanted to ask? No . . .

So I'm asking in His name for Your help. Amen.

Cat wandered across the patio. Straight ahead was the east wing of rooms. So many bushes to hide behind. Would he be hiding?

At the sidewalk she turned right. A few more steps brought her to a stone garden path.

Of course he'd be hiding. He was mad at his dad for putting him off, for hurting his feelings. He would hide from that stern face. Any face that declared, "Not now—I'm working even though this is vacation" would appear stern to a child. And he would want to hide from that uncomfortable feeling of anger toward the one who takes care of him. How do you hide from an uncomfortable feeling like that?

Cat stopped in her tracks.

Well if, like Brendan, you don't watch television, you do it on the inside. You detach within. You use your imagination.

Oh, Father . . .

She hurried along the winding path between bushes and flowers and small palm trees. Although the garden wasn't huge, the vegetation was dense enough to block views from one end to the other. When the stone path forked, she veered to the right. Ahead was the pond. At its most narrow point, the twelve-foot bridge spanned it.

"Brendan?" she called. "Brendan?"

Carefully, she picked her way through stiff junipers and ducked under a drooping palm frond. Reaching the side of the bridge, she knelt. In the small space under the bridge between the path and the pond's edge, a little red-haired boy lay curled like a kitten, fast asleep.

"Hey, Brendan." Glad she was wearing slacks, Cat crawled toward him. The bridge was too low for her height, so she found a fairly flat spot nearby, sat cross-legged, and pressed the button on the walkie-talkie. "Cissy, I found him! We're under the bridge."

She could hear muffled cries before Cissy replied, "Mom and dad are on their way!"

The little boy stirred.

"Hi, Brendan. My name's Cat."

"Cat?" He sat up.

"Yeah. Your mom and dad are coming. Did you get lost?"

He stuck out his lower lip and shook his head. "I know my way back."

"Ahh. Just needed some time alone, huh?"

"Yep."

"Do you like chocolate-chip ice cream?"

He nodded.

"Did you know they've got some in the restaurant? And they've got those humongous," she held out her hands to demonstrate, "waffle cones. And I work here, so I'm going to tell them that you can have one right now for free and they should put extra globs of whipping cream on top. Would you like that?"

"Mom won't let me before dinner."

Cat smiled. "I think she might today. Did you go to the zoo yet?"

They chatted until his parents arrived, accompanied by various staff members. Relief was evident in everyone's smiles as they watched the reunion. Mrs. Lansky cried, and Mr. Lansky swore he'd put the computer away and they'd take a bike ride. Brendan wanted his ice cream first. Naturally they agreed.

Cat waved good-bye, then sat back down on the ground, leaning against the wooden bridge's support beam, holding her head in her hands. *Say thank You. Say thank You,* she told herself. *No. I'll cry if I do. I don't want to cry anymore. I don't want Your love anymore, God.* She wiped at the corners of her eyes and blinked rapidly. *You are so rude, St. Clair,* she thought.

"All right," she spoke aloud, softly. "Thank You."

Above her sniffle she heard whistling, and then Dominick came into view, walking from the other side of the bridge. "Cat, are you still down there?"

She had to clear her throat before answering, "Yes."

He spotted her, then sat on the slats just above her, his legs dangling over the side, under the railing. He wore his paint clothes, splattered jeans, sleeveless T-shirt, backwards cap, sloppy tennis shoes. "We're all having ice cream. It's a celebration. Shouldn't you be there since you found him?" He folded his arms on the railing and leaned over.

"I'm coming. Just had to sit still a moment."

"Does this happen often? Lost kids?"

"Not often. This one was scary. An hour and a half or whatever is a long time."

"How did you find him?"

"God." It slipped out without a thought.

Dominick grinned. "Really?"

She shrugged and pulled at a weed under her leg. "Yeah, I guess. Actually, we're not on speaking terms, but I did ask Him for help."

"I didn't know you could do that. But I'm new at this."

She glanced up at him. "New at what?"

"Faith. Jesus. Praying."

He *was* a Christian then. She found a rock to fiddle with. A stone. A stumbling stone. She'd be one if she opened her mouth.

"Anyway," he continued, "I didn't realize you could talk like that. That you can say you're not on speaking terms with the God who created the universe."

Cat tried to detect a reproof in his low voice. She concluded there wasn't one. What she heard was the wonder of first love. "Well, I don't know if you can, but I am. It's between Him and me. It's—" She laughed nervously and ran her fingers through her hair. "I don't want to talk about it."

"But can you tell me what happened after you asked Him to help?"

She blew out a breath as if she'd been holding it for a long time. "I guess I thought about when I was little and I'd get my feelings hurt. Happens a lot when you're in the middle, you know. The older ones go off and do things. The younger ones need Mom and Dad more than you do." She was quiet a moment, remembering. "I always felt loved and wanted, but I was spoiled. So when my feelings got hurt, I'd go out to the backyard . . ." She met his grin with one of her own. ". . . and sit under the bridge."

He laughed. "No way."

"Yes, way!"

"And do what?"

"Well . . ." Her face felt warm. "I'd just get lost in my imagination, making up wonderful places for families to live in. I'd make up stories about them, and I'd build castles out of rocks and dirt and . . . whatever. Then I'd feel better."

His laughter grew louder.

She grabbed his foot and yanked it. "You can't tell anyone!"

He hooted.

She yanked again. "Promise!"

He caught his breath. "Only if you tell me, were you the little girl who always wondered what happened after Cinderella married Prince Charming and moved into the castle?"

"So what if I am?"

Dominick grinned and stood up, leaned over the railing, and stretched his hand out to her. "It's just perfect—you being manager here at Castillo de Cala."

She put her hand in his, and he pulled her to a standing position. "Assistant manager," she corrected, looking into his gray eyes. When his face dropped its Secret Service expression, like now, it really was a very nice face.

He kept his hand wrapped around hers. "They'll want to thank you. You will go eat ice cream?"

She nodded. Only then did he let go of her hand.

"I have to get back to painting. Don't want to get fired." He walked a few steps, then turned back. "Hey, Cat."

She climbed up to the bridge. "Hmm?"

"He's still listening, isn't He? Even though you're not on speaking terms?" His eyes seemed to bore into her from clear across the bridge.

"Good question. I'll have to think about it."

He waved and strode down the path.

What she'd have to think about was why she so easily opened up to this stranger, Dominick D'Angelo.

~Five~

"I WAS A REGULAR Mr. Motormouth." Dominick concluded his description of his encounter with Cat at the footbridge.

Across the patio table, his friends Adam and Megan Parker stared silently at him.

"I mean, when she said God helped her find the kid, it was like something inside of me clicked on. I wanted to hear all about how she relates to God. I just couldn't shut up. I *have* to shut up."

Meg burst into laughter and thrust an arm above her head with a resounding, "Yes!"

"What?" He turned to her husband, who only contorted his face in reply. "What?" he repeated.

Adam snorted, and Dominick knew he'd have to wait for an answer. As his friend's loud guffaws filled the whole outdoors, he shook his head. The Parkers had moments like these. He didn't know if it was their tendency toward wackiness or an expression of sheer joy. Like now, joy seemed inconsistent with the subject at hand, but they were wacky enough to find it at the oddest times.

He couldn't help but smile at Megan's elfin features all scrunched up in laughter. Except for big brown eyes, she was tiny with delicate features and short brown hair that usually stuck out in all directions. She only sat still on Sunday mornings. Other hours of the week were filled with volunteer work at a homeless shelter and being her husband's best friend. Her wardrobe was down-to-earth, their home modest and miles from the ocean. It always amazed Dominick that, given her talents and inability to have children, she had never pursued a business career or at least spent the good doctor's salary more flamboyantly.

Dr. Adam Parker towered over his wife. He looked like the California native surfer he was—an athletic, blue-eyed, and sun-bleached blond. His nights were spent doing emergency surgery at a nearby hospital.

Which was where Dominick had met him two years ago. He remembered seeing those piercing blue eyes as if from a great distance, just before he lost consciousness. When he awoke three days later, they greeted him. During the weeks he spent recovering in the hospital, Adam befriended him. A relationship developed during follow-up office visits, and as the healing progressed, they began meeting for breakfast, surfing, and racquetball. Dominick owed his life twice to the doctor, once for removing the bullets and once for telling him about Jesus Christ.

Meg dabbed at her eyes now with a paper napkin, and Adam's roar subsided into chuckles.

Dominick tried again. "I'm serious. I can't talk to a suspect like that."

Meg jumped up, ran around the table, and gave him a quick hug. "Oh, Dominick, we know you're serious. Deadly serious." She patted his cheek and looked straight into his eyes. "There's just this new tenderness about you. It's such a joy to see. Don't you think you can have a heart for the bad guys and still do your job?"

"I can't be tender when I'm on a case."

"Why not?" she challenged as she sat back down, her eyes never leaving his face.

"I'm a character who fits a role that's necessary for the moment. If I'm tender, I spill my guts, I'm me, and then I can't be a drifter working a temp maintenance job."

"I think," Adam intervened, "that the something you felt click when Cat— Is that her name?"

He nodded.

"I think what clicked when she mentioned God was His Spirit in you recognizing His Spirit in her. Sometimes Christians sense an ability to communicate about things of faith even when they don't know each other. Does that make sense?"

"Yeah. Go on."

"That's the tenderness Meg is talking about." Adam leaned forward, an eager expression on his face. "It's authentic, and I don't think it's going to go away. But it doesn't have to be specific. A drifter working maintenance as a temp can have a heart for God and a concern for others just as well as he can surf and live in your apartment and drive your pickup and eat pasta until it comes out of his ears. Right?"

"Okay. So far."

"But, understandably, you can't tell her yet exactly just how God got your attention, right?"

"Right, and if I keep running off the mouth like yesterday, I'm bound to."

"Dominick, your discipline is still in place!" His words tumbled out. He was clearly excited, grasping the meaning of this new development. "You've only lost the ability to mask your concern and compassion."

Meg added with a wink, "And besides, I've never known you to talk too much."

"And," Adam continued, "let's back up. In the first place, this is an answer to prayer, remember? You wanted to find this woman. We've been praying specifically for that for months. God's brought you this far. We can trust that you'll have the opportunity to tell Cat everything at the right time."

Dominick looked down at the table cluttered with the remains of Sunday brunch. What they said made sense, but he still felt unsettled. Why would answered prayer so complicate his life? "I just . . . I just didn't anticipate these circumstances."

"Hey, bud, that's when God does His best work. When things are unpredictable, we can't manipulate them as easily."

He thought about what his friends had been teaching him the past few months, that there were many facets to faith and that sometimes there was nothing to go on but the knowledge that God was in it. He gave his friends a small smile. "This is just part of the adventure you keep telling me about, huh?"

Meg grinned and nodded exuberantly. "That's what we think. So what's she like?"

Describe Cat St. Clair? Now here's an easy one. "Friendly. Straightforward. Confident. Professional. Kind. The front desk manager is a little jealous of her, but for the most part the staff seems to like her." He thought a moment. "You know what it is? I just figured it out. She accepts everyone. She makes everyone feel significant, from the little rugrat who tromps on the flowers to the college waiters to the Hispanic maid who never went to school to me, the aimless drifter."

"Oh, I want to meet her!" Meg exclaimed. "And what does she look like?"

"She has eyes . . ." Dominick stopped. If he told them about those eyes that sometimes mushed his insides, or that dimple in her left cheek, they'd go into another laughing fit.

"Good," Meg prompted, "she has eyes."

"Uhh, nice ones. She looks like a Wheaties box photo. Athletic."

"Healthy, all-American?"

He nodded.

Her eyes widened. "This is a suspect?"

"Meg," he said, "looks and personality are not measuring sticks. Believe me, I know."

She frowned. "That is so sad. How do you know whom to trust?"

"I don't. I assume they're all guilty until proven innocent."

"Adam," she turned to her husband, "he can't keep doing this. Talk to him."

Adam squeezed his wife's hand while looking at Dominick. "He's good at what he does, love. And he's needed in that capacity."

"I appreciate your concern, Meg, but I'm all right. I've been at this sort of thing for ten years. After a time, it becomes sec-

ond nature. You and Adam are teaching me to trust. I'm learning to separate work from the rest of the world. I'm learning to
accept the evil in the world and do what I can to fight it without losing sight of a good and trustworthy God. I just can't build
an authentic relationship with Cat St. Clair at the moment.
This operation might take a few weeks. After that I can open up
with her." He paused. "Unless she's behind bars."

Meg's curls bounced as she shook her head in an exasperated
way. "Okay, okay. So I suppose you want me to pray that you'll
shut up?"

"You got it."

Adam yawned loudly. "Isn't it time for you two to get going
on your outing?"

"Sorry, bud." Dominick stood. Saturday nights in the ER
were usually his friend's most difficult. Sunday mornings, like
today, he often went to church anyway, then needed the afternoon for sleep. "Wanna ride with me, Meg?"

"No, I'll drive too. That way you won't have to backtrack.
Adam, leave the dishes."

"You talked me into it, love."

Dominick watched as the two hugged and kissed. An
expression of their obvious love after twenty years of marriage
was always a sight to behold.

He and Meg were meeting a group of kids from the homeless shelter at the zoo this afternoon. It wasn't the first time she
had convinced him paperwork could wait. "See you, doc.
Tomorrow?"

"Sounds good. Kiss the orangutans for me."

"Dominick," Meg said as they walked through the kitchen,
"one thing—you cannot refer to the children as rugrats."

"Megan Parker, you are so persnickety. Can't I keep *some* of
my vocabulary?" She had taken on the challenge of cleaning up
his language with a vengeance these past few months. "It's
authentic, at least."

"It's atrocious. Try lamby-pies."

"I can't say lamby-pies."

"Ha! You just did, big guy!"

"Then meet me on Friday, Mother, at the pot shop." Cat cradled the phone between chin and shoulder as she hooked the strap of her denim overall shorts. "We can eat Chinese at Horton Plaza."

"Will 11 work, honey?" her mother asked. "That'll give me time to do a few errands and—"

"And miss rush-hour traffic and have time to fix dinner before your meeting." She laughed. Her schoolteacher mother's summer schedule made hers seem dull. "I know, I know. Eleven is perfect. I gotta go. Put Daddy on."

"All right. I love you, Catherine. Stanley!"

Still holding the cordless phone to her ear, Cat knelt and rummaged through a pile of clothes and shoes on the closet floor. She found one comfy old Birkenstock and slipped it on her bare foot.

"Hey, Kit-Cat!" her father's voice boomed.

She winced and tilted the phone a few inches from her ear. "Hey, Daddy. How you doing?" Her right hand found the other sandal, and she sat on the floor to buckle the straps.

"Great. We got the Timber Oasis project."

"No kidding? That's fantastic!"

"I think so. How are you? Don't say fine."

Cat smiled. She couldn't dodge a subject for long with her dad, so she seldom tried. "I'm not bad. Trent came by unexpectedly the other day, and I only got a minor, minor headache."

Her dad grunted in reply.

"Anyway, I have a favor to ask. I was roaming around the pond yesterday, and I thought it sure would be nice to sit down and relax and not be sitting on the hard ground—"

"You always liked sitting in the dirt."

"Well, I still do, but I'm thinking of the guests. Can you make us a park bench? Or two? Not elaborate ones like you did for Mother. Just basic, rustic jobs."

"Sure. When do you want them?"

Construction was her father's business, and he'd gladly build her anything. But he was a busy man. "The inspection is two weeks from tomorrow. I thought it'd be a really special touch to have those in the garden for it. I'll come up and stain them."

"Nah. We can do it. Probably have them there early next week."

"Thank you! I'd better go. I'm meeting Elli and Jason at the zoo."

"That's what I heard. Give my grandson a bear squeeze for me. Elli too."

"Okay, Daddy. Bye. Love you."

"Love you, too, Kit-Cat. Good-bye."

She continued sitting on the floor. For a gruff, straightforward kind of man, her dad could be subtle with her, and for that she was grateful. The mention of hugging her sister and nephew, which he knew she always did anyway, was his way of voicing concern about her hug quota. If she didn't get it filled—and that meant at least one good solid wrap every couple of days—a distinct irritableness crept into her personality.

She had always been that way. She didn't know if it came from growing up in a demonstrative, loving family or what, but even through her teen years any grumpy, out-of-sorts feeling had a quick fix in her father's bear hug or her mother's slender arms that gently rocked her. By adulthood she had learned to recognize that feeling and mask it when necessary. But Daddy would always detect it. Thanks to Trent's departure from the relationship and not seeing her folks for the last two weeks—not to mention the upcoming inspection that sat like a barbell on her shoulders—it was probably there today in her voice.

She bit her lower lip, cutting off the sob before it formed, and stood, tossing the phone onto the rumpled bed. It looked as messy as the closet floor.

Oh, well! Her internal voice rose on the *well.*

Cat stepped into the bathroom, shoved aside a wet towel with her foot, briskly ran a brush through her hair, then hurried

through the small apartment. It was a suffocatingly small unit
with only three windows. The combined kitchen and living
room was as messy as the bedroom closet floor. Shoes, clothes,
magazines, and newspapers lay here and there. Two sealed card-
board boxes of books still unpacked after three months were
stacked near the couch. On the floor next to the round dining
table sat a group of brown-leafed plants. The counter, a minimal
dividing line between kitchen and living room, was covered
with various forms of pottery awaiting the final step of sanding
on their rough bottom edges. Today's breakfast dishes were in
the sink inside last night's popcorn bowl that sat atop yesterday's
breakfast and lunch dishes.

Oh, well! Late Sunday nights were good for catching up on
dish washing. She certainly didn't have anything else going on.
What had she heard once? Something about if your desktop was
a mess, it indicated a disordered inner life. Actually, her desk at
the motel was in order. What did that mean about her inner
self—a clear desktop at work but her living space a disaster area?
She didn't think she wanted to know.

Kitchen cabinets above and below a countertop ran along
the same wall where the door was. The one organized spot in the
whole place was at the end of that counter where she always kept
a large celadon-colored platter she had made years ago. In it lay
her purse, keys, sunglasses, pens and pad, a to-do list, and a
migraine prescription bottle. She grabbed what she needed now,
unlocked the chain, two deadbolts, and knob, and headed out
the door, carefully locking up half of what she had just undone.
She strode down the single flight of carpeted steps.

Small but secure. Just what she had wanted and needed.
Security here was expensive and mediocre though. Gone was
her reasonable rent, along with a private front door on a plant-
abundant courtyard. No more patio or assortment of friendly
neighbors, many of whom kept the same strange hours she did.
No more intriguing characters at the twenty-four-hour laundro-
mat across the street or the cafe down the block.

What she had instead was a double set of security doors front and back of the eight-plex that required a key or someone from the inside to open them. Only dense, ankle-height ground cover filled the small green area through which the sidewalk cut. The side drive and carport area was nearby and well-lit. Fellow apartment dwellers were seldom seen. And it was all tucked into a residential neighborhood, the nearest business a gas station three blocks away.

She had needed this, though, needed to get away from the nightmare memories that haunted her other place. The fears. The breakup with Trent.

Maybe she'd outgrow the need in time. If God answered her parents' prayers, she would. They still had hope. At times it was only clinging to their hope that kept her going in between the hugs.

Cat slid into her tangerine-colored, small sport utility vehicle. The Tracker had been a gift from dear Trent, one he insisted she keep. And being utility-minded herself, she did. The higher rent didn't leave much for car payments.

She drove toward the freeway while steering her mind back to her parents. A rush of gratitude flowed through her. In the aftermath of the nightmare, they supported her with loving tact and subtlety, never overbearing in their concern or their opinion on what she should or shouldn't do. Space and hugs. It was a winning combination.

The odor in the children's petting zoo always overpowered Cat's sister Elli, even when she wasn't pregnant. She sat on a bale of hay outside the chicken-wire fence, holding a handkerchief over her nose, while inside Cat and little Jason meandered among the goats.

Her three-year-old nephew resembled his mother. They both had chubby cheeks, brown-black eyes, long black hair, and short legs. Younger than Cat by four years, Elizabeth was the baby of the family but was ahead of her in the marriage and children department. Her husband Jim was out of town on business, which gave the women just a little more time than usual together. Besides being sisters, they were the best of friends.

Jason squealed in delight as a goat nuzzled him. Cat heard a nasal laugh come from Elli's direction and scooped up her nephew before he was knocked down. It seemed a good moment to whisk him out of there. The place was getting too hot and crowded even for her. Although her sister was only about six months along, she was probably suffering.

Tickling him so he wouldn't notice the departure, she carried the boy through the double set of thick screened entrance doors. She pulled open the second and walked right into Dominick.

"Well, hi!" She smiled. Jason wrapped his arms and legs around her and stared quietly.

"Cat! Hi." Sunglasses were perched on top of his hair. Two small children were at his sides, each holding a hand. Someone jostled him from behind, and he moved aside.

A small woman with curly, brown hair walked around him, two youngsters in tow, and laughed. "D'Angelo, you're holding up traffic."

"Blame my boss. She's coming out the wrong way."

"You're his boss?" The woman's voice was incredulous, and her eyes widened. "No, no, no. You're much too pretty and too young to be this ruffian's boss." The two little ones tugged on her arms, and she followed them through the door with another laugh.

Dominick winced. "That's Megan. She's in charge of this outing." He held up his right hand, "This is Mikey," then his left, "and Andy."

"Hi, Mikey and Andy." She noticed they wore yarn necklaces with name tags attached. They were about five or six years old but had a sober grown-up expression behind the grins on their undernourished faces. Similar-appearing children holding adults' hands were making their way around them. "This is my nephew, Jason. Oh, and my little sister Elizabeth behind you.

This is Dominick D'Angelo, the new guy at the Castillo. He's the one doing the big painting project."

"Nice to meet you, Dominick."

He glanced down at Elli. "Nice to meet you. Well, we're off to feed the goats. See you Tuesday, *Jill*." A small smile lifted the right corner of his mouth.

"Bye, *Jack*."

Jason reached for his mother. "Mommy . . ."

"Oh, Jase, let Aunt Kit-Cat hold you. Mommy's too hot in here. Who's Jack and Jill?"

Cat bounced her nephew on her hip and headed down the sidewalk. "Uhh, inside joke. As in jack-of-all-trades. Let's go get some ice cream!"

Jason giggled and squeezed her neck. "I want chocolate!"

"Chocolate!" she echoed. "Elli, are you okay?"

She replied with a wan smile and nodded, wiping her forehead with a hankie. "You spoil this child too much."

"That's what aunties are for, right, Jase?"

"Right!"

"If Mommy says no, then you can always . . . ?"

"Call Aunt Kit-Cat!" Jason yelled.

"Give me five!" They laughed and slapped hands.

A short time later, in the main part of the San Diego Zoo, they sat under an umbrella at a round table. A light breeze gently fanned them as they ate ice cream cones.

"Cat, you never mentioned Dominick to me."

"Yes, I did. I told you we have a new temp who's being a big help with the painting job."

"Like I said, you never mentioned Dominick to me."

"What does that mean?"

Elli wiped Jason's mouth with a napkin. "Well, he's attractive. Really, really well-built. Intense eyes."

Cat shrugged. "Did you see his nose?" She touched her own. "Little askew."

Her sister sighed and made a wry face. She wouldn't press

that it was time for Cat to get on with her life, but she'd come close. "And a few tiny scars. Is he married?"

"No. He's a drifter type, just a temp, just in town a short time. I suspect the man is not the marrying type."

Jason leaned over and licked his aunt's cone. "It's dripping."

"Cat, he's taking homeless kids to the zoo."

She met Elli's eyes. "Is that what they were?"

She nodded. "I saw the name of a shelter on the back of one of their name tags."

"Okay, I admit it. It impressed me to see him holding those two little boys' hands. But I'm not—" She took a breath. "I'm just not interested, Elli."

"I know." Her sister reached over and squeezed her arm.

Jason's sticky fingers grasped her wrist and pulled her melting ice cream to himself. "Aunt Kit-Cat, you should eat ice cream, not fingernails."

~Six~

TUESDAY AFTERNOON CAT absentmindedly brushed a layer of dirt from her desk with a paper towel. Someone must have used her office and left the window open to blow so much of it around. It seemed to her this had happened a couple of other times also. She'd have to ask the Sunday-Monday staff about it. She didn't mind sharing this room, but she had too many other housekeeping and maintenance details to be bothered with tidying up after others.

From a drawer she pulled out a clipboard. Attached to it was the checklist she had created, a combination of her own ideas and the official inspection report. Today she would go through it all again. She would make sure every millimeter of tile grout throughout the lobby was dirt free, every guest room's shower stall sparkled, every formerly leaky faucet was dry, every light switchplate factory-fresh without one fingerprint smudge, every inch of carpet shampooed, every blade of grass neatly trimmed—

She burst out laughing. No wonder her apartment was always a disaster area! She had this place to take care of.

She started with Cissy at the registration desk.

"Uh-oh," the younger woman greeted her. "Denim jumper, bobby socks and tennies, and the infamous, fluorescent lime clipboard. It looks like serious work time. I'd better warn the others."

Cat waved the clipboard above her head. "Right! It is getting-down-to-business day. Hold my calls. And move out of my way!" She scooted behind Cissy and began systematically reviewing the work station. Computer, printer, paper, pens, forms, calendar, telephones, room keys, pamphlets. "Cissy, have I ever mentioned you're welcome to come organize my apartment anytime?"

"Oh, once or twice."

"Thanks for doing such a great job out here."

"You know I love it."

"Maybe we could have fresh flowers on the counter when the big guys come for inspection? And replace that hinge there." Pointing with the pen, she indicated a cabinet door beneath the counter and then the large brass-plated letters on the wall that spelled out Castillo de Cala. "And make sure those are straight. It's a little dusty in that space beneath the counter." She smiled and wrote notes on the clipboard. "Other than that, it's perfect. As usual."

"What about my new reservation program?"

Cat sighed loudly and scrunched her eyebrows together. "I know that's more important. Supposedly it's on its way. I'll try to get an update." She found a notepad on the counter, jotted herself a reminder on the top sheet, then tucked it into her pocket. "Will you call Mandi and ask her to get the restaurant staff together at 3:45 please? And can you find Dominick? He should probably go through this with me."

"Sure."

While Cat strolled through the lobby checking for fingerprints on the knights' armor and dust on the rough-hewn end tables, she heard Cissy speaking into the walkie-talkie.

"Yo, handsome! Are you there?"

The other voice was drowned in static, but Cissy's instructions were loud and clear.

Muttering to herself, Cat finished the lobby inspection and circled back to the counter. "Cissy, that was inappropriate."

"What was?"

"I know the general consensus is he's a hunk, but flirting in public over the walkie-talkie isn't professional."

"Oh, Cat, no one's in here." She flipped back her long blonde hair.

"That's not the point."

"Do I have your permission to go out with him?"

"You don't need my permission, Cissy, you know that. Just keep it on a professional level here."

"Yeah, yeah. No huggy-kissy stuff in the lobby."

"Not even behind a tree. Consider the entire property as being in public and therefore off limits to any display whatsoever of a relationship beyond a business one. Okay?"

"Got it, *Miss* St. Clair." Her tone was borderline huffy, but she recovered quickly and smiled. "Do you want a Band-Aid for that finger?"

Cat glanced at her hands. "What— Oh, that's professional-looking." She laughed at her left ring finger. The jagged end of the nail was covered with blood.

Cissy pulled a box of bandages from a drawer and found one for her.

"Thanks." Cat set down the clipboard. "So, are you going out with him?" She winked.

"Well," she looked beyond Cat's shoulder and grinned, "I'm working on it. Hi, handsome! I mean, Mr. D'Angelo."

Cat raised her brows and leaned sideways in order to intercept Cissy's eye contact.

"Just giving you a hard time." The younger woman held up her right hand. "I'm done. Scout's honor!"

Dominick joined them. "So which is it? Handsome or mister?"

Cissy wiggled the hand she still held in the air. "Just Dominick. Hello, Dominick. Good-bye, Dominick." She meandered down to the other end of the long counter and busied herself.

Cat smiled at him as she picked up the clipboard. "Hi. How are you?" He wore his paint-spattered jeans, but she noticed he had turned his cap right side around and had put on a short-sleeved blue denim work shirt over the T-shirt.

"Fine."

"I'm doing my version of an inspection, and I thought it'd be a good idea for you to come with me. That way you can make your own list and tell me how unrealistic I'm being when I assume it can all be finished by the day after tomorrow."

"No problem." He wore his Secret Service look, his gray eyes never wavering from hers.

She thought he didn't resemble that man who two days ago escorted children around the zoo. "Did you get the goats fed?"

He nodded slightly. "Every last one of them."

"Good. Will it seriously set you back if you leave the painting for an hour or two?"

Cissy giggled as she walked back toward them. "He'll just come in again at 9 A.M." She reached across the counter and tapped his arm with a clipboard. "Here, you'll need this."

"Dominick!" Cat was flabbergasted. "You came in at 9 this morning?"

"Wanted to get an early start."

"But 9 A.M.?" She did some quick mental calculations.

He shrugged. "No reason not to."

"That's six hours' overtime!"

"Miguel and I don't want overtime, just dinner."

"Miguel came at 9?"

"No, he came about noon."

"I can get you some overtime."

"Don't worry about it. Shall we get started?"

"What were you, a Marine?"

"Hardly."

"Don't you have a life?"

"Hey, Cat," Cissy interrupted, "are you going to tell him?"

She turned to the other woman. "Tell him what?"

"About you and your inspection mode. It's starting to show."

For a moment, Cat didn't comprehend. "Oh, right. Dominick . . ." She tilted her head, closed her eyes, and in a singsong tone delivered a prepared speech the other supervisors had already heard. "Don't take anything I say for the next two weeks personally. If I see one blade of grass out of place, I may totally lose it. I'm a little uptight because I failed the last inspection, and I am absolutely determined to pass this one."

"Excuse me, but I thought you were the *assistant* manager?" he asked.

She opened her eyes. "Number two has to try harder."

He burst into laughter. "Weren't you the one who told me to lighten up? Remember, this is southern California."

She was glad to see his face soften. It helped smooth her own edginess. "Let's go. Thanks, Cissy." They walked outside and headed down the sidewalk. "I have to talk to the restaurant staff first. Will you check in the kitchen? They were trying to unclog a sink this morning, and some lightbulbs need to be replaced."

From the corner of her eye, she watched him write on the clipboard. "Dominick, I apologize. Obviously, you have a life. I just saw you with homeless kids at the zoo. Do you spend much time with them?"

"No. Just when Meg comes up with something like that outing and needs an extra pair of hands. I'm not all that altruistic. Left to my own devices, I'd be surfing or moving on down the coast."

She thought Meg must be one special lady to him. If that was his type, Cissy didn't stand a chance. "But you came in six hours early to paint."

"That doesn't involve people."

"Ultimately it does. The guests here are affected, the owners, and me." She chuckled. "Definitely me. Oh, this will be so fantastic if you finish! Promise me you won't move down the coast until after the inspection?"

"Well, I don't know. I don't often plan that far in advance. This may call for another bribe."

"You name it."

"I'll think on it."

"So why *down* the coast?"

He shrugged. "Never been to Mexico. How about you?"

"It's beautiful. Desolate and deserty, but with such friendly people. We used to drive down to Rosarito for rock lobster. I've camped right on the beach further south. And Acapulco is gorgeous. I go into Tecate all the time; it's inland and not far from here. There's so much poverty and sadness. You'd like it, a perfect home for your altruistic heart, Jack."

"Mm-hmm." He opened the door for her. "What about the drug trafficking?"

She walked inside ahead of him. "What about it? If you believe everything you hear, you'd think it was going on right out your back door. It hasn't interfered with my travels at all."

They spent the next hour and a half combing the grounds, then stopped to compare notes outside the back lobby entrance. Sufficient progress had been made on every possible detail. Cat felt confident that things were under control and even caught herself breathing a prayer of thanks.

"That's better," Dominick said.

"What's better?"

"Your dimple's back, and you haven't bitten a nail since we were at the pool."

She laughed. "I'm kind of easy to read, huh?"

He grinned. "Yeah, now that you mention it, you are. If we're done here, I'm going to get back to painting."

"Sure." She watched him walk down the sidewalk, his large frame moving with athletic grace. "Hey, Dominick, thanks," she called. "You're making this bearable."

He gave her a thumbs-up sign as he rounded the corner. "Just doing my job."

He certainly was an interesting character, Cat thought as she turned to go inside. At that moment a man burst through the door. She took a step backwards to get out of his way.

"I'm looking for the manager!" he barked. He was tall and middle-aged, with graying hair and a matching mustache that outlined a frowning mouth.

"I'm the assistant manager, sir. What's the problem?"

"Where's the manager?" His voice rose.

"He's gone for the day, but I'm here." She smiled her sweetest. "If you'll just tell me—"

He made a noise of disgust. "This is not what I signed up for. No room service, no bar, not one !%@#! thing for my teenagers to do, the !%@#! ocean is not at our doorstep, no !%@#! MTV . . ."

Inwardly she winced at his adjectives. "I apologize for the misunderstanding. We try to make it clear that our facilities are on a quiet cove that families with young children enjoy. We will find you a more suitable place and refund your money. Did you just check in?"

"You won't find a place—"

"Apologize to the lady," Dominick's voice cut in.

Cat glanced over her shoulder and saw him striding toward them. His eyes were slits and his jaw set. He was decidedly more intimidating than this irate guest. Quickly she soothed, "It's okay, Dominick. We can just—"

"It's not okay." His voice was a rumble, like a volcano about to erupt. "Mister, I repeat, apologize to the lady."

Cat thought it best to stay out of it. She bit her lip.

The man's mustache moved, but no words came from him. At last he noisily cleared his throat. "Excuse my rudeness. My wife and kids are disappointed."

"Of course they are," she said. "That's understandable. I promise, we can take care of it. If you go to the registration desk, Cissy will help you, and I'll be right there."

As the door swished shut behind the guest, she turned toward Dominick, still glowering behind her. She touched his forearm, an intuitive gesture to defuse the tension. Beneath her fingers the contracted muscle felt like a band of steel. "Hmm," she teased, "I was going to suggest you can borrow the armor from the knight in the lobby." She patted his arm. "But I don't think you need it."

The corner of his mouth lifted, and she felt him relax. "Didn't mean to spoil your fun."

"Oh, this was much more fun. I don't think he can sue us for that little exchange." She recalled Dominick's friend Meg at the zoo referring to him as a ruffian. "If he hadn't apologized, you wouldn't have done anything, would you?"

"Probably just ushered him into the lobby."

"Probably?"

He raised his eyebrows as if not sure.

She caught her breath, wondering how to tell him that combativeness was inappropriate. "Dominick, I can handle these situations. I appreciate your knightly effort, but I really was okay."

"I know you didn't need any help. It was just his screaming at you that . . ." He paused and looked away. "The last time my dad did that to my mom, I punched him. Haven't seen him since."

"I'm sorry. How old were you?"

"Ten." He shrugged. "That's life. You'd better get inside."

"Oh, yeah, right. Thanks."

Hurrying along the corridor toward the lobby, she wondered how in the world God had gotten this guy's attention. It must have been something along the lines of earth-shattering.

He needed a drink.

No, he didn't *need* one, he *wanted* one. A stiff one.

Elbows propped on bent knees, Dominick placed his hands over his face in an effort to blot out reality for just a few moments. It was dark now. He sat on the ground, behind large bushy oleanders against a wooden fence that allowed a cracked view between its slats of the service drive just outside the kitchen's patio. It was where he had hidden the night he surprised Cat after she placed trash in the dumpster.

Father God, help me. Remind me that You are all the reality I need. Help me figure out who's involved. Give me a chance to tell Cat the truth. Soon. In Jesus' name, Amen.

Cat.

She was getting to him. Working in close proximity on Tuesday, scouring the property in her meticulous way . . . He swore he could still feel the imprint of her long, cool fingers on his arm, calming the fire in him with that simple touch, with her gentle teasing about armor.

Why did he tell her about his dad? He had told only two people in twenty-five years about that incident. One was his little brother who had been at the neighbor's at the time. The other was his friend Adam.

Today he had watched her from a distance walking with Carver and Hunter, the manager. Clipboard in hand, she resembled an ad geared toward top female executives. Hair just so, the usually straight layers wavy. Black suit with white silk blouse, small gold earrings, just enough heel to accentuate her shapely legs. She looked focused, in control, not on the verge of a headache. When he questioned Cissy about the different reaction to Carver's last visit, she explained that when Cat had at least a week's notice and the visit was strictly necessary business, she could handle it.

The trial inspection had been conducted early afternoon. He knew when it was over. She came running to where he and Miguel painted, grinning and yelling, "Game time!" She had changed into shorts, T-shirt, and high-tops. A group of girls followed. He recognized them as the twelve-year-olds' softball team staying at the Castillo. From the top of the ladder, he noticed some of the younger staff members—housekeepers, waiters, cooks—noisily making their way down the sidewalk.

She clambered up a couple of the ladder rungs and yanked on the cuff of his jeans. "Come on! The other team wants you cuz you're tall."

"What's going on?" he had asked.

The grin on her face kept the dimple firmly in place. "Trenton William Carver, Jr. has declared we are in good shape, so we're celebrating. We always celebrate around here with basketball. Come on. It's mandatory!"

He spent the next hour enjoying the strangest game of basketball he'd ever played. There were people of all ages and lots of laughter. He soon learned it wasn't a foul to hug someone to prevent them from shooting. Cat hugged everyone. Even him.

He had never met anyone so wholesome who wasn't afraid of him.

Now he mouthed another prayer. *Dear Lord, I pray that she's innocent.*

At the sound of a truck braking on the other side of the fence, he turned silently and looked through the sliver of space between the boards. It should be the Thursday night produce delivery.

He had a good view of the truck because the driver had backed in. Spotlights mounted on the fence lit the driveway. The man unloaded several cartons marked *Oranges*. Around 2 A.M. when the night security guard slept in a corner of the housekeeping room, Dominick would investigate the kitchen to see if indeed oranges were in them.

After a week here, the suspicions were still vague. The Castillo was part of a route, of that much the agency was almost certain. Was it drugs going north, money going south, a collection point? Monday night's bread delivery appeared more than a practical amount in his opinion, but he hadn't been able to search the kitchen. The Friday-to-Monday night security guard didn't nap like tonight's guard. He stayed alert—all night.

Tuesday morning the vending machines were serviced, and laundry was picked up and delivered. He had missed both.

Who helped from the inside? Night security? Daytime maintenance? Registration clerks? Cissy? Not sharp enough. Part-time college kids? They were either users or were too serious about school to risk anything illegal. Kitchen staff?

The driver returned, and Dominick saw that Cat was on his heels. Her clear voice carried. "Bring me some Saturday. Please?"

The man's reply was muffled as he climbed into the back of the truck.

"Well, try hard, okay? I'm going to Tecate early Monday morning. They really need it this time." She accepted a small box marked *Avocados* from him.

"Yeah, I know, Cat," the driver replied. "I'll see what I can find."

Something twisted in Dominick's stomach. *"I go into Tecate all the time."* He remembered her talking about Mexico. Why Tecate? Nothing there but a brewery. And cocaine.

He gritted his teeth and fought down the image of Cat's fresh face grinning up at him, the dimpled cheek.

It was time to sever his emotions from the job at hand. Special Agent D'Angelo had better plunk himself back into the driver's seat and lock all feelings in the trunk. Then he'd better find a place to bury the key, far from any honey-colored eyes and disarming personality that threatened to take up permanent residence in his heart.

He had work to do. *Father, help me do it.*

— Seven —

CAT FOCUSED ON THE heavy freeway traffic zipping eastbound on the 8. The car's top was down, and her hair flew in the wind. She wore sunglasses and visor to protect her face from the hot sun, a white cotton shirt, and khaki shorts.

A box of goodies nestled in the seat next to her. Today it was carrots and potatoes, extras the produce delivery man had managed to scrounge up for her. In the back were gifts from her mother's church circle—cereal and disposable diapers. It wasn't much, but it would be appreciated as much as a rainstorm after months of drought, and it would not go to waste. The orphanage workers were smart managers, and the children ate whatever was available.

She seldom missed one of her semimonthly trips. Two Mondays out of every four she headed down to Tecate, Mexico. Her interest in the place began the Christmas she was fifteen years old. Mother had found an organization that played Santa at one of the orphanages, asking the children what they would like and making their lists available to Californians who then shopped, wrapped, and donated those items. Mother, of course, wanted to deliver them too, and she did, taking along her five children.

The smiles, hugs, game of basketball, and primitive conditions burrowed their way into Cat's heart and stayed there. Mother, disgruntled that Santa received more attention than the King whose birth they celebrated, formed her own loosely knit organization—friends who gave what they could, when they could. Through the years many subsequent trips were made.

Not all the children were orphans. Many just had to live there while parents worked elsewhere. Unable to provide homes for them, they would often visit on weekends.

That above all was what bound Cat to them, but Trent never seemed able to grasp that and often questioned her motives for regularly visiting the orphanage. Many times she had explained, "Trent, I am an orphan. Except for the grace of God and Stan and Betty St. Clair, I could have grown up in that environment."

He would pooh-pooh the explanation, reminding her she was born in the States and it was highly unlikely that environment could have been replicated here. That really wasn't the point she was trying to make. But no matter how she worded it, he just didn't get it.

An image of Dominick D'Angelo came to mind—little boy hands tucked into his large ones. Would *he* get it?

Trent visited the orphanage with her once, cringing the whole time, even while he smiled politely. Another time, just to be ornery, she begged him to let her drive his Mercedes down there. Horrified, he recounted stories of car accidents and the *federalés* confiscating American automobiles. Eventually he joined in her laughter and kissed her . . .

Sometimes she would stare at her reflection in a mirror, noting the complexion a shade deeper than her siblings, the dark hair, eyes "the color of maple syrup," in Daddy's words. And she would wonder what mixture of blood ran through her veins.

Besides the true royal blood, that is. She smiled to herself now. When her parents had explained the concept of adoption into God's family by accepting who Christ was, it was a simple one for her to grasp. It was what they had done for her. They took her into their home and asked only that she accept the gift of love they wanted to give her. The past, where she had come from, didn't make a difference—with her parents or with Jesus.

The green freeway signs now directed the way to Jamul, but

Cat navigated by rote, circling along a couple of exit ramps and onto Highway 94, which soon narrowed to a divided four-lane with stoplights. The roads and scenery had changed drastically through the years, with developments springing up like sage-brush through the dry earth. She turned at an intersection, fol-lowing the highway southeast where it soon left the heavily populated areas, shrank to two lanes, wound up and down rock-strewn hills, and shot through valleys flung with breathtaking vistas. Some S-curves were sharp, and she had to downshift, tak-ing them at thirty miles an hour. Still, it wasn't a long trip. She usually could make it from her apartment and across the border within forty-five minutes.

She moved through Jamul in the blink of an eye, then Dulzura, population all of 700, and Barrett, which was only a sign on the highway.

She took advantage of the sparse traffic and enjoyed the scenery. It reminded her of her childhood home with abundant fragrant wildflowers and scrubby bushes greener than average if the winter rains had been heavy like this year. Distant, higher hills appeared a hazy turquoise dotted with white boulders and an occasional house. The vast expanse of sky was cloudless, the blue unbroken except for an occasional soaring hawk crying in its mournful way.

Seemingly in the middle of nowhere, a border patrol build-ing came into view on her left. It was an immigration inspection checkpoint. A variety of at least ten official vehicles lined the parking lot—cruisers for highway speed, Explorers for off-road excursions, vans for hauling—all painted white with the telltale green stripe and lettering, *Border Patrol*. Two officers stood alongside the road, stopping everyone headed north. That point sometimes slowed her homeward drive.

About twenty minutes later she turned right onto Tecate Road and soon entered Tecate, California, basically just a spot at the top of a hill—a small strip mall, a border crossing, and an intriguing view of Tecate, Mexico. The border consisted of a small building off to the right and a prominent red hexagon sign with the word *Alto* rather than *Stop* on it. She sat for just a few moments as the Mexican guards greeted the occupants of three cars ahead of her before waving them into Mexico.

This wasn't the shoppers' mecca that Tijuana was. Crossing the border here was much less complicated and time-consuming and therefore much easier for her purposes. Even when there was a line of cars when she headed back and each had to be stopped and sometimes searched, it was nothing like that place.

"*Señorita* St. Clair!" The guard's teeth glistened brilliant white against his black mustache. He leaned across the passenger's side. "*Bienvenido!*"

"*Gracias*, Alberto!" Cat chatted with the young man who more often than not was at this post on the Mondays she visited. When another car approached behind her, he sent her into his homeland with a smile. She knew not everyone received that.

It always hit her when she first drove along the narrow street—an immediate sense of being inside someone's private, colorful, cluttered house. Not one inch was unused space. Her eyes couldn't put order to what she saw, bombarded as the scene was with signs, buildings, cars, plants, and people. Even above it all, the sky was crisscrossed with thick telephone and electrical cables.

The median strip was packed with flowers, squatty palm trees, and signs. Along the right curb, cars were parked bumper to bumper, block after block. People—sitting, walking, and standing—filled the narrow sidewalks outside the storefronts. These ran nonstop down both sides of the hill, all different sizes, colors, and shapes with names and descriptions painted in large letters on their stucco walls, rampant bougainvillea twisting between them.

The scene crowded out all thoughts of Trent and the upcoming inspection. Driving toward the orphanage, she knew this was the best way to spend her day off. She'd get her "*abuelita* fix," and all would be right again with the world.

Dominick's soft shoes silently hit the pavement. He spotted the Jeep parked across the street from Cat's apartment building, in view of the carport where that orange car of hers stuck out even in the dark, kind of the way a whale in the Chicago River would. When he opened the passenger's door, the dome light didn't go on. He slid inside.

"She went to an orphanage."

"An orphanage?" Dominick stared at the young man sitting behind the steering wheel. The dim glow from a distant street-light didn't reveal much of his expression.

"An orphanage. Real tough cookie you got here, D'Angelo."

He heard the sarcasm in the other agent's voice. "What else?"

"*Nada*. Little kids, basketball, loud singing in English, a bunch of women. She delivered some boxes. They dug into them outside on a picnic table. Carrots, potatoes, cereal, and—are you ready for this?—disposable diapers."

Dominick leaned back against the seat and rubbed his fore-head. Brent Engstrom, agent-in-training under him, had spent the day tailing Cat. "Orphanage," he muttered again. "What does a good-looking, single woman do on her day off? Drives through miles of desert to an obscure little town in Mexico and visits orphans. Makes perfect sense to me."

"They seemed to know her. You could tell this wasn't her first time. Shoot, the Border Patrol knew her."

"Border Patrol?"

"Yeah. Going down, the guy leaned into her car, laughing and smiling. *I* sure didn't get that from him. Coming out, the U.S. guys just waved her through, a hi-how-ya'-doin' wave. Then she parked, ran over to the Mexican guard, and gave him something wrapped in a napkin. He pulled out a pastry-looking thing and started eating it."

"So she did take something from the orphanage?"

Engstrom shrugged. "Some woman who looked about a hun-dred years old handed her a Burger King bag when she was leaving, then they hugged each other. That's what she pulled the pastry from."

"Did you watch her car?"

"Nobody went near it. I left for ten minutes, fifteen max. Had to find a bathroom. The only stop she made was at a grocery store down the street here, then home by 5. She's been inside ever since. I tell you, it's just all too innocent-looking to be a cover. I felt guilty watching her. Don't you think she's got a wholesome face?"

Dominick ignored the question. Had he ever been that wet behind the ears? Of course he had. He could hear his own voice saying almost the exact same words. *Too innocent-looking to be a cover.*

Fifteen minutes unaccounted for. Regular trips to Mexico. Familiar with border guards. A bag with unknown contents. Attractive, smart, friendly, single woman alone on her day off.

"What's she like?" Engstrom interrupted his thoughts. "Is her personality as wholesome as her looks?"

"You'll find out soon enough. Are you checking into the motel Sunday?"

"Yeah. I'm supposed to be a family man on business from L.A. The wife and kids will be down later in the week."

"Okay. I'll get her car tomorrow, have the crew go over it with a fine-tooth comb. Hadacek relieving you?"

"At midnight."

"Why don't you go get something to eat?"

"Food? I don't need food. This is the fun part. Thirteen hours straight, my eyes glued to one car—"

"Get out of here. Take my truck." He dug into his jeans pocket for the keys. "It's two blocks back."

The younger man opened his door.

"Hey, Brent—about covers."

"Yeah?"

"You never, never know."

Dominick settled back into the seat and glued his eyes to Cat's car. They would watch it until she arrived at the Castillo tomorrow. If she carried anything, it'd be unloaded there. If somehow they missed something between now and then, there'd at least be a clue. False flooring, a hidden compartment, residue. He'd find it. And he'd find her wholesomeness a cover . . . or not.

Guilty until proven innocent. You never, never knew. The one time he thought he knew, he almost got himself and two others killed. She was an attractive bundle of fun, loving and totally innocent-looking. He fell for her hard. That was one scene he wasn't about to repeat.

Not even with this Catherine St. Clair who visited orphans on her day off.

"Dominick, you don't have to do that."

He forced himself to meet those honey-colored eyes across the desk and give her a small smile. "But let me, as a token of my appreciation. Like I said, the car wash has this great deal going today. They did such a good job on the shuttle van, it'll last until inspection next week. And besides, your car's dirty. It doesn't look orange anymore."

"Tangerine." Cat opened the large Burger King bag he had noticed on her desk. "Here, have a *buñuelo*. My *abuelita* makes them for me, and they're the best in the world."

The illogical mental leaps of women never ceased to amaze him, but he tried to just go with Cat's flow. "Thanks. *Abuelita?*" He bit into the crispy, cinnamon- and sugar-coated tortilla-like strip. It melted in his mouth.

"Grandma. Well, she's not really my grandma. Everyone calls her that. I went to see her yesterday in Tecate, which explains one reason my car is so dusty. Had to get my *abuelita* fix." Her half-smile looked absentminded, as if her thoughts were miles away.

"What's an *abuelita* fix?"

"Oh, hugs and food. She prays for me, reminds me to read my Bible." Another half-smile. "Coming from a gentle grandma in Spanish, it gets my attention for some reason."

"Grandmas are like that." A fleeting image from his childhood came to mind. She had been a generous woman, like this
one before him. "Cat, I picked up my check . . ."

She stacked papers on her desk, all business now. "Sorry it
doesn't cover all the time you've put in. I don't have that much
clout."

"Well, I appreciate what you did do. Now can I get your car
washed for you? I'll use my dinner break time."

"Goodness, don't worry about that. We owe you time." She
opened a drawer and pulled out a key ring. "Thank you. I know
I won't get around to cleaning it this week."

He accepted the keys from her. "It'll make the employee
parking lot look better for inspection."

She chuckled and finally looked at him. "And I thought *I*
went overboard. I'll pay for—"

"It's a gift. I won't be gone long."

Dominick headed out the back door. Cat had been preoccupied either with her visit to Mexico or the upcoming inspection but was not concerned about letting her car go. That was a
good sign.

The top was down, as usual. He climbed in and adjusted the
seat.

"Buttering up the boss?" Cissy sauntered toward him across
the lot.

"Can't hurt, huh?" He grinned and winked, buttering her
up, front desk clerk style. How did she know everything? Flighty
as she was, this girl certainly kept her eyes and ears open.

She stopped beside the car. "Did you know Trenton Carver
gave it to her?"

"The ex-fiancé?" That explained why there were no car payments. It sounded better than a hidden stack of cash.

"Yeah. Imagine getting a brand-new SUV for nothing.
Makes me wonder if he let her keep the diamond too. Maybe it'll
show up on a necklace someday." She trailed her fingers along
his forearm. "Got any plans for tonight?"

"Just waiting for you to ask." He slipped on his sunglasses and started the engine.

"There's a big party in PB. It'll go till dawn."

"What's the occasion?"

"Tuesday night. Care to go with me?"

"Sure. How about I meet you there? Gotta feed my goldfish."

"Okay. I'll give you directions later."

He drove off and shoved aside the thought of a party in Pacific Beach. It would mean booze, smoke, deafening music, the whole gamut of drugs, sugarcoating his rebuff of Cissy's advances while his internal antenna tried to pick up leads on dealers.

Forty minutes later Cat's car was torn apart. Seats and doors lying on the garage floor, hood up, tires off. Glove compartment contents were spread nearby. Except for proof of insurance papers and owner's manual, it all looked like the paraphernalia from a woman's purse.

The head of the inspection team ordered the crew to put it back together. "It's clean, D'Angelo."

"No trace of—"

"Nothin'." He chewed his gum harder. "Zilch."

"Okay." He sensed the hope rising inside him and tried to ignore it. "I need it washed, waxed, and vacuumed."

"Nooo problem. Vacuum's over there; hose is outside, around the corner. Junior here will help you." He nodded toward Engstrom and turned on his heel.

Brent Engstrom elbowed him in the ribs. "There's a full-service car wash half a mile from here. How'd you get her car?"

"Long story." He glanced at the younger man. He had a stocky build, deep brown eyes, and a buzz haircut. "Boils down to charm. Thoughtfulness. Human kindness."

"That's not in the manual. Guess that's why I get to hang out with you. Gives me a chance to learn the unprintable stuff. So what do you think?"

What did he think? "The facts are— You know what they are. Unless she made you tailing her—"

"Impossible."

Dominick allowed himself a grin. "You're that good, huh? Okay. You said the office phone tap has come up with nothing. So unless she's simply looking the other way while drugs or money exchange hands at the motel, she's clean. And one extremely naive manager."

"How will you go about figuring that one out?"

Something that felt like the surf pounding in his chest yanked his train of thought off the track. He'd have to get close to her, spend time with her. Catch the nuances in those eyes. Memorize the cadence of the low voice. Brush the hair from her forehead. Hear her heartbeat like his own. God help him. He turned to Brent. "I just have to lay on the charm so thick it'll make a guy choke."

~ Eight ~

"LET ME GET THAT!" Dominick yelled as he hurried across the parking lot.

"I can do it," Cat replied. She gripped one end of a wooden park bench, her ever-present lime green clipboard perched on its seat. The other end was held by a teenage boy, an employee of her father's. "There's another one in that truck."

"Got it."

Cat smiled to herself as she and the boy edged along the sidewalk, the heavy bench sagging on her end. No doubt Mr. Big Muscles could flip the other bench across his shoulders and easily catch up before they reached the garden path.

The benches were great, smooth and clear-stained pine, five feet long, with wide armrests. As promised, her dad had them made. Her dad still spoiled her, but he thought it didn't hurt since she knew it and appreciated it. She should go visit the folks, but this Sunday was out, being the day before inspection. It would have to wait until the week after.

When the sidewalk turned to a stone path surrounded by huge, semitropical plants, she told the young man that was far enough and thanked him. Dominick could move it for her once she decided exactly where to place it. As she suspected, he was right behind them. Catching her breath, she noticed not even an "umpf" came from him as he gently lowered the bench from his shoulder.

He smiled. "Got a new one for you—Jill, heavyweight champ of the Castillo."

"You can have that title, Jack." She flopped onto a bench and picked up her clipboard.

"Why didn't you let me carry it?"

She shrugged and felt a tightness pull across her back. She must have strained it. "I had to do something physical to prepare for the inspection. I helped clean two rooms earlier. I'm thinking of running home to get some paint clothes."

He pointed a finger at her. "That's my department, and it's under control. I noticed the St. Clair Construction sign on the truck. Anybody you know?"

"My dad. He had these made." She patted the wood. "Nice, huh? I'll let you move them."

"Lead the way."

They meandered around the garden, imagining scenarios of guests walking along, spotting a bench, welcoming the opportunity to pause and enjoy the birds and flowers.

Dominick stood under a palm tree. "How about here?"

"No way. Your back's to the pond. Over here."

"Nobody'd even see it there. How about this?"

"Too close to the bridge." She shook her head. "It's gotta be an alone place, for reflection."

"From what I've seen, a hiding place for when the kids get crabby is more like it."

They went back and forth until she finally noticed the corner of his mouth, lost in the 5 o'clock shadow, lifting ever so slightly. He was teasing her. "Dominick! Stop it!"

He laughed. "I'd say you're a little uptight, Jill, boss lady."

"So? I already told you I would be, but you're making it worse! Just put one," she stomped to the edge of the pond and pointed, "here."

"Yes, ma'am."

While he retrieved a bench she walked along the path, then called back, "And here!" She studied the list on the clipboard, waiting for him.

He walked by, balancing the second bench on his shoulder, then reached over and gently pulled her hand away from her mouth. "Cat, I've got a better idea for you than carrying benches and chewing fingernails."

She frowned, bunched her fingers into a fist, and held it at her side.

He set down the bench. "Basketball."

"What?"

"Let me see your list."

"No—" she started to protest, but he whisked it from her hand.

"Let's say you get the benches in place," he winked at her glare, then held the clipboard high, beyond her reach, and read, "and let's see here, call the florist, do this Mandi chat . . . mmm, organize your files—ah, and get the maintenance guy—yours truly—to promise to wax the lobby floor late tonight." He looked at her. "Let's say you do all that, and then you give yourself a break."

"I'll take a break next Tuesday, when this is all over. Now may I have my clipboard back please?" She held her hand out for it, palm up.

Dominick took her hand, turned it over, and examined it. "Your nails won't last until next Tuesday. And the staff won't either without your dimple. That's what keeps us going." He tilted his head, raised his brows, and pressed his lips together, waiting.

The sense of turmoil in her mind stopped. Okay, he had her attention now. She stared back at him.

"One on one, 9 o'clock." He squeezed her hand ever so slightly before dropping it, then gave back the clipboard. "I'll meet you on the court. I'll spot you ten points." He headed down the path.

She found her voice. "You'll spot me ten?" she called. "Ha! You'll need twenty."

At 9, changed into shorts and T-shirt, Cat met him on the lighted court. She knew it was the dimple remark that got her there. Ten sweating minutes later, she knew she should have figured this out for herself. It had been too long since she had pushed herself to physical limits, cleared her head, awakened the endorphins, clarified her perspective.

"Foul!" Dominick held the ball.

"You wimp. I barely touched your arm." She knocked the ball from his hand, but he recovered it quickly and made a layup.

Spectators gathered around the perimeter of the blacktop. Cat grinned when she heard distinct female voices cheering for her.

They played seriously and evenly. Too evenly? He was head and shoulders taller, agile, and obviously stronger than she was. "Time out!" she called. They faced each other, panting. "D'Angelo, is this the best you can do?"

He wiped his forehead with his sleeve and nodded.

"Pretend like I'm not your boss." She dribbled and, seeing his split-second hesitation, stepped around him and tossed off a jump shot. She figured it would be her last one.

The score soon grew lopsided.

He cornered her while she dribbled. "Hey, boss lady," he teased, "shouldn't you get back to work? There's that inspection."

"What inspection?" Cat bounced the ball between his feet and beat him to it but was laughing so hard she couldn't do anything with it. "I quit!"

He braced his hands against his knees, breathing hard. "Mission accomplished?"

She nodded and smiled. "Thanks."

"Thank you. Your dimple's back."

Later that night the thought struck her that maybe God truly was still listening. What an odd way to bring a new friend into her life.

They played again Friday night. After that first game, Dominick noticed Cat had warmed toward him whenever they met, seem-

ingly by coincidence. She was predictable, which made her easy
to find on the property. She responded to his friendly overtures.
His charm.

He rammed his fist into the sand and gazed out at the ocean.
Hints of the morning sun's heat touched his back. In his periph-
eral view he saw a surfboard lowering next to his.

"Morning, Dominick."

"Hey, Adam."

His friend plunked down next to him. "Your words say hello,
but the expression on your face says get lost. Care to talk about
it?"

He shook his head. He really didn't. Adam's concern only
reminded him of how filthy he was. He was grateful the guy
waited awhile before breaking the silence.

"Meg will want to know. Things are pretty bad, huh?"

"I'm getting out. Soon as this is over."

"That's cool."

"Adam, I think she's innocent, but I don't know that for a
fact, and now I'm pretending like I want to be her friend, and
she's falling for it hook, line, and sinker."

"How are you doing that?"

Dominick lifted a shoulder. "Anticipating her needs. Being
there when she needs help. Listening when she wants to talk.
Suggesting ways she can be less stressed out about her job.
Playing basketball with her."

"Just paying attention, huh?"

"Yeah, basically."

"Do you want to be her friend?" Adam asked. "I mean, is she
someone you'd choose to be friends with if you met her in a different setting?"

He didn't respond.

"You don't know, do you?" Adam's voice sounded exasper-
ated. "Take a minute and think about it. Just be a man, not
Dominick D'Angelo, special agent for the Drug Enforcement
Administration. Here you've got a woman who, from your

description, makes others feel special, and she's attractive in a Wheaties-box way. Athletic. She knows Christ."

Cat doesn't matter, he thought. *She isn't the point.* The point was, how could he separate himself from what he did? Impossible! He had no other identity.

"And her eyes do a number on you."

"I didn't tell you about her eyes."

"You didn't have to."

Dominick laid back on the sand, arm propped under his head, and stared at the blue sky but saw only dark lashes and honey-colored eyes that crinkled when she laughed. He had it bad, and Adam could tell.

"Look, Dominick, I know you got taken one time, and it hurt. But you now have a relationship with God, and you can believe that He brought you to this situation. If you like her, then like her and stop feeling guilty about it. If she's responding, maybe she needs a friend just like you."

"She doesn't even know who I am."

"I don't think that matters at this point. She knows you better than you know yourself. She's seeing you from the inside. That's where your real identity is. And you want my opinion?"

"No."

"You're seeing her from the inside. You're seeing the real Cat St. Clair. That's what's drawing you to her." Abruptly, Adam stood. "The bottom line is, it's just too weird that you found her under these circumstances. God has put you there for a reason. Now answer the question."

"What was the question?"

"Would you want to be her friend if you didn't have to be?"

Dominick sat up and brushed sand from his hair. "I think if I think too long about it, I'll think I'm falling in love with her. Does that answer your question?" He squinted up at his friend.

A smile spread slowly across Adam's face. "I wonder why I had to ask it."

By Saturday night Cat admitted to herself that Dominick's shaggy good looks and friendly demeanor were growing on her.

She lived and breathed inspection preparations that week, neglecting her apartment more than usual, the pot shop, Elli, and eating. At least the basketball games had provided a stress outlet. That helped along with manager Ron's kudos. Visiting Tecate had helped. She had even read a few Psalms. But she was still knotted up inside. The Castillo was her life, and if it didn't pass inspection this time, she and Ron would be standing in the unemployment line come Tuesday morning. Maybe she could go to Dominick's temp agency.

She drummed her fingers on her desk. This line of thinking was going nowhere.

It was late, almost time to go home. The painting was done, except for some trim work in the southeast corner. Dominick had promised to come in tomorrow and finish it. The man really went overboard helping out. Where had he come from? It was such a pleasure to meet someone with his work ethic. The funny part was that from his looks, you'd expect the exact opposite. On the other hand, impeccably dressed, polite, and wealthy Trent should be a role model for gracious, overboard giving.

He probably billed the hours he spent on dates with her.

She caught herself smirking. *Oh, let's not go down that road.*

Cat headed outside. She might as well try to walk this off with one more round of the property.

She followed her usual route but didn't go inside the restaurant. Instead, she breezed passed its patio side, then down along the west wing and beach area. As she neared the equipment booth, she heard glass breaking and loud voices from the direction of the pool. She ran toward it. In the distance, shadowy figures crashed through the gate. Since it was after-hours, the lights were dimmed. *No one should be in that area!*

"Hold it!" she yelled. Nobody stopped.

Another figure stood near the pool. Cat ran that direction and realized it was a girl. When she reached her, she heard her crying and saw she was holding her upper arm. "What happened?" she asked. A quick glance about the area told her what had happened. Turned-over chairs, a table, and broken glass glimmering in the low lamplight. Simple. Kids had been breaking rules. "Are you hurt?"

The girl whimpered, and Cat helped her sit in a lounge chair. Her hand felt something warm and sticky. "Let me see." She moved the girl's hand and bit back a gasp. Even in the semi-darkness it was obvious she was bleeding profusely. "Lie down. I'll get a towel."

She ran the length of the pool to the bathhouse, a doorless concrete block. There was no time to use the phone. She flipped on the interior lights and the exterior spots, grabbed a towel, and ran back. She held up the girl's arm, wrapped the towel around it, and pressed firmly. Why hadn't she carried a walkie-talkie?

"Cat?" It was Dominick.

"Oh, thank God! I think we need an ambulance."

"I'll call."

She soothed the girl, who continued to cry. She appeared about thirteen. Cat finally got her name, but she didn't give a room number. The towel was soaked through. "Dominick! Bring more towels."

He returned, knelt beside her, and helped replace the towel. "Guess a tourniquet won't help." The cut was too high underneath her arm. "What's her name? I'll go call the front desk, see if we can find her parents."

She continued soothing the girl, never letting up on the pressure. At last she heard the sirens.

"Cat, are you okay there?" Dominick rushed past. "I'm going to meet them, direct them to this end of the parking lot."

"Go."

It seemed an eternity. The girl stopped crying, and her eyes closed. Cat prayed. At last the paramedics arrived. They nudged her aside and took over. Another eternity passed.

"Is she okay?"

"She'll be fine, ma'am."

Cat and Dominick followed them to the ambulance. As the

EMTs were lifting the stretcher into it, the parents showed up. It seemed like they hurried from the parking lot; they must not have been in the motel.

Cat's job was over. Silently she and Dominick returned to the pool. "I'll hose it down," he said.

Cat tried to nod, but there was a rushing sound in her head, and she couldn't make it stop. She went into the women's changing room and stood at the sink before the mirror. Blood streaked her face, soaked the front of her chartreuse silk blouse and beige slacks. Her hands were red. She turned the hot water on full blast, vigorously pumped the liquid soap onto her hands, and held them under the stream. The water turned pink and then blurred before her eyes.

"Why can't people just follow the rules? No glass in the pool area. Do not enter after-hours. Do not run. Simple, simple rules! Why can't they just follow them?"

As he hosed down the pool deck, Dominick heard the sobs above the spray whooshing across the concrete. He knew she was coming unglued.

He lowered the hose, directing the cleansing stream toward the grass beyond the fence, and hurried into the open bathhouse.

"Cat . . ."

She was talking to herself, tears falling down her face harder than the water from the faucet that she held her hands under. In between sobs he heard "rules" and "stupid" and "AIDS."

He found a towel and went to her. "Cat, let's dry your hands." He turned off the water and clasped her hands within the towel. The front of her blouse was almost completely covered with blood.

"Dominick, why can't people just follow the rules? They're so simple! No one would get hurt—"

"It's over, Cat." He unbuttoned the denim work shirt he

wore over a sleeveless T-shirt. "Here, get rid of your blouse and put this on."

He went back outside to put away the hose. He could hear her still crying.

She emerged, buttoning the shirt that looked like a big robe on her. In her hand was a rolled-up white towel with a corner of her bright green blouse poking through. She shoved them into a nearby trash can. "What was I supposed to do?" Her voice rose, her words rushed together. "Tell her to stop bleeding for a minute while I go hunt up some latex gloves? 'Maybe there's some down in Housekeeping, I'll be right back'? Why can't people just follow a few stupid rules? I should have had a walkie-talkie! Oh, why don't I carry it all the time? I always think I can handle everything! Idiotic—"

He went to turn off the lights. She was scared. He thought of her broken nails and cut skin and hepatitis and HIV. As he walked back outside, he prayed, *Dear Father, protect her.*

She stood hugging herself, whining managerial-type orders to him in an unnaturally high voice. "You know, we have to scrub the deck with special—"

He wrapped his arms around her, cutting off the flow of hysteria-edged words. "I know. It's all taken care of. You probably saved her life, Cat. Everything's all right. Shh."

It felt right to hold her, to press her forehead against his chest, to tighten his arms around her trembling shoulders. When her crying slowed in only a few moments, a twinge of disappointment surprised him.

"You okay?"

She nodded against him.

"Come on then. It's time for you to go home." He released her.

She was quiet as they walked through the courtyard, abnormally quiet after such an outburst. In the brightly lit lobby she mumbled a thank you. He watched her walk rigidly down the hallway, arms crossed over her stomach and head held at a stiff angle. It was the way she had walked that time after Carver's visit. Cissy had given her something for headache pain, but Cissy wasn't here tonight. Was this the same thing?

He stopped to tell the desk clerk that the girl's parents had arrived, then hurried to Cat's office. She was digging through a large handbag on the desk. "Want me to get you something?" he asked.

Her breathing was labored, and the tears were spilling over again. "No." She rummaged in the bag, her obvious frustration growing, then groaned and sank into the chair, leaning her forehead against the bag. "It's not here."

"What isn't here?"

"Migraine stuff. I don't need it because I don't get them anymore."

"Have you got one?"

"Mm-hmm."

"I'll take you home." He helped her to her feet.

Without protest she leaned on his arm all the way to his truck. He half lifted her up into it, where she immediately laid down on the bench seat.

Ten minutes down the freeway he remembered that he knew where he was going, but he hadn't been given that information by her. He had been to her place that night with Engstrom, but she didn't know that. "Cat, what's your address?"

She mumbled something.

There, that was covered. *Man, what a night!*

Not wanting to have his truck towed away, he parked in the carport slot where her car had been, then flicked on the dome light. "Cat, where's your key?"

She pushed herself up, unsnapped the handbag, and slid it toward him. Her hair was mussed and her eyes puffy slits.

He hesitated. He was accustomed to searching personal items that did not belong to him, but for the first time it seemed like an invasion of privacy.

Gingerly he picked up the large purse and peered inside. The scents of leather, minty gum, and her subtle, citrus-like perfume wafted out. It was so like her, basic and wholesome. And, so like her, a ring of keys was attached to a clip just below the opening. Miss Jill Assistant Manager was organized. He almost smiled in relief.

He helped her out of the truck and to the back of the square building, where he unlocked the door. Inside, as they climbed a flight of stairs, she leaned heavily against him, clutching his arm. They stopped outside a door on which was a peephole with a silver number 3 attached above it. He unlocked it with another key. The doorknob turned, but the door didn't budge.

Cat, leaning now against the wall, pointed to another lock, a deadbolt. He fiddled with the keys again and at last got the thing unlocked and ushered her inside.

She flipped a light switch, opened a kitchen cupboard, pulled out a prescription bottle, and handed it to him. He twisted the cap off and poured two capsules into his palm. She took one and disappeared around a corner.

He swept his gaze over the combined kitchen and living room, trying not to feel as if he were snooping, which he knew was exactly what he was doing in this case. Ever since that moment he held her at the pool, it seemed professional habit kept bumping into a mishmash of feelings. He wasn't sure how to act. Friend or DEA agent on duty?

Familiar with the appearance of her office and now her purse, her home was surprisingly a cluttered place. Dishes were in the sink. On the other side of a counter covered with an assortment of pottery, he saw clothes and reading material strewn around the living room. He looked in cabinets, stepped to the half-empty bookshelf and read titles of hotel-related books, peeked through the blinds and saw the top of the carport.

Cat came from a short hallway that must lead to the bedroom. She still wore his shirt and now white sweatpants. She trudged on bare feet to the refrigerator, a cloth bag in her hand. He realized it was an ice bag and offered to fill it for her. While he did so, she picked up a cordless telephone and started punching in numbers.

He took it from her, handed her the ice bag, and pressed the off button. "It's after midnight, Cat. Who are you calling?"

She closed her eyes. Her voice was barely a whisper. "Trent."

"Why?"

She turned away and shuffled to the couch.

He knew this was none of his business, but he followed her and repeated, "Why?"

She rested her elbows on her knees, pressing the bag against her forehead. Tears slid beneath her lashes. "To come hold me."

The two steps it took to reach her side crossed something more significant than the short distance between them. Dominick knew it the instant he sat next to her and she leaned into the circle of his arms.

~Nine~

RED LIGHT DANCED behind her closed lids.

Cat groaned and rolled over to her other side, burying her face against the back of the couch.

Couch? She groaned again.

Awareness came slowly, as it always did after a migraine. First was the obvious giveaway—that drugged feeling. Thoughts formed like cobwebs in a dark closet, threads hanging with no form, so little to grasp and comprehend. The metallic taste on her tongue begged for a toothbrush scrubbing, the first thing she would do as soon as her legs and brain connected.

She rolled over again and let the sunlight tease open her eyelids. Why was she on the couch facing west, not in her bed facing north? Sunlight . . . west . . . Good grief! It was afternoon. Whoa, back up. What *day* was it? Sunday. At least she wasn't late for work. Normally this would be a day off, but with the inspection coming . . .

She felt warm, peered down at a blanket, and kicked it off. Why was she wearing sweatpants and—and— Her eyes were wide open now, and she clutched the large piece of denim she wore. Dominick's shirt?

Last evening came back to her now. The accident at the pool, herself in the bathhouse, nearly hysterical, throwing away her blouse and the towel. Soaking the beige slacks in her tub. They would never be the same.

She studied her hands, the cracked skin around the short

nails. *What kind of germs had seeped in there?* A sense of dread washed through her, then settled like cold fingers clutching some inner part of herself, a fitting companion to that other constant fear, the one that was now over seven months old.

Oh, God, where are You?

She had been feeling better, coping better these past couple of months. How could she still so totally lose it?

She groaned again and willed herself to ignore the frustration and instead consider the facts. The past two weeks had been the most draining she'd put herself through in a long time. She had felt up to the task and so pushed herself to the limit. When Ron wasn't paying attention, she had put in a few twelve- and ten-hour days. But by last night she was running on empty.

Tears of frustration smarted her eyes. When would she ever just get over it? When would she not succumb to a migraine over some accident that truly was beyond her ability to prevent? When could she throw away the prescriptions, those drugs she couldn't function with or without?

She wiped the corner of her eye with the shirt sleeve. A faint scent of soap cut through her thoughts. Irish Spring maybe?

The cordless phone rang on the coffee table at her side, but it was ringing for a third time before she managed to pick it up and push the on button.

"Cat, it's Ron. You're not coming in, are you?"

Well, she had planned on it. "I thought—"

"Stay put. Dominick told me about last night. The girl's fine. And I mean she's fine, Cat. She's an extremely healthy young girl, okay? And everything is under control here. The painting is even done. How are you?"

"All right," she lied.

"Well, I know you got one of your headaches, so I want you to promise me you'll stay home and not push it. You know you'll be better for it in the morning, and *that's* when I need you."

She closed her eyes and imagined the Castillo. It had looked perfect yesterday, but would it stay that way without her there today? Had Dominick completely cleaned up the pool area? Her head throbbed. "I promise."

Deep laughter filled the receiver. It wasn't just the manager's. "She promises not to go anywhere!" More laughter.

"What's so funny?"

"You *can't* go anywhere. Your car's here in the lot!" he roared. "Oh, sorry. We couldn't help it. Dominick's here—he wants to talk to you. Don't worry about anything. I'll see you tomorrow."

"Hmm."

"Hi, Cat. You feeling better?"

"Uh, yes. Thanks for bringing me home."

"You're welcome. I'll come pick you up tomorrow, unless you want your car today? Never mind, Ron says you're not going anywhere today, so your car stays put. So, what time tomorrow?"

"Uhh." What was his schedule? What was hers? Why—

"Eight o'clock early enough? The bigwigs are coming at 10."

"Okay."

"Need anything else?"

"Uhh, no. Thank you."

"See you in the morning then." The line went dead.

She clicked the phone off. Maybe she'd just sleep until tomorrow. Maybe it'd all go away between now and then.

She turned back on her side and smelled the soap again.

Dominick D'Angelo. Jack-of-all-trades to the rescue. At the pool. In the office, understanding that she was in no shape to drive. At home, unlocking the door, opening the bottle, filling the ice bag, not letting her make a fool of herself by calling Trent. At her side. Holding her until the fear and the pain floated away on the drugged sea.

She hadn't been aware when he left. Now she glanced around the apartment. The lights were off; the ice bag was on the counter, cap off. The quilt from her bedroom covered her; a pillow was under her head. He was like that, attentive to details. Attentive to her needs.

Trent wouldn't have come anyway. He had stopped coming

a long time ago. His voice would still have been a comfort, but nothing like—

Cat tried to stop the thought from forming, but it kept coming, riding the coattails of a warm, snug, carbonated fizzy feeling.

Nothing like those massive arms of Dominick holding her gently against his chest. Nothing like his deep voice laughing just now through the telephone, scattering any discomfort or embarrassment she might feel over last night, anticipating and promising to take care of her need for a ride tomorrow.

She combed her fingers through her hair. He was a drifter sort, had a good friend named Megan, and drove a pickup truck. And Cat was, as the phrase went, on the rebound.

She wrapped his shirt tightly around herself. This could be dangerous territory, and she had absolutely no business entering it.

At 7:55 the next morning Cat found Dominick outside her apartment building, arms crossed, leaning against his truck. What she had thought was a nondescript exterior now looked bright emerald green. He seemed to be into clean vehicles this week. It wasn't bad looking for a pickup—full-sized cab, short bed, a model of fairly recent history, not many dings.

As she approached, he slipped off his sunglasses and slid them into his shirt pocket, another denim like the one she carried. He wore neatly pressed khakis, and his thick black hair was damp and almost looked as if it had been brushed.

He smiled. "What would you do if I whistled right now?"

"Fire you."

"That's what I figured." His ice gray eyes were twinkling in the sunlight. "What if I said you're looking especially lovely and professional this morning?"

"I'll buy that." Her ears felt warm. "I mean— Oh!"

"A little nervous, are we?" He chuckled and opened the passenger's door for her.

"Thank you. Here's your shirt." *Duh*, she thought to herself, *like he can't see.* She laid it and her bag on the seat and realized

she was stretching upward. She eyed the height of the floor-
board. Her ivory suit skirt and heels were not going to make it,
but she lifted a foot anyway, then set it back down on the
concrete.

"Need a boost?"

Cat turned toward him. "I could just stay home."

"And miss all the fun?" He placed his hands around her
waist, bunching up the suit jacket. "Duck your head."

She balanced her hands on his shoulders as he lifted her
onto the seat. "Thank you."

He shut the door and leaned through the open window, his
face sober. "You forgot something."

Her breath caught in her throat; a mental checklist raced
through her mind. Everything was done. "What?"

"Your dimple."

"That's not funny. Just get in the truck."

He laughed and walked around to climb in the driver's side.
"You'll be fine." He started the engine. "You look terrific, the
epitome of an assistant manger. The Castillo is in tip-top shape.
Ron says everything is under control. I do have one question
though." He glanced at her as he stopped at a red light.

"What?" She heard the exasperation in her voice.

"Your files." He turned to her, his brow furrowed. "I hope
they're not as messy as your apartment?"

Her jaw dropped.

Dominick smiled and drove through the intersection. "I
mean, that could be a problem, you know?"

"You're fired."

"For what?"

"You can't talk to me that way."

"What way? Just stating a fact?"

"My housekeeping habits are off-limits, bud."

"Well, if they're related to this inspection, for which I have
put in almost as many hours as management—"

"For three weeks!"

"Three *crucial* weeks." The corner of his mouth lifted ever so slightly.

"Dominick, stop it! If I laugh, I'll start crying."

He glanced at her. "Take a deep breath."

She did as he suggested while keeping her eyes on the freeway traffic. "Okay. I'll be fine." It sounded like a whimper. She cleared her throat. "I'm fine." She took another shaky breath. "Anyway, why are you here? This is your day off. Ron could have picked me up."

"He's busy." He paused. "With your files."

She burst into laughter. The carbonated fizz bubbled again. If she had made this trip by herself, she would have been a mess by the time she reached the Castillo. "Thanks. I think you're making this less difficult."

"Good."

From the corner of her eye, Cat peered at him. "And thanks for, umm, for taking care of things Saturday night. And me."

"No problem. A guy's gotta look after his boss. Especially since she promised to take him to dinner."

The painting challenge! "Oh, yeah, dinner." He was serious about that?

"Miguel and I thought tonight would be good, since the three of us have it off."

"Tonight?"

"Unless you have some other plans to celebrate passing inspection?"

"No. I was just hoping not to be having a pity party."

"You're sure? Carver won't want to take you to dinner?"

"N-no." She looked out the side window. "It was stupid of me to want to call him. We won't be going for dinner. Or anything."

Dominick reached over and nudged her hand from her mouth. "I bet you'll want to celebrate. So, how about you, me, and Miguel? What's your favorite Italian place?"

She thought for a moment. "I have a few, in the Gaslamp District downtown. Have you been there?"

He had. For the remainder of the drive they discussed the variety of menus and the ambience of the district's sidewalk dining. They decided on a particular restaurant. As he parked at the motel, he said, "Shall I pick you up about 7:30? I'll get Miguel first."

Miguel or no Miguel, this resembled a date, which was more than she wanted to try to handle just now. "I'll meet you there. At 8?"

"All right. Wait, don't move." He ran around the truck to open her door. "If you jump out on those heels, you'll be in the emergency room instead of on the inspection tour." He grasped her waist again.

"Thanks." She retrieved her bag from the seat and glanced up at him. "And, umm, well, thanks." Her heels clicked across the parking lot.

She had considered wearing flat shoes and slacks, but the thought of what Trent liked nagged at the back of her mind. Trent and the other testosterone-type owners. There was a very real possibility they would admire her in a skirt more than they would the completed painting job. At the very least this suit would make a favorable impression. Was she being unfair, manipulative, untrue to herself . . . or just plain practical?

"Hey, Cat!" Dominick's voice broke through her thoughts.

She turned around.

He placed a finger on his left cheek and smiled.

She returned his smile and gave him a thumbs-up sign. *Dimple. Okay—dimple, skirt, and high heels. And my best efforts. Let's do it.*

~ Ten ~

CAT RAN ACROSS THE downtown street, then hurried along the sidewalk, dodging passersby. No heels tonight. She moved freely in an ankle-length black knit dress, her bare feet wrapped in comfortable espadrilles, the long purse strap across a shoulder. It was 8:10, and she had parked three blocks away.

Even if she had been early, she would have raced. It was as if fireworks were exploding inside her, ricocheting great bursts of energy that sent her legs flying, her heart laughing, and her arms aching to be flung around someone. She had hugged Ron and the housekeeping ladies, but that was hours ago. Elli hadn't been available all afternoon, and Cat hadn't had the time to drive to her parents' home.

At the restaurant she stopped near the maitre d's outdoor stand. A group of people blocked the entrance to the sidewalk dining area, which was surrounded by a three-foot-high wrought-iron fence. The typically beautiful, cool summer evening meant that even a Monday was crowded.

"Oh!" she cried aloud in frustration. Stretching, she peered over heads and spotted Dominick standing and waving at her from the far corner. "Oh!"

She couldn't get through. And she couldn't wait another moment. She stepped back out of line and ran along the side-walk. "Dominick!" she squealed when she reached him. Balancing with a toe on the fence crossbar between them, she reached over and threw her arms around his neck. "We did it!"

He hugged her back and laughed. "Told you so."

"Help me over this thing." She bent her knees, lifting up her heels.

His arms tightened, and he hoisted her smoothly over the low fence. "Do you always make such a grand entrance?"

She smiled at nearby diners who chuckled in their direction and slid onto the chair he pulled out for her. "I'm sorry I'm late. Where's Miguel? I need to hug Miguel too."

Dominick sat across from her and folded his hands on the small, linen-covered table. A votive candle glowed from a glass bowl between them. "He couldn't make it. At the last minute one of the grandkids got sick, and they needed him at home. I was at his house when it happened, too late to reach you. I hope you don't mind?"

She was struck then with his dark good looks. He wore a black suit, white shirt, and red tie. In the dim light cast from the restaurant's interior through a large window, his black hair shone. It was combed off his forehead. She knew it wouldn't stay there. "Uhh, no, of course not. That's, umm, too bad. You look really different. Nice. Really nice."

The right corner of his mouth tucked itself into the recesses of his shadowed jaw. "Thanks. Bet you thought I didn't own a suit."

"Never thought about it. Oh, I feel like I'm going to pop," she giggled.

"Here comes the maitre d'. You could hug him. Then maybe he won't throw you out for climbing over his fence."

A man wearing a tuxedo and a small, formal smile appeared at her side. "Good evening, ma'am, and welcome." He handed her an oversized menu, then turned to Dominick, eyebrows raised, and said something in Italian.

Dominick replied, and the man left.

"You speak Italian?" she asked.

He shrugged. "My grandmother spoke nothing else, so I know phrases. And I can read a menu."

"What did he say?" Why had she never noticed his thick eyelashes before?

"He said you were worth waiting for."

"He did not."

"All right. Truth. He said you were prettier than I described you, and he hoped I was proposing tonight because any woman who climbed over fences would not be available for long."

"Dominick!"

He chuckled. "I asked him to bring you an S. Pellegrino."

That he knew which sparkling water she preferred was more unnerving than his compliments. She held the large menu in front of her face. He placed a finger on it and pulled it down.

"I haven't said congratulations yet. Congratulations." He smiled.

"Thanks. I tried to find you when it was all over."

"I saw the entourage leave and heard you scream, so I knew the verdict. I left. After all, it was my day off. What'd you do?"

She touched his arm. "I appreciate your coming in when you didn't have to. Well, after I finished screaming, I shopped for staff gifts. And—" She pointed a finger at him. ". . . and, no wise-cracks now, I cleaned my apartment and got ready for my—for dinner." Again she held up the menu. She had almost said "my date." It must be the adrenaline still pumping from the excitement of passing inspection that caused this fluster. It had nothing to do with the S. Pellegrino set before her now or the attentive friend sitting across the table. Wearing a suit.

"Cat, do you know yet what you'd like?"

She shook her head. "I can't think straight. What do you recommend?"

They discussed a few items, and then he ordered for them, the Italian flowing from him without hesitation.

He listened to her babble on about the inspection, through the soup and salad courses, until at last she ran out of breath. As steaming dishes of pasta were served, she held up her hands. "Okay, I'm done. This was a major ordeal for me. Sorry."

"Don't apologize. I've enjoyed watching it all come about, and I'm glad you succeeded."

"Well, we do have to make some changes in order to meet the budget. Umm, this is great."

"It is. My *nonna* would be impressed. Are you firing me for real then?"

"No. Actually, we want to hire you full-time, permanent. Are you interested?"

He raised his eyebrows.

She rushed to add, "I don't have to know tonight." The thought occurred to her that the word *permanent* wouldn't be in this man's vocabulary. No doubt he'd be moving on soon. But she didn't want to hear those words just yet.

He gave her a small smile. "I'll think about it. So how's the conversation with God going?"

She shrugged. "I was wondering, how did He get your attention?"

Dominick looked down at his plate. "I was in an accident about two years ago."

"A serious one?"

"Yeah. Anyway, the doc and I became friends. He surfs with me sometimes." He looked at her now. "Remember meeting Megan at the zoo? He's her husband."

"Oh." *Ohh! Megan has a husband.*

"They sort of adopted me, and I just sort of kept watching the way they lived. I admired them, and they told me about Jesus. How about you?"

"Nothing so dramatic as a serious accident. My parents included Jesus in every decision, every meal, most conversations. He was part of our life, and I understood at an early age what He had done for me and that I could accept Him or not. I saw no reason not to or to put it off for later. Even now . . ." She toyed with her fork. "Mother and Daddy think it's a faith-stretching time for me. I haven't turned my back on God—I just don't want to look Him in the face. I feel as if He let me down."

"So it's hard for you to trust Him?"

She nodded.

"What happened?"

She met his eyes. The gray was melted ice tonight, concerned, curious. She hadn't noticed the Secret Service look about him for a long time. "I call it my nightmare. You really want to hear it?"

"I really want to know all about you, Cat St. Clair."

That fizziness bubbled inside her again. "Well, since I already offered you dinner and a job, I guess you're not just being polite, huh?" she teased.

He grinned and pushed aside his empty plate. "No, I'm not just being polite."

"Okay." She took a deep breath. "About seven months ago, right after Christmas, Elli—you met my sister at the zoo—Elli and her little boy and I were at Bay Village, that outdoor mall just off the freeway on Friars Road. Jason's favorite place is the fast-food restaurant there, so we stopped in. They got in line, and I headed toward a table in the back. This—this big guy with a gun . . ." She stopped and bit a fingernail.

Dominick gently pulled her finger away from her mouth, placed her hand on the table, and covered it with his own. His thumb stroked her wrist.

She cringed. "All of a sudden I felt a yank on my ponytail. Then there was this gun in my face. People were screaming, and he was shouting at me. A policeman yelled something about the wrong one. They ran off. It was all over within a split second." She let out her breath. "I guess I fainted. My head hit the floor. I've been a basket case ever since." She shook her head. She'd spare him the details, about how fear had totally affected everything she did. "It's no big deal. I should be over it by now."

He squeezed her hand. "Of course it's a big deal. You weren't seriously hurt, but I imagine you were scared to death. That doesn't go away overnight. What did he look like?"

"I don't know. It happened too fast. He wore sunglasses and an army green jacket. He had a full beard. He was just . . . just big. When he turned, I saw hair pulled back in a ponytail. It's pretty much just a blur."

"Where does Trenton Carver come into the picture?"

She stared at him. *How did he—? Oh, probably Cissy.* Although Cissy didn't know this story, she would have told Dominick something about her odd behavior and the broken engagement. "Trent didn't want to be engaged to a basket case. It didn't fit the job description." She bit her lip. "No, that's unfair. I became extremely fearful. I had nightmares. I got my long hair cut off. I moved out of my apartment to another one. I had migraines all the time. I still haven't set foot in that mall again. I wasn't the woman he had proposed to. He couldn't or wouldn't go through it with me. Probably a little of both. We decided not to get married."

"I'm sorry."

"The hard part is, I've always followed God's rules, and this is what He let happen. I wanted to marry Trent and have a big family. What was so wrong with that?"

He squeezed her hand. "What happened to the guy with the gun?"

She shrugged.

"Didn't you tell the police?"

"No. In the first place I wanted to totally forget it ever happened. And I know he just made a mistake. Elli and I figured he was an undercover cop and I happened to fit the description of somebody he was after. He was just trying to do his job. Phoning the police wouldn't change what had happened. God could have taken him another direction."

He removed his hand from hers. "Do you want some coffee?"

It seemed an abrupt change of subject. "Uhh, sure." Her hand felt empty.

He signaled the waiter and ordered it. "The bottom line then is that God let you down." He looked at her. "What do you think it would take for you to get back on speaking terms with Him?"

She fiddled with a spoon. "I used to think if Trent changed

. . . you know, and we got back together . . . But it's more than that. I'm just so afraid. Of *everything*. If I weren't afraid—if God could rewind that split moment when my life fell apart, like— oh, I don't know—walk me back through it and swing His divine sword at all the fears and banish them and tell me *why* it had to happen . . ." She looked back at him. "That might do it. In the meantime—ice cream!"

The waiter set silver bowls of spumoni before them along with the coffee.

"Thanks, Dominick."

He grinned. "You're paying for it."

She grinned back at him, then sobered. She had just told him everything, including her innermost feelings. "Not many people know my story. Only Trent and Ron and my family."

He reached over and brushed hair from her brow. "It's safe with me, *mi gatita*."

Later, after dinner, they both drove to the Castillo. Cat was pleased that Dominick wanted to accompany her. It seemed only appropriate after his weeks of hard work that he would be nearby while she personally thanked staff members. And she wanted to give his gift to him there.

She smiled to herself, watching him saunter toward her across the parking lot. *Appropriate* had little to do with it. She was enjoying his company, probably beyond what was appropriate, given his drifter status and her rebound status. But that exact combination made him less of a threat. He'd be leaving, and she was just taking advantage of an available male shoulder to lean on, no strings attached. Maybe that was what had granted her heart permission to notice his manliness tonight and to trust him with the nightmare.

A shiver went through her. She didn't know why she had done that, told him about that day.

God knows. Her mother's voice popped into her mind. The phrase was from a children's book she had often read to them, something about mysteries in nature. Every page asked the question, "Who knows how this and that can be?" The only answer of course was, "God knows, that's who!" Mother used it to answer the countless unanswerable questions that arose in the lives of her five children. It wasn't a flippant retort; the four words were packed full of assurance.

It reminded Cat of something from the Proverbs. "There are three things which are too wonderful for me. Yes, four which I do not understand: the way of an eagle in the air, the way of a serpent on a rock, the way of a ship in the midst of the sea, and the way of a man with a virgin."

That last one she certainly didn't understand. Dominick strolled toward her now, and that carbonated fizziness effervesced through her. Absolutely, totally illogical.

His demeanor was nonchalant with suit coat open and flapping in the breeze, hands stuffed in the pockets of his slacks.

"For a temp," she teased, "you sure act like a permanent employee, coming in at all hours, any time of day or night."

"Maybe it's the company." He winked.

"Mm-hmm." She turned to go inside. "You sure know how to make points too."

He opened the door for her. "Did I mention names?"

"No, you didn't. Excuse me for assuming it was present company."

"Did I say it wasn't?"

Cat laughed and stopped beside the door to Housekeeping. "I'm going this way."

He waved and headed down the hallway. "I'll be in the lobby."

Her first hug and gift certificate went to a second shift housekeeper. Afterwards she meandered through the courtyard toward the pool and sports equipment shed where Kevin should be. She and Ron had decided they wanted to give tokens of their appreciation to the staff. It would strain the budget, but this moment called for it. Cat had spent the afternoon shopping for the people she knew well enough to make their certificate a little more personal by purchasing it at a favorite store of theirs. Tomorrow she would see Miguel and Mandi and others, but tonight she wanted to catch a few who wouldn't be around then. And of course she wanted to hug Cissy as soon as possible because she played such a major role in keeping things running smoothly.

The Castillo felt like Cat's to care for again. It had passed the test. With the inspection cloud no longer hanging over her, she could relax in maintaining the status quo and could pursue the creative side of making the motel a memorable place for guests. The owners had approved a new ad campaign of hers, something that had slipped through the cracks after she and Trent parted ways.

She gazed up at the stars. Saturday's migraine indicated it wasn't over yet. But it was *almost* over, of that she was certain. *Thank You, Lord.*

Where had that come from?

She continued down the sidewalk and, out of habit, made her rounds, greeting a few guests along the way. Since she hadn't brought her keys, she skipped the restaurant. Dominick met her as she came around the front of the building.

"Cat, who else delivers on Monday nights besides the bread guy?"

"Nobody. Why?"

"I just saw an unmarked white van fly out of the service drive."

"Maybe the bread truck was out of commission and he used a private van." She glanced at her watch. "And came early."

"I think we should check it out. I got the keys from Cissy."

They walked to the back and entered through the kitchen door. Cat flipped on the lights. "No bread yet."

After a quick search inside and out, they concluded that nothing appeared out of place. "Probably just kids out cruising," he offered.

Back in the lobby Cat hurried around the front desk to hug Cissy. "Oh, thank you, thank you, thank you, Cissy."

"Hey, just doing my job."

Cat gave her an extra squeeze. "No, you're not. Here—a token of my appreciation and Ron's." She pulled an envelope from her tote bag.

When Cissy opened it, her usually aloof appearance melted away. "Cat! This is—this is unbelievable. Thank you!"

"You're welcome." She handed an envelope to Dominick across the counter. His certificate, too, was a larger amount than one would commonly refer to as a token. She and Ron had added their own personal funds to these two.

He didn't open it. "Cat, dinner was more than enough."

"Ron and I don't agree. So there. You're welcome." She replaced the kitchen key in a drawer and pulled out one to her office. "Now I'm going home. I'll see you two tomorrow." She smiled at them and left.

As she walked away she heard Cissy say something about a party to Dominick. As she unlocked her office, he strode up.

"Cat, thank you." He held up the envelope's contents. "This is . . . I don't know what to say."

She smiled at his loss of words and opened the door. "It's not enough for a new longboard, but— Why is my light on?" She dropped the shopping bag on the desk and noticed a trace of grime. She wiped her finger through it. "Whew! Now I know I'm tired. Tonight this place can stay dusty."

He followed her back through the door and pulled it shut behind them. "I can take you home."

After locking her door, she patted his arm. "I'm fine, Dominick. Just walk me to my car. And could you put this back at the front desk for me?" She handed him her office key.

"I'll follow you home."

"No."

"For my peace of mind."

"You must watch too much television."

They walked silently until they reached her car. "You said you were afraid—"

"I said I'm getting better."

"You should be afraid, after what happened at that mall, and this time of night. Let me—"

"Dominick! I drive home every night at this time."

He let out an exasperated breath. "But are you afraid?"

She opened her door and climbed in. "That's not the point."

"Then what is the point?" He leaned inside, preventing her from shutting the door.

"That I do it by myself." She stared at him with clenched jaw, suddenly feeling very tired.

He didn't blink or budge.

"I'm just getting used to doing it by myself. Don't make it easier for me."

"I'm following you."

She placed the key in the ignition and turned it. "You're fired if you do."

"Compromise. I'll call you."

"All right." She pushed his shoulder. "Now close the door."

"At least you've got the top up. Lock the doors. Thanks for dinner. And the gift certificate."

"Dominick!"

"Bye." He smiled and shut the door.

Cat drove quickly from the lot and toward the freeway. Her mind begged for sleep, but a dizzying anticipation won the debate. She'd rather talk on the telephone with Dominick D'Angelo into the wee hours of the morning.

"Want me to follow her?" Brent Engstrom's soft voice came from near the employee entrance. His black sweater and slacks blended into the shadows.

Dominick stopped just outside the door. "She'll be fine. We have to check something. Wait, let me make sure Cissy's not headed this way." He cracked open the door. If the desk clerk saw him again, he'd have a difficult time dodging another party invitation. He'd rather run into the security guard than that little spitfire.

He motioned to the other agent to follow him inside. They quickly slipped into Cat's office and shut the door.

"You're lookin' pretty spiffy, boss." Engstrom spoke in a stage whisper.

"Hmm," he grunted. In the dim light coming through the closed blinds, Dominick maneuvered his way around the chairs and switched on the desk lamp, then climbed on top of the broad desk, pushed up the attic covering, and slid it aside.

"The charm must be working," Engstrom continued. "All dressed up, cozy dinner. Sounded like you even had a little disagreement. Must be serious if you're having a spat already."

Dominick poked the top of his head through the attic opening and stretched his arm into the dark. "Rule number one, Engstrom—shut up." His hand fell on something soft, covered in plastic. "Got a flashlight?"

He handed a tiny one to him. "When do I get to be the charming guy instead of a married dork with an imaginary wife— What'd you say?"

Dominick didn't bother to repeat the expletive. "It's here." He eased himself down from the desk. "Take a look."

He listened at the door while the younger man peered inside the turret.

Why did Cat come in here? Just to drop off that tote bag? She was surprised. Of course she was surprised. I was right next to her. What's she gonna say, "Oh, they've left attic dirt on my desk again while digging into the stash"?

Engstrom let out a low whistle. "Five kilos?"

"Let's go."

They quickly replaced the cover, turned off the lamp, and made their way out to the edge of the lot and stopped in the shadows near Dominick's truck.

"Brent, were you around when that white van was on the service drive?"

"Yeah. It just pulled in and made a U-turn. Odd thing, though, its lights were off. Couldn't get the plate number."

"You okay checking out the bread delivery? This guard's thorough."

"But predictable. I got his routine figured. If he changes it, my cover is the wife and me had a spat, and I needed some milk to calm my nerves."

"And knew how to pick a lock. Okay, whatever. I'm leaving then."

"Better make that phone call, clear up your little spat."

Dominick walked around his truck.

"Hey, D'Angelo, the stuff in the turret?"

He paused and looked over his shoulder.

"It still doesn't prove anything, right? Miss Wholesome Athlete maybe is just incredibly dumb?"

Dominick wanted Cat to be innocent. Truth was, the other agent was right. Over 200,000 dollars' worth of cocaine hidden a few feet above her desk didn't prove a thing. Something inside of him relaxed. "Could be, Engstrom. Could be."

~ Eleven ~

TWENTY-FOUR HOURS LATER, Cat and Dominick had again lingered in the parking lot. Instead of discussing whether or not he would follow her home, they discussed meeting at an all-night coffee shop. Sleep was the furthest thing from her mind and, apparently, his.

Twenty-four hours after that, they skipped the discussion and just met in the same booth they had sat in the previous night.

Sitting across the table from him, she figured maybe he felt sorry for her the night of the pool incident. Then, just to be nice, he called her on that dinner bet. After that enjoyable evening, it was a natural—albeit quick—progression to longer conversations when they met on the job . . . his wondering if she ate after getting off work at 11 . . . a mutual craving for stuffed French toast . . . inside jokes . . . Jack and Jill completing each other's sentences. Something had clicked between them. She couldn't deny it.

Cat's internal monologue tape was stuck on replay when she wasn't near him. *Go slow. Just be friends. Temp guy, temp relationship. Go slow. Just be friends.* When she saw him looking at her, though, with that slight lift of the corner of his mouth, it was as if the reverse button clicked on, and static filled her head.

Of course she was at a disadvantage. He caught her attention at an incredibly vulnerable moment, when the migraine had struck that night. Before that he was just another person.

No, not quite. His hard work, gentle teasing, and basketball challenge pruned the weeds choking the path that led straight to her heart. When she looked up, he was standing on the path, staring at her.

A shiver went through her now.

"Cold?" he asked and rubbed her arm. "You've got goose bumps. I've got a flannel shirt in the truck. I'll get it."

She shook her head no. Truth was, she'd rather have him across the table from her. His wild black hair fell across his forehead and in the back touched the top of his short-sleeved gray sweatshirt. His shoulders filled the booth, blocking from view the occupants at the table behind him.

Already his face had etched itself into her mind's eye, and she could see it even as she read the menu. There wasn't the symmetry of Trent's handsomeness here. It was rather . . . craggy. She suspected his nose had been broken at one time. There were scars—a slit just below his left eyebrow, and on his forehead a ridged line with stitching marks. The shadow of a thick beard never lessened. His lips were a bit off center because the right corner always tucked itself up when he smiled. There was not a spare ounce of flab. His face was a solid extension of the rock-like muscular shoulders and neck. Discipline and character, yes, but this was not a small-castle-in-the-suburbs future now staring at her.

"Where's your dimple?" His gray eyes crinkled.

"Same place as your Secret Service look."

His hand went still on her arm. "My what?"

"Your Secret Service look. You probably don't even know you do it. Cissy and I noticed it right away. Of course your build has something to do with it, but your eyes get kind of serious now and then, like they're watching out for the President."

"I see. And where does that put your dimple?"

She smiled. "I don't know."

He moved his hand aside as the waitress served their food.

In between bites, Cat added, "We have a couple of other theories about you. Are you interested?"

"I didn't know I warranted theories."

"You're so different, it makes you mysterious. We assume you came to California all on your own without friends or family or job. And you're old enough to know better. It's not as if you're a young kid trying to find himself. We've never met anyone like you."

"Hmm."

"You're either a rock singer incognito or a convict."

His eyebrows shot up. "I don't think I want to know any more."

She laughed. "Okay, tell me something about yourself. Then you'll be more real to me. Tell me about, umm, when you were a little boy."

"Like . . . ?"

"Like remember I asked you where you felt safe? I said I did in the backyard, and you said your backyard was a dark alley. Think of a place."

Dominick sipped his coffee.

She saw his eyes go cold but decided against telling him she had found his Secret Service look.

"Okay," he said, "but this is just between you and me."

"Agreed."

"The safe place was in the kitchen with Ma hugging me while she cooked. And with Vince, my little brother, at the table doing homework. He'd be doing *my* homework while I was busy explaining why I'd had another fight."

"You'd been in a fight and your mother would *hug* you?"

He chuckled, and his eyes softened a little. "After she yelled at me for fighting."

"And your dad wasn't around?"

"Not after . . . not after I was ten."

"I'm sorry."

He gazed over her shoulder, his jaw locked. "It's okay. It was safer after he left."

She remembered what he had told her when that guest had shouted at her, when she thought Dominick would punch him.

He had told her the story of punching his dad. "Are your mom and brother still in Chicago?" she asked.

He smiled, and the ice melted again. "Vince is a hotshot stockbroker with a beautiful wife and two great kids. Ma lives in a condo in a nice neighborhood. I try to get back at least once a year."

"When did you leave home?"

"Ahh, too many long stories, Cat. Another time. I was wondering, are you and Cissy friends?"

She shrugged. "We have fun together at work. She's perfect as the front desk manager, and we have a good rapport. But outside of the Castillo our interests are so different, we don't socialize. She's kind of on the wild and crazy side, in case you haven't noticed. And I go to Padres games."

"And Lakers?"

She smiled. "Maybe once a season my dad and I make it there."

"Your voice just got real soft. Sounds like you and your dad are close?"

"Yeah, we are. Besides the fact that my brothers aren't as crazy about basketball as I am, Daddy and I just get along in general. He's a special man."

"Obviously. He makes park benches for you just in time for inspection. I imagine you're spoiled rotten."

She heard his teasing tone. "So what if I am?" she countered.

"No problem." He grinned. Then his face sobered. "At first I had a hard time calling God 'Father.' You know, with my background. But I have glimpses now of being spoiled rotten by Him."

"You do?" Surprise raised her voice.

"Did you see the sunrise this morning?"

She laughed. "No! You did?"

"I was surfing. How about the sunset tonight?"

The chuckle died in her throat. At the display of such tenderness on his strong face, her breath caught.

"And those are just the little things He gives me."

Somewhere from deep inside a warmth began to grow. It was as if a flood of liquid sunshine washed through her. Dominick heard God's whispers. He shouldn't. He was too independent, too unsettled, too scarred by the childhood he hinted at, too *physical*. But he did hear! Why couldn't she?

"Your French toast is getting cold."

"What? Oh." She turned her attention back to her plate.

"So tell me what else you do. What would you be doing right now if we weren't here?"

She glanced at her watch. "I'd be sleeping."

"It is getting kind of late."

It was after 1 A.M. Last night she had gotten home at 1. She peered at him through her eyelashes. He didn't motion for the check. She didn't hurry her eating.

"What will you do tomorrow before work?"

Again she glanced at her watch.

"Sleep," he answered for her.

She laughed. "Yes. And I'll go to the pot shop."

His eyes narrowed.

She grinned. "You know, pot shop—where potters make pottery. Need a bowl or a vase?" She told him about her friends there and her love of shaping clay.

"And what do you do on your Mondays off?"

She imagined him in a kitchen in the middle of a rough neighborhood, his mother hugging him after he'd been in a fight. He was a good candidate to join her. "This week I'm going to Tecate. Will you come with me?"

"To visit your, what was it, *abuelita?*"

"Oh, there's much more than my *abuelita* in Tecate." She would surprise him.

Before Monday came, Cat and Dominick met two more times at the coffee shop after work.

They also met at the potters' studio. On Thursday morning he came, and she helped him throw a pot. Her hands on his, she guided them round the wet lump of clay on the wheel, shaping what she called a man-size cereal bowl. She was surprised at the agility of his large hands, surprised that her heart beat in sync with the spinning wheel.

And they met on Saturday morning at the pier. They ate breakfast at a nearby outdoor cafe, his hair still wet from surfing. He made her laugh with his stories of how he had learned to surf. She asked if he had been athletic in high school, if he had played football. She realized her inability to comprehend his childhood when he smiled softly and mentioned something about fighting and hanging around street corners. She wondered then about gangs but did not ask.

All these hours together were in addition to the eight they spent in close proximity at the motel. It seemed a natural progression of a new friendship. Neither hesitated when the other suggested a meeting.

On Sunday they went their separate ways, she to see her parents, he to see his friends Megan and Adam. Cat didn't know what he thought, but she knew she needed a breather by then. It was getting more difficult to tell herself to go slow. She admitted to herself she felt an attraction that went beyond friendship. Dominick crowded out her fear and loneliness, Trent, and sometimes even sleep. He made her laugh, held her hand when she started unconsciously to bite her nails, and made her think about God.

It wasn't that he directly questioned her struggle with faith. It was that she caught glimpses in him of such pure awe at comprehending the fact that the Creator of the universe knew him, Dominick D'Angelo, by name and cared about him. She was intrigued by that, perhaps almost envious of that in him.

On Monday morning he parked his pickup at her apartment building. She insisted on driving. He sat beside her in her open Tracker, wearing shorts, T-shirt, baseball cap, and a wary look in his squinting eyes.

"Where are your sunglasses?" she asked.

"Forgot them at home. Now what exactly are we doing in Tecate?"

She smiled. "Hmm. I thought you had an adventuresome spirit, one that doesn't need to know the outcome."

"Sure, I'm adventuresome. That's why I let you drive this go-cart with me in it on the freeway."

"Ha, ha. Just wait until we get on the winding two-lane. That's the best part."

Less than an hour later she parked and escorted him through an unmarked gate. When the shouting children ran across the dirt courtyard toward them, he grinned at her. "A school?"

"Sort of. An orphanage."

He fit in easily. They delivered canned goods, sang songs, joined in their lunchtime. The children as well as workers adored his antics and his halting attempts at their language.

Sometime later Cat sat under a shade tree with Rosa, the elderly woman she called *abuelita*. They watched Dominick kneel on the ground while the children wrestled with him. When they knocked him over, something deep within Cat broke apart, and the laughter she hadn't known for so many months was at last released. It was a cleansing, unadulterated delight that flowed from her in tears and loud unladylike bellows. He lifted his head between the small arms that hugged him and smiled.

She had hoped for a favorable response to the children. Her hope was a mere fraction of what he gave. This was compassion, boundless and glorious.

Rosa put a hand on her arm. "He makes you laugh, Catalina."

She looked at the white-haired woman whose aged face crinkled in a smile. "*Sì, Abuelita.*" As always, they conversed in Spanish.

"The other one didn't."

She patted the woman's hand. She had often sensed that Rosa did not care wholeheartedly for Trent.

"This Dominick has known pain. It's in his eyes. That is why he can give such joy."

He approached now. She wasn't embarrassed when Rosa said to him in Spanish, "You are the man for Catalina. Take good care of my little one, and do not forsake your Father's word."

To Cat's surprise, Dominick leaned over and tenderly kissed Rosa's cheek.

When they left, a tiredness filled Cat, the comfortable kind that comes after a hard physical workout, like hiking up a mountain. She handed him the keys, which he accepted without a word.

"Dominick, did you notice a restaurant all by itself, on the highway just this side of Jamul? It's called El Coyote. Shall we stop?"

"Only if we have enough time to get to the pier before sunset."

"What?"

In reply he simply touched her face. "Catalina. It's pretty in Spanish."

He drove, and she napped until the sound of gravel under the tires woke her. They were at the restaurant.

As they ate in the quiet courtyard surrounded by colorful potted plants, she told him about her first trip to the orphanage and how she fell in love with it. It seemed a small thing to bring gifts and spend a little time with the people there. She was sure she received more than she gave. Dominick understood. She didn't have to tell him more.

He asked for the check instead of coffee and stood. "Let's go."

"Where to?"

"The sunset. I think Rosa told us to watch the sunset from the pier."

She laughed, glad he didn't ask what Rosa had really said because she couldn't tell him and she couldn't lie to him.

They made it in time. She closed her eyes as he maneuvered her car into a tight squeeze of a space she never would have attempted. They hurried along the sidewalk to the pier, glad to see the white wrought-iron gate still unlocked at the entrance. Although open to the public during daylight hours, the Crystal Pier was private property. Dominick grabbed Cat's hand, and they ran between the rows of white motel cottages that lined both sides of the first half of the pier.

He slowed down when she couldn't keep up. At last they reached the far end where a small crowd had gathered to await the sunset. They spotted an opening at the wooden rail. He nudged her forward into a tight fit between others standing there.

"Kind of like parking the car," she mused.

He stood behind her, his hands resting on her shoulders. Nothing but the railing and the vast expanse of ocean separated them from the sinking sun. They observed it silently. She thought of how he had described this as a gift from God. It was obvious. Low on the horizon, all shades of purples and pinks streaked through the clouds. Below them, the red-orange sun dissolved into the ocean. Day turned into night. On the other side of the earth, night turned into day.

The crowd began to disperse, but she stood still, not wanting to break the spell of the sunset's beauty—or of this physical and emotional closeness to Dominick.

He dropped his hands and moved to her side. "It was a good day, Cat. Thank you."

"I'm glad you went with me." *More than glad.* The mental cobwebs were at last swept away. She was all right. There was abundant life after the nightmare. She smiled at him. "Thank you for being a friend."

In the deepening twilight they stared at one another for a few moments. He leaned toward her and hesitated.

Cat held her breath. "This wasn't supposed to happen."

"You're telling me," he murmured. And then he kissed her.

Maybe Rosa had told them to watch the sunset after all.

~ *Twelve* ~

"YOU'RE CLEANING!" Elli exclaimed as she stepped into her sister's apartment. "*Cleaning?*"

Cat shut the door and hugged her. "Well, hello to you too. Where's my nephew?"

"With his dad. Jim's working at home this morning, so I'm doing errands without my little appendage."

Cat cleared books from a dining table chair. "Sit down. How's the littlest appendage doing?"

Elli patted her abdomen and propped her feet up on another chair. "Just fine. He or she was kicking half the night."

"Want some iced tea?" Cat busied herself in the kitchen.

"Thanks. Hey, nice tabletop. I haven't seen it since you moved in."

Cat served the tea and asked small-talk questions while scrubbing the sink. That lasted less than five minutes.

"Okay, Cat, what gives?"

"Nothing."

Elli giggled. "That was a quick response. Sit down and look me in the eye and say that."

Cat wiped her hands on her gym shorts, then fiddled in the silverware drawer.

"C'mon, sis, you haven't really cleaned or organized this place in the four months you've been here, so I take this little spurt as a significant development. What happened?"

She opened a cupboard and began rearranging spice bottles.

Fourteen years of sharing a room with this sister and a lifetime of being there for each other through all the highs and lows meant she couldn't hide from Elli. She had been up since 5 A.M. hiding from herself.

Not that she had slept much, trying to make sense of her totally emotional, illogical response to a man who was in no way, shape, or form her type. After last night's sunset there were whispered words of going slow, a silent ride home. At the apartment door they had simply stared at one another, still speechless. It was as if the kiss ended everything. Or just began—

"Catherine Michele!"

She sat down. "Dominick went with me yesterday, to Tecate."

"The big guy from the zoo? The one you had dinner with after the inspection?" Her dark brown eyes danced with anticipation.

Cat nodded.

"And?"

"Well, I don't know exactly, except I like him." She sucked in a breath. "A lot."

Elli clasped her hands to her chest. "Oh, Cat, that's wonderful! It's time. Go ahead, be excited and care about yourself again and clean your apartment."

"I'm *cleaning* so I don't think about him."

"Why not think about him?"

"Elli, I'm on the rebound. It's like he's just there instead of Trent. I'm barely standing on my own two feet again. If I care about him, then when he leaves I'll fall flat on my face. I can't handle that again. I can't even *think* about trying to handle that again. I'd be lost. Probably forever. I'd never be—"

"Whoa! What do you mean 'when he leaves'?"

"He's just a temp and not just as in employee. We're going to offer him a permanent position, but he's a drifter. It sounds as if he's lived all over, and he talks about heading south, I'm sure before winter. Just him and his surfboard. He probably lives in a room with his board and a sleeping bag and a hot plate!"

"Cat, slow down. What do you know for a fact? Other than he's lived beyond San Diego and he now works as a temp?"

"I know his hair is as long as mine and he drives a pickup!"

Elli burst out laughing and reached across the table to put an arm around her. "Well, I'd say we know for a fact that he's no Trenton Carver."

Cat rested her forehead against her sister's. "Maybe you better pray about this, El. I get that fizzy feeling whenever I see him. Or think about him."

Her sister sat up. "You haven't prayed about this? Oh, Cat, Cat, Cat! When are you going to talk to God again?"

"I don't know."

"He knows what He's doing!"

"I still don't like what He did. I played by His rules, and . . ."

Elli sighed in a frustrated way. "Life is not a game of basketball. You know better than that."

"You have everything you want or need."

"I know. And I understand that I cannot fully appreciate what you feel. I didn't lose what you lost that day." She squeezed her hand. "I am just so thankful no one was killed."

Cat looked at her. She could still read terror in her eyes whenever Elli remembered that day at the fast-food restaurant in the mall. Her sister had heard the screams and from a distance turned to see a man pointing a gun at Cat. She had described it as a split second with the feel of an eternity, torn between rushing toward her or racing away with her son.

"You know I'll talk to God for you. For *now*."

She nodded, slightly calmed after unloading on her sister.

"Fizzy feeling, huh?"

Cat rolled her eyes.

"Remember the house rules?"

"Of course." House rules were their parents' boundaries set when they were children. They had been fair as well as permanently engraved in their minds.

"Number 12?" Elli asked, examining her fingernails.

Cat's jaw dropped open in surprise.

"Aha! He kissed you!"

"El, I'm thirty years old!"

She laughed. "Number 12 is forever. First kiss, you gotta bring him home for a Sunday dinner to meet the fam."

Though non-interfering, they were a close-knit family. And despite her independence Cat knew she needed their support. She met Elli's challenging glare with one of her one. "If you breathe a word of house rule number 12, I'll tell Mother about you-know-what."

"You wouldn't dare."

"Would too."

Their semi-serious argument eventually disintegrated into giggles. It felt so good to laugh again.

"D'Angelo, you with us?"

Smitty's sharp voice cut through the cottony sensation in Dominick's head. "Yeah." He pressed the heels of his hands against his eyes. Nothing would focus this morning just twelve hours after one sunset and one kiss had plunged him into an ache he wouldn't have imagined was possible. But almost simultaneously with that plunge, he had skyrocketed into an overpowering sense of total release from that ache. After a sleepless night, he knew the two were inseparable. And he knew that Catherine St. Clair was responsible for opening his heart to both the ache and its release.

"D'Angelo!"

"Huh?" Dominick sat in the Drug Enforcement Administration's field division office. Across the table sat Brent Engstrom, the newest recruit, and Robert Smith, the Special Agent in Charge or SAC. Smitty was a lean and mean type and at the moment short on temper.

"I want it tied with the AFO," he insisted again. The Arellano-Felix Organization, also known as the Tijuana Cartel, was responsible for importing multi-ton quantities of cocaine through the Baja area, from Colombia to Mexico to San Diego.

Dominick shook his head. "Who doesn't want it tied to them? We told you, we're done. The Castillo is small potatoes, Smitty, the end of a route before a few kilos hit the street. It's gotta be umpteen steps removed from the Cartel. Combined with this," he riffled a stack of papers, information collected from the DEA, FBI, Border Patrol, and Customs, "we can shut down a very short string of very small potatoes, but that's it."

"Let's say," Engstrom interjected, "I stick like glue to the bread man."

He gazed at the young agent and recognized the attitude. When had his own adrenaline stopped pumping when he looked evil in the eye? When had he given up on saving the world? Rather than one turning point, it had been a slow chipping away by life's realities—evidence turning to jelly in the hands of an inept prosecutor. A woman he thought he loved setting him up. Relocating at the drop of a hat. Eating and sleeping according to some sleazeball drug dealer's schedule. Submitting to random drug-testing because handling coke and meth and weed meant you had easy access and maybe you forgot how to say no. Learning never-ending new twists on money laundering. Posing, fusing fact with fiction, lying . . .

Grabbing an innocent bystander by her bouncing ponytail and sticking a gun in her face.

He had to get out. His debt was paid.

"Engstrom," he explained in a quiet voice, "think it through. Say you follow the bread man. He goes to his brother-in-law's for Sunday dinner, backs his car into the garage, picks up five kilos. You know where it's going, you found it in the turrets at the Castillo. So you follow the brother-in-law. His source is some friend's garage. Let's say you keep going and eventually are led to a warehouse and someone delivering. You hang out with that guy a few weeks until he drives into TJ.

"You decide to break the rules big-time—this isn't watching a woman on her day off visit an orphanage two miles across the border—and you go into Mexico. If you've talked with the wrong authorities—and nine out of ten times they're on AFO's payroll—you're dead. If you haven't talked and no one's looking, you find this guy's taking orders from someone who doesn't have a clue who the bread man is or AFO's phone number, let alone a face from the inner circle.

"If after all these months you should by some quirk happen to get close enough to prove a link, some Mexican official will have egg on his face and they'll want to extradite you in order to prosecute you. In the meantime, your proof gets lost in enough red tape to wrap up the Rose Bowl."

Smitty and Engstrom stared at him in silence, and then the younger man raised his hand. "What about the one out of ten times?"

Smitty burst into laughter and clapped Dominick on the back. "You need a vacation. It's all true, but," he turned to Engstrom, "tell us, Boy Wonder, what's our mission?"

"To combat drug trafficking, sir!"

"Right. First I need you to help wrap things up in Logan Heights, probably by next Monday. Then go shut down the Castillo operation and the two others related. Coordinate it with Rehder and Frenell. How many arrests?"

Engstrom counted on his fingers, "Bread man, two bus boys, one security guard, one kitchen staff. The assistant manager is an unknown."

"Cat's not in on it." Dominick's stomach knotted.

"We can't rule her out yet," the younger agent disagreed. "I don't want her to be part of it either—she's the straightest-looking chick I've ever seen, so wholesome I don't even want her to *know* what's going on. But the stuff's in the turret above her desk."

"She's not in on it." His adamant tone left no room for doubt.

Smitty frowned. "This isn't personal? You're sure beyond anything you've ever been sure of in the past?"

He knew what situations his boss referenced. One was years ago, but the lesson from being set up by a woman he cared for had been well ingrained. The second one Smitty had been involved with, the incident from just seven months ago, the one that had forced him to order Dominick off the street for a time.

"Yes, sir, I'm sure. It's not personal, not related to anything in the past."

Oblivious to the undercurrent, Engstrom continued, "Then the front desk manager must be. One of them has got to be coordinating efforts."

"Cissy?" Dominick turned in surprise. "She's too flaky."

Engstrom grinned. "Someone once told me you never, never know about covers. I take it that includes flakiness."

~ *Thirteen* ~

DOMINICK THOUGHT CAT was avoiding him. The fact was, he was avoiding her. The boundary line had blurred, the line that kept authenticity out of reach in order for him to role-play the charmer. Blurred? After that kiss he couldn't even find it anymore. It was probably far behind him. He had unconsciously, easily stepped over it somewhere between a pickup basketball game and stuffed French toast in the middle of the night. Until he got his bearings, it was best that he avoid her.

Therefore, they hadn't talked much at work this week, hadn't spent any off-hours together, had agreed after the sunset that . . . that what?

That it wasn't supposed to happen.

He glanced now at his truck's sideview mirror, signaled, switched freeway lanes, and rehashed Monday night.

"Dominick," she had whispered. They stood at the end of the pier as the sky darkened.

He leaned toward her again, to catch her words before the wind flung them out to sea.

"I— I can't get involved."

"I know." He knew she was fragile, and he of all people knew exactly why. He knew she wasn't ready and would never be ready for the likes of him.

But then she had brushed her lips against his cheek. Her soft hair touched his face, filling him with the sweet, citrus-like scent of her perfume. In his mind he cried out to God, begging for her healing, begging that he would be a new man in Christ, one she could trust.

If he didn't step away, he would kiss her again.

He took a step back. "Cat, I care for you. I can't ignore that any longer. But I won't pressure you. Tell me what you're comfortable with."

"Just being friends. Going slow?"

"Seeing what happens?" Tentative solutions.

"Yes."

The early evening stars were twinkling by then, and he couldn't see those honey-colored eyes, but they were branded into his brain. They would always be a part of him. Not to confess his sin and his love at that moment had demanded a discipline from him that he had never before known. Even now he could still feel a splinter in his hand from clutching the pier's old wooden railing.

The day in Tecate had been magical. No, Meg would say it had been supernaturally orchestrated. Any lingering doubts of Cat's wholesomeness, any professionally sound restraints were swept away that afternoon at the orphanage when he heard her laughter.

Given that discussion of five days ago, that agreement to go slow, why was it that at this moment she sat in his truck as he drove them to her parents' home for Sunday dinner?

It was first, of course, because of those eyes. And second, it was because when he was with her he was that new man, more alive than at any other time. He was like the grimy city, and her smile was a cleansing rain shower and the pristine sunlight all rolled into one.

"Why do you drive a pickup?"

He diverted his eyes now from the freeway traffic for a fraction of a second. Her knowing smile told him she understood that he loved his truck. He grinned. "Why wouldn't I drive her? She's an F-150 four-by-four with regular cab, short bed, rad set of chrome wheels, and thirty-inch tires."

Her laughter filled that regular cab as well as his heart, and he wondered how he was supposed to go slow.

"Daddy will like it."

Twenty minutes later he met "Daddy," and he prayed the man would like something about him.

"Nice to meet you, Dominick!" Stan St. Clair was his height, barrel chested, steely-gray-haired. The man's forearms were as thick as his biceps. As he held Dominick's hand in a vise-like grip, he announced in a foghorn voice, "If you hurt my Kit-Cat, I'll kill you." His blue eyes twinkled, his mouth smiled, but there was an air about the man that said he was serious.

Dominick had never felt so intimidated in his life.

"Stanley!" Betty St. Clair pushed aside her husband and took Dominick's hand in hers. There was a softness about the petite blonde that gave him an immediate sense of being in first grade. "Aren't you glad you're not a sixteen-year-old boy? He always greeted the girls' boyfriends like that too—scared the living daylights out of them. Welcome to our home. I want to hear all about how you and Catherine met."

Cat rescued him before he had to answer. She showed him around the house and introduced him to siblings and in-laws and children. His mental camcorder, normally second nature to him, took a while before clicking on. Stan St. Clair had shot normalcy right out of the water.

Eldest sister Anne had medium brown hair, height, and weight. Husband John was occupied in the garage assembling bicycles. Felicia and Grant were the cutest identical twins he had ever seen. Today was their fifth birthday.

Brother Ben was tall, skinny, red-haired, married to someone in the kitchen. He worked with his father at the construction company and, like Anne, had three children.

That made six kids.

He remembered Elizabeth from the zoo, the short, raven-haired, pregnant young woman. Friendly husband, salesman-type, Jim. Shy little Jason.

Seven and one on the way.

Doug was in the Navy, in Japan. His wife Penny was here, a studious-looking mother of two.

Nine kids, all under the age of eleven. And one on the way.

Cat steered him through the house. It was a rambling, hacienda affair with a red-tiled roof, U-shaped with a covered porch that ran the length of the inside of the U. In the center of that was a flagstone patio, with a fountain and potted flowers everywhere. Distant hills were visible.

Inside the house was dark wood, Spanish style with high, beamed ceilings, a cool oasis in the desert's hot afternoon. Walls were covered with family portraits. He lingered over an area devoted to Cat. Definite Wheaties box material from the age of five when she wore a shiny pink athletic shirt and white shorts, a soccer ball tucked neatly in the crook of her elbow, the other hand propped on bent knee.

"Dominick . . ." She pulled on his arm. "I want to show you the bridge before the game."

"What game?"

"Basketball. It's a family tradition whenever most of us are together."

He followed her across the patio and noticed a basketball court off to one side.

"Daddy built that for Ben, but of course I was always under my brother's feet. All of my free time was spent either on that court or down at the footbridge."

They trudged down an incline full of scrub brush and large boulders. The rock-hard soil was blonde, as if the sun had bleached out the earth itself. Desert heat dried his throat and warmed him all the way through to the bone marrow. It took only a few minutes to reach the bridge, but it wasn't visible until they were almost upon it.

"Isn't it great?" she asked.

He smiled. It was about six feet long, simple wooden planks placed crossways over two beams, all covered in flaking red paint, without a railing. It spanned a dry creek bed that looked about five feet deep at this point. "Uhh, sure. It's fantastic."

"Come on!" She punched his shoulder. "It really is. Here, you have to sit beneath it to get the full effect."

He scrambled down the bank behind her. They sat cross-legged, facing each other in the dirt. It wasn't as hot here in the shade of the planks and a nearby tree.

"If you follow the creek bed," she pointed to her left, "it winds up into the hills where the avocado groves used to be. It's a housing development now."

"So, this is your safe spot?"

"Mm-hmm. Except for the occasional rattler."

He looked over his shoulder.

"Don't worry. We always keep a snakebite kit in the house."

He peered over his other shoulder. "I was hoping you'd have a Daddy-bite kit."

She laughed. "Oh, and this," she pointed to an arrangement of stones near her feet, "is a castle." Her tone was final, as if she had shown him everything.

He knew that in contrast to him, she *had* shown him every-thing. She had opened to him the corners of her heart.

"Dominick?"

He saw concern on her face.

"I know they can be overwhelming at first. I just . . . I just wanted them to meet you."

Oh, dear God. "Cat . . ." He exhaled. "I've never . . ." He swallowed. "This is like a foreign country to me. All those peo-ple under one roof, related and laughing. All this space. With my background, I don't exactly fit in."

"Yes, you do." She shifted her weight to her knees, braced an arm against him, and quickly kissed his cheek. "Thank you for reminding me how special this place is. I sometimes forget. God has given us so much, not just in material things. Did you figure out we're all adopted?"

"What?"

"All five of us are adopted."

There was no resemblance between the siblings! Where had his mind gone? It had turned to mush somewhere between Stan

St. Clair's handshake and these honey-colored eyes now just inches from his face. "That's why you don't look alike."

She smiled. "Duh."

"All five of you?"

She nodded. "Pretty amazing when you think of all the biological families represented here. Mother and Daddy weren't able to have children, but they desperately wanted them, and so they found us. We're all two years apart, all came here as babies, all California natives."

He brushed hair back from her cheek. "Where did they find you?"

"In a crack house in Los Angeles."

For a split second his mind hit empty space, quickly displaced by a rushing wind of incoherent thoughts. *Born in a hell. Fresh. Wholesome. Suspect? How could I ever—? Honor student. All-star athlete.*

"Well, the police found me. Daddy knew somebody who knew somebody on the force. Actually, I might not be two years behind Ben. The doctors guessed at my age. There was an unidentified dead woman, but there were no records of her giving birth, no relatives found. They really couldn't figure out where I came from. I was just this scrawny little thing—can you imagine me a scrawny little thing? Daddy held me for twelve months straight. It was the only place I was content. I think that's why he still gets a little overprotective."

Dominick listened to her matter-of-fact description, and then coherency fled again. He cupped the back of her head with his hand and could think only of that dimple and the generous mouth that made it appear. Tenderly he kissed both.

A distant bell clanged, slowly bringing him back to the present.

Her lips brushing his, she murmured, "Game time."

He lifted his head. "Cat, I can't go slow. Do you know what you're doing?"

She frowned.

"When you sit close and kiss me and thank me and tell me everything about yourself?"

"Just being friends?"

He pulled her to himself. She could be so frustratingly . . . *wholesome.*

"Dominick," she said, her voice muffled against his neck, "this is my safe spot, and you're sitting in it. That makes you part of it."

Straightening, he placed his hands on her shoulders and looked at her. "You feel safe with me?"

"Completely. Maybe God doesn't want us to go slow."

He blinked. "You're talking to God?"

"Well, I'm thinking about it. I don't understand how I can feel so close to you when if I'd had my way, I'd be addressing *wedding* invitations today. Maybe that guy with the gun was an angel in disguise, saving me from a huge mistake with Trent."

His heart skipped a beat, and he closed his eyes. *Angel in disguise?*

"I mean, I don't think anymore that you're just filling up the hole that Trent left."

He forced himself to meet that shimmery honey. "Why do you think that?"

"I brought him here once. He never sat down in the dirt. And he never ever asked where they found me."

The obvious way God was answering his prayers was almost frightening. No doubt about it now. It was time. She had to know the truth.

Dominick traced her jawline with his finger. Did she truly feel safe with him as she'd said? He would push her to the edge and see. She wanted a divine sword to banish the nightmare. He knew God would hand it to him, but he could not wield it until she totally placed herself in his hands. If she did that, the plan he had devised could work. If it did, the fears would be gone, and their relationship would find its one chance of moving forward.

And he really wanted it to move forward.

With a quick prayer and great effort, he slipped his voice and his facial expression into professional mode. "Catherine Michele St. Clair, do you trust me?" He saw in her eyes then what he knew he could put there, a flicker of fear.

"Y-yes."

"You're absolutely sure?" He touched the worry crease between her brows.

"Dominick . . ." She swallowed. "I trust you. Even when you get that icy, Secret Service look on your face that reminds me I really don't know a whole lot about you."

"Good girl. I want to walk you through the nightmare."

She stared back at him.

"We'll go to the mall, into the restaurant, stand on the spot."

"I can't," she whispered.

He held her with his eyes. "I'll stay with you."

"I can't."

"I know you can't. But if you trust me, I can do it for you. Do you trust me?"

She laid her head on his shoulder.

"Please. Let me do this for you."

"Why?"

He kissed the top of her head. *Because I'm the only one who can.* "Cat, you know I'm new at this faith business. But I do understand that God loves you, and He doesn't want you to be afraid of this anymore."

"I'll . . . I'll pray about it."

He wrapped his arms around her. "All right."

—*Fourteen*—

IT WAS FRIDAY MORNING. Cat meandered through the quiet pot shop, rolling up the sleeves of her oversized denim shirt, idly inspecting other potters' work. The place resembled a library. But instead of books, the floor-to-ceiling shelves were stacked with mugs, bowls, platters, vases, and knickknacks.

In the five days since Dominick's offer, she had successfully avoided praying about it. To a large degree she had avoided even him. Whenever she'd catch a glimpse of him in the distance, she'd turn and go the other way, then tell herself how silly her behavior was. And then her heart would race while her practical mind shouted, *He's not your type!*

Yesterday she had joined Elli at her Lamaze class and afterwards for lunch. Her sister, of course, launched a full-court press before she even had time to open the menu.

"Cat, he's perfect."

She rolled her eyes. "Who?"

It was Elli's turn to roll her eyes. "Dominick!"

"Hmm," Cat grunted as she studied the menu. "He's . . . He's . . ."

"He's what?" she prompted.

"Perfect. Except for the fact that he doesn't in any way, shape, or form fit any dream I've ever had for my life!"

"You're not still on that kick about a North County castle-type house and a big family of athletic, straight-A kids and never a financial concern?"

"Wellll . . ."

"Did you see him talking to Dad? Going over each other's pickups like a couple of mothers talking about their babies? And then Dad skipped his usual twenty-questions routine during dinner. Mother thinks he's wonderful. All the kids liked him—"

"Jason was standoffish with him."

"Jase is going through a quiet period. He can't figure out the deal with my big tummy and the baby talk. Anyway—"

The waitress interrupted them at that point, but Elli got right back to it after they gave their orders.

"Mother and Annie and I think you two make a striking couple. You look better with a guy bigger than Trent. He's just too slick to go with your earthiness, you know, your bone structure."

Cat stared out the window.

"So when are you seeing him again, I mean besides at work? Like as in a date?"

"El, slow down! If I think this way I'll just get all fizzy-feeling inside again."

"What's wrong with that?"

"I can't see where I'm going. It's like I used to feel life was a garden path. All I had to do was keep the rules and skip on down it. Then out of the blue it gives way to this abyss and I'm clinging to the sides. So I've decided that's real life, not the garden path garbage. Only I'm not plunging headfirst without looking anymore. I'm holding on and taking it one step at a time so I can see where I'm going."

"God knows where you're going."

"God says we can make choices, right? Well, I choose to trust only as far as I can see. If I start praying about it all, I know what He's going to do. He's going to make me let go of the grip I've got and then I'll feel like carbonated soda and not in control, and when Dominick changes his mind, I'll lose mine for sure." She covered her face with her hands.

"Whoa, Cat. Maybe you'd better slow down. You're that crazy about him?"

She nodded.

"Ladies," the waitress boomed, "need some Kleenex here?"

"No, thanks," Elli answered.

Cat sniffled and lowered her hands. "We're fine. Just a couple of goofy females talking about men."

The waitress chuckled and refilled their iced tea glasses. "Coulda guessed that. Have a nice day."

Her sister studied Cat's face, waiting.

"El, he . . ." She pressed her lips together. The words refused to form.

"He what? Good or bad?"

She lifted a shoulder.

"Cat, it's obvious he's attracted to you. If he cares about you, it's probably more on the good side."

"The mall. He wants to take me there."

Elli's eyes widened. "You told him about that?"

She nodded. "He thinks I should get over the fear."

Elli blinked and thought a moment. "And get on with your life." She slapped the tabletop. "He's right! You can't really get into a new relationship until you let go of all that past horror. You're so much stronger than you were a few months ago, Cat. Maybe you're ready for it now."

"I guess that's what I thought, the part about a new relationship. If I do it, then Dominick will mean even more to me and— Oh, can we just change the subject? I have to think more about it."

"And pray about it. You know they're usually one and the same when you know God." Elli caught the frown on Cat's face.

Now, in the pot shop, Cat pushed her sister's words to the back of her mind. She'd mull them over later.

She picked up the bowl she and Dominick had formed together. She smiled, remembering how they laughed at his attempts. Despite its dubious beginnings on the wheel, it had survived the first firing and was in the bisque stage, ready to be dipped in the glaze. With deft strokes, she wiped a sponge around the bottom, spreading a liquid form of wax to prevent the glaze from adhering to it. That breathing space would keep it intact during the next firing.

As often happened here in this artistic, creative environment, Cat's logical thought processes tangled with a fanciful slant. She liked clear-cut rules to follow, and when something like this lopsided bowl caught her attention, she had to admit that not keeping the rules sometimes worked.

The ill-formed piece should have exploded in the kiln.

Dominick D'Angelo didn't fit the form she had decided upon long ago. He was too tall, too muscular, from *Chicago* of all places, not interested in a salaried professional career, evidently had not grown up in a church. And he drove a pickup. His influence over her should have fizzled by now. He shouldn't be this close to her thoughts. *All right, heart.*

She would apply the glaze to the bowl—there was nothing else she could do—and see if it endured the second firing.

If she allowed their friendship to be glazed, to be coated with the attractive things—laughter . . . candlelight . . . hand holding . . . anticipation—would it survive the unknown, inevitable changes?

Only time would tell.

She studied the string of colored tiles, trying to choose one for his bowl. The grayish green of celadon? His gray eyes came to mind . . . his green truck. A red? She thought of the tie he wore to dinner . . . the rose he had laid on her desk last night.

Obviously the glazing of the relationship had already begun. And she was decidedly enjoying the process of it.

She grasped the bowl with long-handled tongs and stepped to the barrel of deep blue liquid. Blues brought absolutely nothing to mind about Mr. D'Angelo. She quickly dipped the bowl in and out, then set it on a shelf and headed down an aisle toward the huge plastic bag that held the clay.

She disagreed with Dominick and Elli. The nightmare didn't fit in anywhere. It had nothing to do with what was going on here. It was in the past; she was getting over it. Five years from now that mall would be no big deal to her. She was fine with her life as is. No reason to complicate matters with prayer and working through some ugly fear. If she prayed about it, she knew she would agree to walk with Dominick through the nightmare because . . . because she trusted him.

Cat halted in the aisle, her eyes focused internally. That was it. Why did she trust him? Because she sensed that somehow he really could absorb her fear. The only way he could do that was supernaturally. He believed in God as she did, in the supernatural power of God walking in human form as Jesus, bringing the kingdom with Him for the here and now and forever, to replace all their fears with His love.

Dominick reminded her of what Jesus must have been like to the people who lived with Him. As a man who built things and walked great distances, His physical strength was a given. People would be attracted to His friendly demeanor, His attention to detail, His concern for others, His storytelling that made them think as well as laugh.

Dominick was all of that. He showed concern for things Trent had never noticed about her. He even mentioned her middle name, which she hadn't told him—he'd probably seen it in her mother's cross-stitched piece amidst the mass of photographs he studied. Photographs that Trent had merely glanced at once.

Her family had enjoyed him. He made them laugh with his stories. Mother learned that his family called him Nicky, his brother was two years younger, his mother knitted for the needy, he attended a church downtown. Other than that, they knew only that there was integrity in the way he spoke of others and observed the world, humility in the way he listened to the little ones and helped in the kitchen.

And Cat sensed there was a divine sword available to him, and he would fight with it for her.

Which was why she was *not* going to pray about it. If her fears were banished, what would she cling to? She'd lose *all* control and race headlong into the emotional upheaval of falling in love and planning the future with hope, this time knowing full well that God could nix it at any point. If she had a choice in the matter, she didn't want to ever be in that position again.

She wiped her eyes with her sleeve and strode over to the bag of clay. She dug inside and pulled off a fistful, slapped it onto a tabletop and viciously pressed the heels of her hands into it, kneading it, crushing air bubbles.

Trent seemed still full of air bubbles, as if he hadn't been crushed enough by life. When the intense heat came, he didn't look so good. His character was splotchy; there was not enough depth in him to care for her above himself. He had never made her feel *cherished* or *safe*. When Dominick kissed her under the bridge, she was the most special woman who ever walked the earth. When he wrapped his muscular arms around her, it was his inner strength that protected her from the world.

Cat lifted a shoulder to rub the sleeve against her eyes again. *Uh-oh.* Tears were a bad sign.

Oh, Lord!

The following afternoon Cat pushed open the door marked *Housekeeping*. As usual, bleach-scented humidity and a dull thumping of the industrial-sized clothes dryer greeted her.

With hesitant steps she walked between floor-to-ceiling shelving units packed full of linens, cleaning supplies, and miscellaneous hotel room items. She heard a radio, soft strains of jazz mingled with the laundry noise. Where the room opened into a wider area, she stopped. Dominick sat writing at a desk, his back to her. His broad shoulders dwarfed the desk and chair. She noted that his black, rather shaggy hair was probably longer than hers, long enough even for a ponytail.

He set down his pen and folded his hands on the desktop. He seemed to be waiting, and she wondered if he sensed her standing six feet behind him. He was like that, attuned to details most people missed. A whiff of her perfume, a shadow, a slight shift in the air, even the pounding of her heart. Like Jesus, he knew her, probably knew she stood there, but he was the consummate gentleman. He would wait for an invitation before speaking.

"Dominick?"

His shoulders drooped, as if he exhaled a breath held for a long time. He swiveled in the chair to face her. "Hmm?"

"I've thought about it." On its own accord, her forefinger slipped into her mouth. "I—I don't want to do it."

"Did you pray about it?"

"Sort of."

"Doesn't count."

She bit harder on her fingernail and turned to leave. "Well, it has to."

"He's waiting to talk to you, Cat." Dominick was immediately beside her. He braced his right hand on a shelf near her head, cutting off her escape. "Just like I've been waiting all week. What's holding you back?"

She leaned against the shelf and stared at the top button of his plaid shirt. If she just didn't look at his face . . . "I like it where I am."

He placed his other hand on the shelf above her and leaned toward her, tilting his head until she had to meet his eyes. "I don't think we can move forward until you deal with this situation."

She blinked rapidly and whispered, "I know. That's just it."

"Are you saying there's nothing between us?"

No! Yes! No! "I don't *want* anything to be."

He smiled. "I think that's a moot issue at this point, *mi gatita.* We'll take it one step at a time, and this is the first step. A necessary one. Uncomfortable, I know. We'll get it over with tomorrow."

She bit another nail. His deep, whispery tones were doing something to her spine.

He pried her hand away from her mouth and gently kissed each fingertip one by one. "Would you like to go to church with me first? We'll let God adjust our perspective, ask for His blessing, eat lunch, and then just do it. Hmm?"

She winced.

He held her hand against his cheek and took a deep breath. "Cat, this is for me as much as it is for you. Will you do it for me?"

In his gray eyes she saw something new. Somewhere between the ice and the meltdown was pain. How could he care that much for her welfare? She nodded.

His eyes closed. "Thank you."

"Elli was with me."

"Is she afraid of that mall or shadows in the dark?"

She shook her head. Neither was her sister afraid of prayer.

"I'll pick you up at 10—"

"Well!"

They turned to see Cissy just inside the door.

"This is certainly professional!" The sarcasm in the young woman's voice was unmistakable. "Or does it mean inappropriate behavior is appropriate as long as it's done in Housekeeping?"

Dominick chuckled as he lowered his arms and straightened up. "It probably means you'll uninvite me to your party."

"You got that right, mister!"

Flustered, Cat finally found her voice. "Cissy, did you want something?"

"There's a phone call for you, *Miss* St. Clair." She turned on her heel and walked out.

Cat moved toward the door. Her head was beginning to pound.

"As I was saying," Dominick's voice held traces of laughter, "I'll pick you up at 10:15."

"All right. I think I'm going home now, after I take this call."

"Are you okay?"

She turned, her hand on the doorknob. "Yeah. It's just been a long week."

"Call me if you need anything."

"I'm supposed to say that. I'm the manager who's leaving five hours early."

"Don't worry. We'll take care of things."

"Maybe *you* will, but you'd better keep an eye on Cissy. A scorned woman is not nice." She opened the door.

"I didn't mean to scorn her. I'll tell her. Hey, Cat, will you wear your red jumpsuit?"

"I don't have a red jumpsuit."

"I thought you were wearing a red jumpsuit?"

"Oh, I threw that thing out. I knew I'd never wear it again. Bye."

"See you."

As she strode across the hall to her office, she dismissed the idea that she had never mentioned to Dominick what she had worn the day of the nightmare. She must have told him and just forgotten. Instead, she replayed his comforting "Call me if you need anything." That would get her through the night.

~ Fifteen ~

SITTING IN THE PEW NEXT to Dominick the next morning, Cat felt as if life were rushing along a roller coaster track with some unseen person at the controls. Forget slipping along a steep slope—this was turning into a totally unpredictable wild ride.

Here she was sitting in a church of all places with some guy she barely knew, thinking about doing something she desperately did not want to do. Why was that?

Because Dominick D'Angelo had lovely eyes and treated her respectfully and obviously cared for her welfare and made her laugh when she didn't want to and gave her space and hugs in just the right amounts? Probably.

Dominick now slid the hymnal into its place on the back of the pew in front of them. His shoulder brushed hers. The sheer solid presence of him flooded her with security.

She looked around and felt another reassurance in the grandeur of the stately old church. Located downtown, it exuded a different ambience from what she had known growing up, but Jesus was here too, and people worshiped Him. Was it His sheer solid presence that reassured? Was it okay if she just basked in that for a while?

This roller coaster ride must be what it was like to be carried on the updraft of someone else's prayers. She knew, of course, whose prayers those were, and she knew Whose hands were at the controls.

Cat felt Dominick's finger brush at the corner of her eye. She blinked back the tears.

"You all right?" he whispered.

She nodded. "I'm ready."

He tilted his ear toward her.

"I'm ready," she repeated.

He smiled and reached for her hand.

Goodness, she hadn't held hands in church since she was a teenager and her dad wasn't looking.

A short time later they stood on the sidewalk outside at the edge of the crowd, waiting for Dominick's friends to make their way over to them. She remembered Megan from the zoo. Her husband towered above her, decidedly more surfer than doctor in appearance.

"Meg, Adam, this is," Dominick paused and stared at her as if unsure of exactly who she was. ". . . Catherine St. Clair," he finished softly with a smile.

They greeted her warmly, both shaking her hand.

"I'm so glad to see you again," Megan exclaimed, her brown curls bobbing. "We've been hearing about you for such a long time. He calls you Cat. May we?"

"Yes."

"Will you two come for dinner tomorrow night? Please, please? You're both off from work, right?"

"Well . . ." Cat glanced at Dominick who raised his eyebrows, leaving the decision to her. "Yes," she said, "I'd like that. Thank you."

"About 6 then? Here . . ." Meg scribbled on a business card. "Call me if something comes up. Our number is unlisted." She handed it to Cat with a smile and leaned toward her. "I didn't think there was a woman alive who could get Dominick's attention. You must be very special, and I really want to get to know you. I'm glad you're coming."

They parted ways with promises to talk at length tomorrow.

As Dominick and Cat strolled to the parking lot, they discussed where to eat lunch. Their halfhearted conversation finally convinced them they weren't hungry. They shrugged at each other and climbed into his truck.

The mall was tucked between two freeways, its entrance off of Friars Road. Cat hadn't driven on that road for almost eight months now, often taking circuitous routes to avoid it. When Dominick signaled for its exit from the freeway, her heart raced.

"My dad," she gasped, "tried this once."

He shifted as they came to a stop at a light.

"We got as far as that next light." She remembered screaming.

"Was that a while ago?"

"In January." Begging. *Daddy, take me home!*

"Long, long time ago. Another lifetime."

Crying. *I can't do it!*

They approached the next intersection. Dominick reached over and squeezed her hand. "I'm with you now."

Screaming until Daddy had no choice but to turn around, take her home.

"And I'm bigger than your dad."

Cat's breath caught in a strangled giggle.

"Well, sort of. Take a deep breath. Younger anyway."

She closed her eyes as he turned into the parking lot, a tightness in her chest allowing only shallow breaths.

"Back in January," his low voice soothed, "I don't think the divine sword was ready yet. It was still in the blacksmith's shop, getting shaped for today."

She unhooked her seat belt, scooted across the bench seat toward him, and buried her face between his shoulder and the back of the seat, crossing her arms against her midsection. The truck came to a stop, then the engine cut.

"This is a big day for you, Cat. And it is going to be as bad as you imagine, but you will get through it. Trust me?"

She nodded.

"Let's go to that fountain in the center, then you go on

ahead, into the restaurant. I'll follow you. I think you need to do it by yourself."

By myself? She didn't answer. From the fountain to the restaurant? There were too many storefronts in between. It was too far.

He kissed the top of her head. "I'll be nearby."

"It's too far." Her voice was muffled against his shoulder.

"It's where you walk with God. There's no other way."

She looked up at him. "You said you'd do it with me."

His eyes held hers. "When you get inside the restaurant, I'll be there to hold you, and you won't have to be afraid anymore. Ready?"

She shrugged.

"You can do this, Cat. I'm with you, and God is right here with us."

They sat quietly for a few moments. She sat up and nodded. He took her hand as she slid from the truck.

On that day almost eight months ago now, the wide walkways along the mall had been filled with festive Christmas trees and fake snow villages. Silver garlands and red bows entwined the lamp poles. The winter weather had been its midday warm in the sunshine, sweater cool in the shade. The store windows displayed after-Christmas sale signs.

Cat had worn a favorite red jumpsuit, her hair pulled casually back in a ponytail. A new diamond sparkled on her left hand as she and Elli swung little Jason between them, entertaining him through the inevitably tedious ritual of returning wrong-sized gifts alongside hordes of post-holiday shoppers.

Today the crowd was sparse. Cat wore a simple white dress. In spite of the summer heat, goose bumps covered her arms. Dominick walked beside her, his dark hair set off by a white polo shirt tucked into black dress slacks, a somber warrior look on his face. She edged closer to him, trying to breathe deeply and calm the dread that filled her, trying not to remember that day. She wasn't successful.

At the fountain located halfway down the sprawling mall,

they stopped. Dominick took both of her hands in his. "Doing okay?"

She shook her head no.

He wrapped his arms around her and gave her a quick bear squeeze. "You go on ahead now." He glanced around.

"Walk with me."

"Then it wouldn't count. Let God walk with you, Cat. Talk to Him." He rubbed her arms, smoothing the chill bumps, and smiled. "I'll be close by, but I can't do what He can."

"But you'll come into the restaurant?"

"I'll come into the restaurant. That will be the toughest part." Quickly he kissed her cheek. "Go."

She took a backward step, then a few sideways steps. He gave her a thumbs-up sign, and she turned. *Oh, God.*

The fear was tangible. It was as if window shades in her mind were being pulled down one at a time. Darkness closed in.

Father! I can't do this alone!

The black lightened to gray.

Cat looked over her shoulder. Dominick wasn't there. She stopped and turned around in a full circle. Nowhere. He was nowhere!

"I'll be nearby. I'll be nearby."

He had to be there—he promised!

She crossed her arms over her waist. Thick blackness crept in again, now blocking even her eyesight.

"I will never leave you nor forsake you."

Promises. God was here just like Dominick. Unseen but here. And available. If she cried out, Dominick would come. She knew it. And so would her Father.

Oh, God, I need You. I don't want to be afraid anymore. Help me!

The mental shades lifted. A flower bed at her feet came into focus.

Cat continued down the sidewalk. God was as real as Dominick, and even nearer. He had always been there, waiting to answer her because He loved her . . . more than her parents, more than Trent . . . more than Dominick.

A hymn from the morning service sprang to her mind, and she began humming. *"Prone to wander, Lord, I feel it, prone to leave the God I love; here's my heart, O take and seal it."*

The scent of greasy french fries slowed her steps, churned her stomach. It was her little nephew's favorite place. How many outings would she miss with that child if she kept avoiding it?

With a shaky breath she walked to the glass front of the fast-food restaurant. It was an innocuous place, as usual full of friendly faces, all ages, talking and laughing at tables, in aisles, in line at the counter located at the rear, not far from a straight line of colorful booths shaped to look like train cars.

Eight months ago as they had entered, Elli and Jason went to stand in the food line while she headed to save a place on the "twain." He liked the locomotive the best, but it was most often taken. When its occupants that day began gathering their things, Cat bounded between tables toward it and then . . .

Not yet. Go inside first, she told herself.

She noticed a family approaching the restaurant. When someone opened the door, she stepped behind the group and followed them through it.

She was inside.

The crowd noise and the greasy smells were overpowering. Her heart thumped erratically. The sides of the room slipped from view as if she had tunnel vision. She saw only the path that led to the spot where terror had first entered her life.

Terror is not from Me.

It wasn't a voice but a distinct impression. *Dear Lord, dear Lord, dear Lord. Help me!*

A child bumped into her. Unintentionally, she moved.

Her breaths were shaky and her steps unsteady, both taken beyond her own willpower.

She reached it, that spot halfway between the counter area and the train, at the end of an aisle alongside a post, amidst people coming and going and eating and talking. She stopped.

An urge to turn around assaulted her. If she had turned that day, perhaps things would have ended differently. But she hadn't turned, she hadn't known there was a reason to turn . . . She resisted the urge.

The memory flashed vividly now. She sensed that she shouldn't fight it. It had to be replayed step by step.

She remembered the vicious tug on her ponytail. Her hands going to her head. Her cry of shock. Her body bending, turning slightly into the pull. The gun barrel inches from her face. The massive army green jacket filling her vision. The harsh voice barking unintelligible words.

Her screams.

Another voice. "Wrong one!"

Wrong one, wrong one, wrong one.

The pressure released. The gun was removed. The army green retreated.

His face. Nothing. A glimpse. Full, dark beard. Sunglasses . . . wire-rimmed, aviator shape. Red and white bandanna across the forehead, covering the hair.

The back of his head, bandanna tied above a ponytail. Blond? Dark? Red?

In less time than it took to tell the story, the intruder had crashed into her world and then vanished. With him fled all comprehension of God. A great nothingness engulfed her.

And then the blackness.

The blackness didn't come now. There was no escape.

Oh, God! she prayed. *Oh, dear Father! I lost You here. Let me find You again. Please let me find You again.*

Tears streamed down her face, and she felt a softness inside that hadn't been there for a long, long time. She wiped at her eyes. Things were going to be all right. They really were. Now that she was actually standing here, she knew the nightmare could become just a frightful memory. Over time even that would diminish.

Knowing she would cry, she had tucked a hankie into a pocket. Now she took it out and dabbed at her eyes. There was one more step. She had to turn around and see that nothing was there, prove to herself that the ghosts were gone. She heaved a sigh and peered over her shoulder.

Dominick stood directly behind her.

She smiled at him. "I'm okay," she whispered.

"Good. We'll finish it then."

She saw then the army green jacket he carried.

Her smiled faded, her skin prickled. What was he doing? Did he think they had to reenact the whole scenario complete with props?

As he shrugged into the coat, his head tilted, revealing the black hair tied into a short ponytail at his neck.

It was black hair! Black hair. Black hair . . .

He reached into a pocket, pulled out sunglasses. Wire-rimmed, aviator shape, reflective lenses. He slipped them on.

Blood pounded in her ears.

"Cat, you forgot to tell me about the bandanna." He wrapped a red and white kerchief across his forehead, over the top of his head, tied its corners at the back. "But I was wearing it, wasn't I?"

He caught her before she fell, his arms around her waist, bracing her against himself. Her knees refused to lock.

"I'm sorry," he whispered in her ear. "I am so sorry."

The nightmare terror bombarded her. A battle raged in her head; lightning flashes pierced thick blackness. Her heart thumped in her throat, choking her until all breath was gone. Still she saw his face, the glasses and grim mouth just inches from hers.

"Breathe, Cat. It's okay. It's okay. Come on, sweetheart. Breathe."

At last she emitted a strangled, "No!"

"Hold on, it's okay." He pressed her head to his chest.

She clutched his jacket. Against that rough olive green cloth that had haunted so many of her hours awake or asleep, she sobbed. "Not you! Not you!"

"Hey, mister!" a gruff voice exclaimed behind her. "What's going on?"

"My wife's not feeling well." The lie came swiftly. "Can we use the back door? I need to take her home."

"Yeah, sure. This way."

Across the floor and into the parking lot she moved awkwardly beside him, his arm around her waist, her face buried against his shoulder, her hands clinging to the jacket. Her sobs deepened. Each breath became a strangled gulp for air.

He lifted her into the truck. She huddled against the door, helpless to stop the flow of tears, unable to think coherently.

"Cat, please."

The next thing she knew, she looked up, and the truck had stopped.

"Talk to me?"

Talk! She didn't even know who he was! Her eyes were almost swollen shut. He was a watery blur across the seat. "Who are you?" She choked on the words. They sounded garbled to her ears.

"Let's go inside your place. I'll explain everything. Please."

"Who are you?!" she shrieked now.

He pulled off the bandanna and sunglasses. "I'm Dominick D'Angelo. I'm an agent with the Drug Enforcement Administration. I work undercover. Last December I was after a dealer who was spotted in that mall. I heard the description. Female, tall, red jumpsuit, ponytail. And then I saw you. Cat, I am deeply sorry and . . . I love you."

She opened the door, jumped out, and ran to her apartment building without a backward glance or thought, intent only on getting away.

~ Sixteen ~

WAS EVERYTHING a lie?

Of all the questions disturbing her head since yesterday, this was the one they all came down to, the one Cat needed answered. Now, at 7 o'clock Monday morning, she asked it again as she stood on the pier watching distant surfers bob in the ocean's gentle roll.

Dominick was out there somewhere. She had to ask him.

After leaving him outside her apartment, she had cried uncontrollably for a long while. In time she sensed a cleansing effect. Everything poured from her—eight months' worth of bot-tled-up disappointment and fear and anger, the hardness of her heart built on her willfully turning her back to God day after day.

She faced Him finally because there was no one else to face. Nothing made sense, and so she read the Bible, the book of Job, reminding herself that whatever happened, God deserved her trust and devotion. It was the only thing that mattered in life. It *was* life. At long last she prayed again.

There was no question of forgiving Dominick for his initial mistake, the incident at the mall. Despite the fact that her life had been turned upside-down and she had been angry at God, she knew the nightmare occurred for some beneficial purpose. She truly believed the gunman was an angel in disguise.

But that Dominick had betrayed her was beyond compre-hension. When had he first recognized her? Why hadn't he told her? How could he behave like a concerned friend—actually *promote* their relationship!—while concealing his true identity? How could he *kiss* her? And how could she fall for it?

And what in the world was he doing at her Castillo working maintenance?

Again, though, there was no question of forgiving him even for this. The Bible's teaching was clear. But it would take a long, long time.

She had called Elli, but there was no answer. She could not talk to anyone else. Angry as she was that she didn't understand, only Elli knew her well enough to let her vent her confusion and not hold her responsible. Daddy was out of the question. He really would go after the man.

Megan Parker.

Cat had found her phone number tucked in her purse. Did she know who he was?

The woman answered midway through the first ring.

"Megan? This is Ca—"

"Cat! I'm so glad you called! How are you?" The compassion in her voice said she did indeed know who he was and then some.

Fresh tears sprang to Cat's eyes as she clutched the phone. "Who is he?"

"Didn't he tell you?"

"Yes, but . . ." She bit her lip. "Why?"

"First, can you tell me what happened this afternoon? He promised to call but hasn't. That means he's very upset. He told us he was going to walk you through that horrible situation at the mall."

"You knew about that?"

"Oh, honey, it was a major event in his life. He didn't have anything to do with Jesus until that happened."

Cat sat down on the couch, pulled her knees up to her chest. "Was everything a lie?"

"No, no, no. He loves God. He is everything he appears to be except a temporary maintenance employee. He cares deeply for you. He has been in agony these past six weeks or so, not being free to tell you what he does for a living."

"Why couldn't he tell me?"

"I don't know. He doesn't tell us the details of what he's working on."

Her breath caught. "He's at the Castillo *working* on something? Some *drug* thing?"

"I assume so."

Dear Lord! "I'm so confused, Megan."

They had talked awhile. Cat was thankful for her new friend's comfort, for encouraging her to just talk to Dominick. Megan gave her his unlisted phone number, but Cat couldn't even make the effort to get up for pen and paper. Last night had been too soon to speak anyway. She needed time to absorb the shock of yesterday. She needed distance between learning the truth and deciphering what to do with it.

Megan also reminded her of his surfing habit. Now, this morning, she had become almost frantic to ask him that one question: Was *everything* a lie? She scanned the ocean for Megan's description—a black wet suit with faded red short sleeves, on the north side. Elbows propped on the wooden rail, she leaned over and focused far below the pier on the long, staggered row of surfers who waited patiently under a gray sky. The possibilities of finding him or not finding him both filled her with a dreadful anticipation.

Images of him flashed like a mental slide show. Dominick teasing her about picnic benches, playing with the children at the orphanage, painting on the ladder, dribbling the basketball, holding her while the migraine pounded, celebrating the inspection over dinner, sitting under her bridge. Dominick kissing her on this pier, agreeing it wasn't supposed to happen.

But all along he must have known who she was while she didn't have a clue who he was!

She saw the beginning of a wave, like the humpback of a whale underwater rolling toward the surfers. Many paddled with their hands, moving into position to catch its curl at just the right moment. Some missed it and turned back out to sea. Some stood for milliseconds, then plunged below the water's surface, their boards flying skyward. Some stayed with it, racing just ahead of the crashing foam, a sheet of fiberglass keeping their bare feet atop the water.

It was impossible to tell where he was. Cat hurried along the pier, now dreading the thought of missing him. She should wait on the beach until he came out. Megan said Adam assured her that he would be here this morning.

She finally spotted him in the shallow water carrying the board under his arm, tugging at the back zipper's string. He stopped in the sand near a pile of clothing, set down the board, and peeled the wet suit from his arms, shaking water from his hair.

She approached as he bent and picked up a towel.

"Cat!"

"You sound surprised. That's probably a first."

In spite of her bitter tone, his slow smile lifted. "The first time was when I walked into your office."

She blinked, turned her head sideways toward the pier. "You knew me then?"

"Oh, I knew you. I had been looking for you for six months. It was your eyes I could never forget. I used to hold up a jar of honey in the sunlight, trying to catch their color."

She bit her lip. "Daddy always called them maple syrup."

"Well, I was looking at them with different eyes."

"I don't understand." She looked at him now. He was standing very still, watching her, the towel in his hand, water dripping from him. "I don't even know where to begin to ask *how* to understand."

"I know. I'm sorry. You have every right to hate me—"

"No, I don't have that right. I know you made a mistake, and I forgive you, but I don't know you, and you know all about me. I am just so confused and angry. Was *everything* a lie?"

"No, ninety-nine percent of it wasn't. Let me start with the incident."

"Just tell me the one percent! What's not true?"

"Please. Give me five minutes? Please?"

"Don't manipulate me." She didn't hate him, but she knew she didn't trust him either.

"I won't. Just hear me out."

She waited, jaw clenched.

"Adam had been telling me about God for a long time. I listened to some of what he said, but I didn't really hear. When I held a gun to you and looked in your eyes, then I heard."

Her anger melted.

He took a deep breath. "Your beautiful, expressive eyes, Cat. I saw you asking, 'Why are you doing this to me?' And that's what I heard Jesus asking. You know, kind of like Saul on the road to Damascus? Why was I persecuting Him? Every day I chose to go my own way without Him, I was persecuting Him. I always hoped you would call the police, so I could thank you. I've been loving you for a long time, Catherine St. Clair, for that reason alone. You gave me a priceless gift, and I know what it cost you." His voice cracked.

She closed her eyes. This was too much.

"The only way I could make it up to you was to help you get over your fear at that place. I thought you were ready yesterday. I needed you to be ready because I was falling in love with you in a different way, not as the stranger who had changed my life forever. I mean, after I got to know you . . . well, what was there not to love?"

"Please don't say that. My life was ruined that day."

Dominick briskly dried his arms with the towel. "I think God only 'ruins' what He wants to rebuild into something even more beautiful." He bent and picked up a white T-shirt. "You know that."

She did, of course. "But it doesn't change my feelings, what I went through."

"No, it doesn't. Why don't you want to hear that I love you?" He placed his arms through the shirt sleeves, then gathered it in his hands.

Before he could slip it over his head, she reached out and touched a scar on his chest, toward his right shoulder. There were two short, pink, jagged slashes, close together. "What is this?"

"I was shot. That's when I met Adam. He saved my life."

"I thought you said you were in an accident." She met his eyes for a moment, and then he pulled on the shirt, breaking the contact. "Dominick, I don't want to hear it because I don't know you. It means *nothing* from a stranger. And you are still a stranger to me."

He swallowed. "Can we fix that?"

"I don't know. What are you doing at the Castillo?"

"It's almost finished. You don't have to worry about it."

"Tell me!"

"It's part of a drug run. Cocaine is dropped there, picked up by a few dealers."

"No!" she cried and covered her mouth with her hands.

"Cat, everything will be fine when it's over. We'll do what we can to keep a lid on the publicity."

She peered at him over her fingertips. "Who . . . ?"

"I can't say."

"Dominick, not my castle!"

"I will take care of it. You understand, it's imperative that you not tell anyone who I am. Absolutely no one. Not Ron or Trent or Cissy. Not your dad."

She nodded. "Do you have a gun?"

"It's part of the job."

"You can't take a gun to my castle!"

"We can pray I won't need to. Okay?"

She closed her eyes.

"Cat, will you meet me at Adam and Meg's tonight? They know me better than anyone. They can fill in the gaps. Please come?"

"I don't know." She lifted a shoulder.

"Think about it?" His head tilted in that gentle way that had become so familiar. "Pray about it?"

She winced, knowing at last one thing for certain. "Yes, I will do that," she agreed, then hurried away as quickly as she could drag her feet through the sand.

It was after 7 P.M. that night. She sat outside in a cushioned patio chair at Megan and Adam Parker's home, her legs curled up, wrapped in a sweatshirt to ward off the early evening cool that settled in with the chill that had lingered inside her all day.

"Is he always this late?" she asked.

Adam and Megan exchanged glances. Adam answered, "Dominick's schedule is unpredictable. We usually try to grab him after church."

"But he's always at work on time, sometimes early—" Cat realized it was his other job that got him there. "Does that mean he's working now?"

Adam nodded. "If it would help for you to ask us more about him, go ahead."

There was no pretense with these two, she had noticed soon after her arrival. They welcomed her like an old friend, offered her appetizers and drink, skipped weather talk, volunteered information about themselves. They asked her about the Castillo de Cala, about her family, her school. "Well," she raised her brows, "I guess that's why I came tonight. He said you could fill in the gaps. And there are gaps. I'm having a hard time fig-uring out how to process all this."

Megan stepped over to her and squeezed her hand. "I can't imagine how difficult this is for you. Do you remember when we met at the zoo? Dominick said you were his boss. I just assumed you were his DEA boss. He wouldn't let me near you after that. But I've been praying for you, that you can forgive him and trust him again. I don't like what he does, but they tell me it's neces-sary, that he accomplishes good." She returned to her seat.

"Mind if I start, love?" Adam winked at his wife. "I'm sure Cat has enough emotionalism to deal with."

Megan waved a hand at him and pulled a tissue from her pocket.

Adam chuckled. "Well, about two years ago I was on ER duty, middle of the night. A few guys were brought in, a couple of them in pretty bad shape. There had been a drug bust, a shooting. I worked on the one I figured was the bad guy. You know firsthand how grungy Dominick can look—long hair, unshaven, dirty, torn jeans. He was in tip-top physical shape, but still it was touch and go for a long time. When he woke up, we hit it off and began spending time together.

"He was, to put it mildly, an emotional wreck, and the recovery period was good for him that way. It gave him time to begin unwinding. He grew up in Chicago and has a younger brother. Did he tell you that?"

She nodded. "Did he live in a poor neighborhood with an alley for a backyard? And did he punch his dad, who left them afterwards?"

"He told you that?" Adam's tone was surprised.

"I didn't know that," Megan interjected.

"Cat, I can guarantee that whatever Dominick told you was the truth—he just didn't always tell you everything." He locked his eyes with hers. "Can you accept that?"

"I—I'll try."

"I don't know another man with as much integrity as he has. That's why he chose to do what he does. His childhood was harsh. He got into drugs early on. When his best friend died of an overdose when they were sixteen, he quit cold turkey. I don't think he's taken an aspirin since then. He almost killed the guy who sold them the stuff. Fortunately he got connected with some big-brother types, went to college, became a Chicago cop, then joined the DEA, trained at Quantico, lived various places doing undercover type work.

"I know he feels he's paying off a debt to his friend. He has a love-hate relationship with what he does. I don't know how long he can keep it up. What he did to you at the mall almost put him under. They forced him to take two weeks off, then stuck him behind a desk for a while. The whole time he kept searching for you. He hung out at the mall, kept checking with the police, hoping you'd report the incident."

"I went to an emergency room."

"Emergency room?"

"I guess I blacked out. My head hit the floor. I went to one up in North County. I didn't explain the incident."

Megan blew her nose.

Cat shrugged a shoulder. "It's okay. I mean, it—it wasn't. I had migraines for six months, but now I know God was working in me."

Megan's curls bobbed. "He was doing His work in Dominick too. He wouldn't have been ready for you back then. When God finally brought the two of you together, you were a suspect again, so—"

"Suspect? *I* was a suspect? At the Castillo?"

Megan threw Adam a look of panic. He intervened. "Cat, he has to distrust everyone until he figures out who's involved."

She felt blindsided again, hit with another incomprehensible facet of Dominick D'Angelo. "But how . . . how could he think I was . . . ?"

"A long time ago he loved a woman who double-crossed him. He learned the hard way that no matter what someone appears to be, it may be just that, an appearance, not the truth."

She closed her eyes. "When did he stop thinking I was a suspect?"

"I don't know."

Her lids flew open, and she pleaded, "*Did* he stop thinking that way?"

"Oh, yes," Megan assured her, "yes, he did. Otherwise he never would have told you who he was. The last time I talked to him, he told me about your trip to Tecate. He even told me what the grandmother said to him, to take care of you. He wouldn't have told me that if he wasn't thinking the same thing."

"He told you what Rosa said? How did he know what Rosa said?"

"Didn't she talk to him?"

"In Spanish! She doesn't speak English, and he doesn't speak Spanish!"

The Parkers exchanged glances.

"He does speak Spanish?"

They both nodded.

"Oh, I can't think this way. It's just too complicated and confusing."

"Adam," Megan cried, "say something!"

He sighed. "It *is* complicated and confusing, Cat. None of us would deny that. The bottom line is, kids are dying from drugs. Dominick fights that day in and day out. He works with incomplete information. Sometimes he knows only that the bad guy is wearing a red jumpsuit or works at a motel. He betrayed you because he didn't know how else to protect those kids on the street. Every time he told you something like he lived in Chicago but didn't tell you he was a cop there, or like he knew some Spanish words but didn't tell you he was fluent, he died a little inside. And I know that's true because he told me you're the most significant person in the world to him."

He stood. "Now, Meg, are we going to eat dinner or not? I'm famished." He walked over to Cat, pulled her to her feet, and hugged her. "That's from Dominick, God bless his rude soul."

She gave him a small smile. "Thanks. I was beginning to think your bedside manner is really lousy."

Megan hugged her then. "And this is from us."

— Seventeen —

"SO WHERE'S YOUR *'friend'*?"

Cat swiveled around in her desk chair to see Cissy just inside her office door. "Cissy! You startled me. I wish you'd knock when the door's shut."

"It was open." She sat in a chair, crossed her legs, and propped an elbow on the desk. "Pardon the expression, but you look like something the cat dragged in. Do you have a headache?"

"No, I just didn't sleep well last night. I'm a little tired. By the way, I need the to-date August figures for a meeting with Ron on Thursday. Can you get your stuff to me tomorrow?"

"Sure. Did you and your 'friend' have a spat?"

"What 'friend'?"

"Dominick." She flipped her long blonde hair off a shoulder.

Cat massaged her forehead. Maybe she did have a headache. So much had happened since Cissy had seen Dominick holding her hand in the Housekeeping room. She had gone from trusting him to total confusion regarding everything about him except the fact that his subtle Secret Service air was for real, just clothed in a different name—DEA Special Agent. And she wasn't supposed to tell. "He's just a friendly, hard-working temp. We're not *'friends'* as you say."

Cissy laughed. "Things didn't look just *friendly* and temporary with the two of you all snuggled up in Housekeeping." She threw up her hands at Cat's frown. "Hey, it's okay. He really isn't my type. I'm just a little surprised he's your type."

"It wasn't what it looked like." *Well, not exactly what it looked like . . . certainly not anymore.* "He was telling me something about God."

Cissy guffawed loudly. "God? Man, is he yanking your chain. Two weeks ago he was at a big party, smoking dope and drinking tequila at 2 in the morning."

Inwardly she cringed. Was this another side of Dominick D'Angelo . . . ? *No! Not drugs!* Nothing was as it seemed. What was it Adam had said? Dominick dealt with incomplete information. This was incomplete information. Could he *appear* as if he were smoking, drinking—

"Don't worry." Cissy leaned across the desk and patted her hand. "This rebound season will pass and you'll be fine. No more Trents or Dominicks. Anyway, he's not here. And he hasn't called us or the temp service. Maybe he's not so hard-working."

"He's still not here?" Cat glanced at her watch. It was 6 o'clock. She hadn't seen him since yesterday morning at the beach. He had never shown up last night at the Parkers'.

"Aha, you checked! You *were* looking for him."

"Cissy . . ." She stopped herself from accusing the younger woman of crossing the line of respect toward her boss. What made her think she was above reproach just because she happened to be in an assistant manager's position? "Cissy," she repeated in a different tone, "I apologize for not behaving professionally. We weren't snuggling in Housekeeping, but it was close enough to be just exactly what I told you not to do. I'm sorry."

The younger woman stared at her.

Cat saw behind the mask of bravado then. Cissy's face resembled a little girl's, a hurting little girl's. "Do you know God loves you?"

"Save it, Cat." She stood. "I've been on my own for a long time. We've got a couple of maintenance-type problems in rooms. What do you suggest?"

"Where's Miguel?"

"At home. Family emergency."

She sighed. "I'll pull Chris from the restaurant after they slow down. He's handy with tools. Can it wait an hour?"

"Yes." Cissy shut the door behind her.

Cat distinctly remembered closing the office door before sitting down at her computer. Cissy often popped in, as if the door were open. Their good rapport had allowed her an easy access that had become Cat's biggest help during the unbearable days after the nightmare. There were times that if she hadn't covered for her, found her medication, led her to an empty guest room, or arranged a ride home for her, she would have been in trouble. Had she ever thanked Cissy for that? Really thanked her?

Probably not. The past eight months had been an intense focus on herself. Who else had she ignored or hurt along the way? What all had she missed?

Besides cocaine dumped at her castle?

She covered her face with her hands and held back a sob.

Who was involved? Everybody was so nice!

Oh, Father, please just fix it. And take care of Dominick, wherever he is.

By the next evening at 6 o'clock the strain was wearing on Cat. She pulled a compact from the desk drawer and applied more makeup, trying to cover the dark circles under her eyes and to press away the crease between her brows.

Dominick still hadn't been heard from. She had called the Parkers four times. Megan assured her this morning that it wasn't uncommon for him to be gone a week or two without communicating, but she promised to let her know the moment they heard anything. She made Cat promise the same, as if he would call her first. As if she were his friend.

Friends wasn't the word. Neither friends nor *"friends"* the way Cissy said it. Not even *acquaintances* described the weird set of circumstances that allowed them to meet. Twice. Only God could design such a crisscrossing of paths.

She snapped shut the compact.

Whatever.

Cat buried herself as best she could in work. There was enough to keep her occupied as long as she could force herself to concentrate on it. At 11, unable to keep Dominick from the center of her mind any longer and not yet ready to go home, she walked around the grounds one more time.

Where was he? Was he all right? How did she feel about him? How could she know what she felt when the only Dominick she knew was the temporary maintenance employee? And what was going on at her castle? She tried to turn all the questions into prayers. Her attempts felt like dismal failures. The old fear kept getting in the way, pointing the questions back into herself.

Back in the lobby, Cissy was waiting for her. "Well," she smiled, "it seems you have a new admirer already!"

"Admirer?"

"Someone named Adam just called. Ni-ice voice."

"What did he say?"

"He said, 'Please tell her that her angel in disguise is waiting.'" She waggled her eyebrows. "So, why is he your angel in disguise?"

Adam wasn't. Dominick was. She had called him that once, before she knew who he was. He must be there then, at the Parkers'. Cat took a deep breath. "Umm, I didn't recognize him as—as someone I'd care for." She shrugged. "But now I do."

"Wow, you work fast."

"Prayer works, Cissy. Not always fast or the way I want it to, but it works."

Angel in disguise. In a sense that was what she did know of Dominick. He was God's way of preventing her from marrying Trent . . . of smashing the imaginary castles she had built with her own hands without His blessing . . . of wounding her in the hope that she would turn to Him for healing. If that were true, it made Dominick D'Angelo a rather significant person in her life. That seemed a good place to begin knowing someone.

Before she could ring the Parkers' bell, Megan opened the front door and greeted her with a hug. "He's all right."

Cat heard tension in her new friend's voice. "But?"

"Well, he was hurt." She shut the door and tried to smile. "Adam thinks a couple of cracked ribs, says no big deal. He taped him to ease the pain. You know, I always imagine the good guys yell 'Halt, you're under arrest', and the bad guys freeze and hold up their hands."

"What happened?" A vision of Dominick being rammed hard enough to crack ribs flashed through her mind. "No, on second thought, I don't need details."

"Me neither. He's down there, in the den." She pointed at the hall that led from the entryway. "He showed up here about 10:30. Adam's gone to the hospital now and wanted him to go, but you know Dominick. As long as he's awake and breathing, he doesn't need a hospital."

"Megan, I don't know Dominick. I don't really know the first thing about him."

She squeezed Cat's hand. "You can start now, if you want."

She hesitated a moment, eyeing the closed door at the end of the hall. Dim light outlined it; muted television voices came from beyond it. Walking toward it was more intimidating than going through the mall the other day. There at least she knew the fear that lay ahead. Now there was only an injured stranger, but she sensed that her attraction to him could very well turn her entire world upside-down. And that was the greatest fear of all.

Cat brushed her knuckles against the door.

"Meg, you don't have to knock." His voice was strained.

She pushed open the door and caught a glimpse of white bandaging where the top of his flannel shirt was unbuttoned. It was the sight of the rest of him, though, that halted her just inside the door and flung her flippant reply back against her throat. In a recliner, footrest raised, her big, dark-alley type sat motionless. With each breath he took, pain etched a new furrow across his face.

He closed his eyes and pressed a remote clutched under his

hand on the armrest. The low volume on the television was muted. "What are *you* doing here?"

"Hey," she swallowed, "you were supposed to meet me at Adam and Meg's two nights ago."

He didn't reply.

"Not to mention, Jack, that faucets are dripping all over the motel and I've had to drive the shuttle van twice."

"Sorry. My schedule changed. My real schedule." He struggled with every word. "That feels good." He looked at her now through half-closed eyes. "To say that to you. 'Real' schedule."

She went to him and, taking his hand, sat on the floor beside the chair.

"Don't cry, Cat." With a small grunt as if the effort hurt, he reached over with his other hand and gently stroked her cheek.

Oh, how could she care for this guy she didn't even know?

"No more lies or half-truths. I promise. What are you doing here?"

"Adam called. I've been pestering him and Megan since Monday, asking about you. He knew I was . . . concerned."

"What'd he say?"

"He left a message—"

"You didn't talk to him?" Barely audible as his voice was, it had an anxious tone.

"No. Cissy did. She thinks I have a new beau named Adam."

"What'd he say?"

"My angel in disguise was waiting."

A small smile lifted the corner of his mouth. "Good old tight-lipped Adam."

"Why did he say that?"

"So that only you would know it was me." He brushed hair from her forehead. "I told him about it the day you said it. It was my first ray of hope . . ." He stopped.

"Hope? For what?"

"That you'd want to get to know me. Who wouldn't want to get to know their angel in disguise?"

Yes, who wouldn't? She smiled softly. "I guess that's why I came tonight."

"Well, this is it." He leaned his head back against the chair, breaking eye contact. "This is my life. Gone for three days without a word. No regular sleep or meals. Still fighting, like when I was a kid. Sticking a gun in the face of an innocent woman."

"Dominick . . ." She laid her cheek on his hand. "I forgive you for that."

"For that." He looked down at her. "I've been lying to you since the moment we met." His honesty was brutal.

A tear slid from the corner of her eye onto his hand. "Give me time."

He turned away. "Next week I could be told to move to New York, and I'd go. It's my work, what I signed up for. Impressed yet? I can tell you your dad would not be impressed." He rubbed his eyes. "I need to sleep."

"What about the Castillo? What's going to happen?"

"I don't know the timing—no, I do know, but I won't tell you. You'll be fine. It's nothing like what this just was. Please don't worry."

"What do I do?"

"Nothing, Cat, nothing. Just promise you won't worry."

Not answering, she stood, tired and more confused than ever. How could he hope that she wanted to get to know him and practically in the same breath consider moving across the country?

"Promise me."

She nodded.

His eyes closed. "Be careful going home."

"Bye."

She found Megan in the kitchen.

"Oh, Cat . . ." The woman took one look at her face and hugged her again. "He hasn't slept for forty-eight hours. Whatever he said, don't take it to heart."

"When exactly can I take to heart what this guy says?"

"I don't know. Leave it in God's hands. He's a potter, like you. And I suspect He's creating something exquisite."

~Eighteen~

CAT SLEPT BETTER THAN she expected, probably in relief that Dominick was safe. When she awoke, she lay in bed and tentatively directed her thoughts to God, thanking Him for those two things, sleep and safety. To her surprise, she immediately realized that something was missing from her usual morning awareness.

Fear.

The nightmare had lost its power. Trent and her castle dreams had been obliterated. Dominick D'Angelo was one big question mark on the horizon. She was a lump of clay and not the potter . . . And yet there was cause for hope. Her trustworthy Father had better plans than she could ever design.

She'd have to tell her parents their prayers were answered. They would be thrilled. But that would mean getting into who Dominick was. Who he was at the mall . . . who he was at the Castillo . . . what he did for a living. It would have to wait.

That decision made her uncomfortable. She didn't withhold from her parents. Maybe she could tell them only that Dominick had helped her go to the mall and that she wasn't afraid anymore. That could cover it for now.

A thought struck her. Was this just a hint of what Dominick dealt with day in and day out?

Dear Lord, please give him strength for this day. And how about a new job while You're at it?

She bounded from the bed, eager to start living without being afraid.

Cat wished she could talk with Elli, but that was out of the question for the moment. She was glad her sister would assume that as usual this week was keeping her necessarily occupied. Other friends came to mind, ones she had let drop by the wayside through the months. Some had offered help during the really tough time, but she had only wanted Trent and only allowed Elli. Now she felt like throwing a party in her ugly new apartment. Perhaps sometime soon.

Knowing the best outlet for her excess energy was a few extra hours spent in preparation for the Castillo's upcoming party, she left early. A few years ago she had created an end-of-summer festival, to attract families before they returned to school routines. Sign-ups were scheduled for a week from Friday. That Saturday would be filled with games and tournaments, ending in a hog roast and ice cream party and a swashbuckling fencing demonstration. Sunday offered an informal church service on the beach and late checkout time.

Later that afternoon she strolled around the property, writing notes to herself about what was needed for decorations. At the pool she stood and watched giggling children splash in the water. It was a beautiful, warm summer day. She hadn't noticed for a long time how refreshing it was to work outside under the bright blue sky. That was another plus for her job, being able to come outside at will, or for that matter stay inside when the winter drizzles came. Another was to wear whatever suited the role her agenda called for. Today, as assistant-manager-party-coordinator, she wore casual, multicolored overalls and a fuchsia T-shirt without a second thought as to whether or not it was appropriate for the managerial half of the title.

Until she saw Trent walking toward her.

She scribbled furiously on the clipboard. The overalls were ditzy, faddish, definitely not classic, not *haute couture*, not— *Oh, dear Lord, do we really have to do this today?*

"Hello, Cat." All the blue from the sky and the swimming pool gathered in Trent's eyes. "You look great, like an end-of-summer festival, all wrapped up." He smiled.

She swallowed the *Huh?* and said, "Thank you."

"Do you have time now to talk with Ron and me? We're going over some budget items and need your insight. I realize you were scheduled to do it later—"

"No, now's fine."

Trent opened the gate for her, and they walked side-by-side through the courtyard. She noted with surprise that he was minus the usual suit coat. He and Ron must really be into the figures. But as usual he looked good in his long-sleeved white shirt, dark tie, and trousers. His light brown hair, neatly trimmed above the ears and across the neck, was cut so straight it could be used for a ruler.

"How are you?" His tone was sincere.

She stuck a hand in front of his face and wiggled her fingers. "Nails are growing."

"That's a good sign."

"Mm-hmm. And I went to the mall this weekend."

"Ah, shopping?"

She stared up at him. "*The* mall."

"*The* mall?" He thought for a moment, then his eyes widened. "You haven't been there?"

She turned away and bit her lip.

Trent pulled her arm through his and crooked his elbow. "I'm sorry, Cat. I'm sorry I didn't know, and I'm sorry I've let you down in so many ways."

She didn't reply. They had been through the apologies months ago.

He squeezed her hand. "It's the end of August."

She knew the date, of course. Because it was almost time for the festival, she knew the date, but she had buried the connection to the fact that it was almost September. Five weeks from tomorrow was to have been their wedding rehearsal and dinner. She had planned it to take place after this busy time at the Castillo—after the late summer's heat, when her parents' backyard captured that subtle shift of seasons and would provide the perfect early evening reception atmosphere.

He loved her, had loved her anyway, in his own way. It was his wedding too, his future.

She leaned her head against his arm. "I'm sorry too, Trent."

He stopped and drew her close.

With her arms wrapped around his neck, Cat felt she was in essence releasing him. She knew the headache wouldn't come this time, knew she could let the emotional pain go. She could forgive him.

He held her tightly for another moment. "Wanna have dinner?"

She leaned back to look up at him. "No."

He winced. "Maybe another time?"

"Maybe." She smiled. "Sometime."

"You have the most beautiful smile, Catherine. I will never ever find another smile like yours." With a dramatic sigh, he kissed her cheek and let go.

When they reached the lobby Cissy beckoned to her. She told Trent she'd meet him in Ron's office in a few minutes and walked over to the registration counter.

Cissy grinned. "Did you see Dominick?"

"Dominick's here?" Cat glanced at her watch, hiding her expression while she did some quick mental gyrations. What was she supposed to do? What exactly did she know, supposedly or otherwise? What didn't she know? What was he doing here anyway? Was it time *now*?

"Yeah, he looks like he's been partying a little too hearty."

"So," she searched for a nonchalant tone, "where's he been?"

"When I asked him, he just winked, you know like he does, shrugged, and asked what needed to be done first." Cissy giggled.

Cat interpreted the giggle to mean that the young woman's on-again, off-again Dominick infatuation was on again. "And you said?"

"He was fired." She giggled some more. "Seriously, I told him about the handrailing in the west wing."

"Okay, that's good." He was *working*? "I'll be in Ron's office." She hurried off, called "two minutes" as she darted past Ron's open door, then ducked into her office and shut the door. She had to compose herself.

What was he doing? She didn't think the charade needed to continue now that she knew. Wouldn't he just come unexpectedly, wearing some sort of official-looking suit and tie, flash a badge and announce who was to get into the paddy wagon?

Cat crossed her arms over her head and slid along the door until she sat on the carpet. No, he wore a ponytail and grungy army jacket and flashed a gun. And he got his ribs broken while fighting. The old terror engulfed her again.

Lord, I don't understand. I can't do this.

There was a soft knocking.

She stopped breathing.

Another knock. "Cat . . ."

It was Dominick. She stood, opened the door wide enough for him to step through, then shut it again.

"Cat," his voice was a low whisper, "sit down." He steered her toward a chair, then knelt before her, rubbing her hand between his. "It's all right. Relax."

She couldn't catch her breath, couldn't stop shaking.

"Relax." He smiled. "It's just me."

Me? Who is me? "Your smile," her breath came in a hiccup, "isn't right. The real one tucks in." She touched the right corner of his mouth. "Here."

His eyes closed briefly. When they opened, the ice had frozen over. "Undercover smile."

"Dominick, don't!" She threw her arms around him.

"Ouch!"

She sat back. "I'm sorry! I'm sorry! Oh, I can't do this."

Through clenched teeth he growled, "You don't have to do *anything!* Go about your business. I'll get a hammer and screwdriver and go about mine, and I will avoid you for the remainder of the day. That's all there is to it. Got it?"

She shuddered.

"Dear Father . . ." Dominick stared back at her, but he was praying. ". . . we need help here. She can't lie. Everything shows on her face. Please calm her so others won't be concerned and ask her what's wrong. In Jesus' name—"

"Amen," she whispered.

Gingerly he rose. "You could just go home. The place will stand without you here watching over it for one day. The budget can wait."

How did he know so much? She took a deep breath. "If I lose it again, I will. I promise."

"I was concerned about your initial reaction. You'll be fine, Miss Jill-of-all-trades." He winked and quickly slipped through the door.

Cat wondered if God answered Dominick's prayer with a gift of anger instead of peace.

The fact alone that he prayed confidently with her had a calming effect . . . until she thought of his pretend smile or his wink or not telling her what to expect. With those thoughts, the anger flooded her.

At least no one seemed to notice her condition, and that itself *was* the answer to prayer. She had made it through the meeting with Trent and Ron more or less intact. There were no surprises in their budget discussion, so she was well-rehearsed for that interchange. Twice, though, Ron did ask her if she felt all right, mentioned she looked pale. And Trent remarked that her hair looked fine, she needn't keep toying with it. She mumbled something about crepe paper for the festival.

Afterward he followed her into the hallway. "Cat, you will tell me if you change your mind? About dinner?"

She felt a vague notion that he interpreted her distraction as a hopeful sign for himself. If she weren't so unnerved, she probably would have laughed.

For the remainder of the workday she wasn't put on the spot. Thankfully she didn't see Dominick. No one saw panic on her face and asked what was wrong. She didn't have to decide how to circumvent the truth, which was that she was worried out of her mind because this man who was an undercover agent who carried a gun was the complete antithesis of Trenton Carver and yet had captured her attention in a way that Trenton Carver never even approached.

Not to mention that someone at her castle was dealing drugs.

No wonder she was angry. And where was God? According to Dominick, He was right there in the midst of it all, listening to a prayer about how she needed a peaceful countenance so Dominick's work would not be hampered.

It was after 11 now, and she should be going home. Instead she strolled down the dimly lit courtyard toward the pool. *This* was her home too! She had always felt a personal responsibility to the families who stayed here. Like a mother, she would make her rounds, locking doors, shutting off lights, symbolic to her of tucking everyone in.

This drug business added a whole new dimension to her usual concern. She had to make at least one more round, linger awhile, reassure herself that everyone was safe. If a room had been available tonight, she would have used it. If she had a couch in her office, she'd even consider sleeping on that. She simply could not leave.

It was anxiety that kept her here. And truthfully it wasn't anxiety *just* about the threat of what Dominick, probably along with other agents and the police, might do at any moment. It was about standing last night in the Parkers' hall and realizing that she was falling in love with a man she knew innately but not practically. It was about wondering what he was going to do about their relationship, what she wanted him to do. It was about not knowing if there was even enough between them to *do* anything about.

Yes, she was anxious, and she knew what to do about that, but still she hesitated to pray. This was the type of thing to leave totally up to God, trusting Him to work out the details.

The clincher was that a relationship with Dominick was out of the question. It was totally unimaginable, and totally unimaginable relationships did not fit her agenda. There were certain things she expected to occur in her life. A house, which her dad would build, inland. Three babies, hopefully a boy and two girls. All the sports for all of them. Car pool . . . make that minivan pool. Season zoo passes. Part-time work at the Castillo. She had a timetable, albeit about eight months behind schedule at the moment.

Well, she had come a long way in those eight months. What had she learned exactly? Following preconceived rules of the Christian life did not guarantee fulfillment of the agenda. Obviously God wanted more of a say in her agenda choices, wanted more of a hand in shaping her.

How would Jesus respond if He were in her shoes—those of an adopted daughter in a loving family, who enjoyed a job that utilized her talents and gave pleasure to others, who was afraid of the love she felt for a man because it might hurt, who didn't want to let go because God might have something else in mind?

Jesus would pray. He'd pray a lot about everything. He'd give love to others and accept love in return. He wouldn't worry about possible future wounds, because each day every need would be met. He wouldn't make up rules about if He did this, His Father would have to do that. He would trust in His *Father's* agenda.

She remembered the first time Dominick had talked about God, when they were by the garden footbridge. She had seen the look of awe on his face, the wonder at knowing that the Creator of the universe loved him. Had she lost that somewhere along the way? In the comfort of being able to talk to God as her Father, she had become casual, her worship routine. She had even had the audacity to snub Him for a time.

Now she strolled along the sidewalk that paralleled the small beach. Bay water lapped gently against the sand. Except for the reflection here and there of the few lamps that lined the walk, the water was black. The misty air obliterated the stars from view.

Obliterating the stars . . . but only from her point of view.

They were still shining. She knew that. She had always known that. She had just ignored the fact.

As she followed the walk, Cat began humming. Soon the words took shape, words asking for forgiveness, words uncurling her fist that clutched her perfect agenda, her castle dreams. It was so hard, but for the first time in her life she wanted to do it.

She reached the far northwest corner of the grounds, the pile of boulders that served as an informal boundary. Beyond, the sidewalk continued through a group of low buildings owned by some community group. This time of night it was always deserted, lending the Castillo an air of a large private estate.

Cat paused near the boulders, remembering her dream as a young girl of being a princess who lived in a castle and spent her days dispensing outrageous gifts. In a sense it was fulfilled, even if Prince Charming had fled the scene and business was precarious. For the time being she could still create a respite for others from the harsh world. Perhaps that should be enough. And as for Dominick— Well . . . ?

Well, he was still one big question mark.

Dominick crouched in the night shadows next to Brent Engstrom. They were behind the tall wooden fence at the end of the service drive, in the oleander bushes where last week he had trimmed away some of the thick leafy branches.

He shifted his weight and stifled a groan. It was at times like these that he considered thirty-five an old age, too old for this line of work. Each breath he took punctuated the sharp pain on the right side of his rib cage. That coupled with one good night's sleep out of the last five left him running on empty.

And then there were his emotions, like a field of land mines he didn't have the wherewithal to inspect. The mere thought of Cat set off internal explosions. The image of her tears last night spilling from those honey-colored eyes wouldn't leave. No one had ever cried over him like that before; no one had grieved over his pain, forgiven him so freely, accepted him for who he was, unafraid.

Engstrom nudged him. Dominick peered through the fence. An unmarked white van was backing down the service drive.

He tried to snap his mind to attention, slam shut the doors to all other thoughts and feelings that did not pertain to this moment. None of the old tricks worked. He knew he was in dangerous territory. Somebody could get hurt.

Dear God, I'm at the end of myself. Isn't this where You do Your best work?

Engstrom began videotaping through a tiny knothole. The exchange would be recorded. Later, somewhere down the freeway, the driver would be stopped by CHP officers for an imaginary broken taillight. And then they would read him his rights.

In the meantime, Dominick and Engstrom would monitor those involved at the Castillo. They knew the coke would be stashed in the turrets—

He heard off-key humming. His heart skipped a beat.

He touched Engstrom, silently motioned his intentions, then slid from behind the bushes.

He couldn't see her. Slipping from shadow to shadow beneath the trees, he hurried toward the sound.

What was she doing here?

Reaching the maintenance garage, he saw Cat strolling toward it, undoubtedly heading around it on her way toward the fence at the end of the service drive. The reverse of her usual route and two hours beyond it, she was about to walk into—

They would hurt her.

Unless they were expecting her.

He rushed to her.

A large shadowy figure came into Cat's view, just a few yards away. No sooner had she halted than she knew intuitively it was Dominick. Before she could react, he was beside her.

"Dom—"

He pressed his fingers against her lips, gently but firmly.

She got the hint to be quiet, but when his other arm grasped her around the waist, she wriggled. He squeezed her to his side and nudged her along the sidewalk. She stumbled. He lifted her, and her feet skimmed the concrete, then slipped through the sand as he urged her toward the boulders. When they reached the far side of them, he released her.

"Cat!" It was a hiss. "What are you doing here?"

"Oh!" She leaned toward him and hissed back, "Can't you just walk up to me like a normal person?"

"Answer me! What are you doing out here?"

"I don't have to answer you!"

"You're supposed to be gone by now." His voice was husky, almost threatening.

"So are you!" In a flash she realized that when he was pressed against her side, she had felt the gun beneath his jacket. "I'm dealing drugs, Dominick!" Her voice rose in anger. "What do you think?"

"Cat!"

"That's what you think! That's what you've always thought!"

He sucked in his breath. "Talk to me."

The light was too dim to read his eyes, but she could discern the ice in them. She couldn't communicate with that, wouldn't even try. "No." She spun on her heel, but he grabbed her wrist and twisted her back around. "Dominick!"

"Talk to me," he repeated.

"Not when you sound like that."

"I'm working, Cat; this is how I sound when I'm working. Now for the record, talk to me. Why are you here?"

"You're hurting my wrist." She yanked it away. "Why do you think I'm here? I work here! I live here! I care about this place. It's my castle, my home! You know all that. Why are you like this?"

He leaned back against a rock and pulled her to himself, held her head against his neck.

She resisted, but he didn't let go. His chest heaved, and she realized that he still hurt, physically and emotionally. She stopped struggling. Unsure where to hold him between injured ribs and a gun, she just nestled her face against him, laid her hands on his shoulders. They stood, silent except for his labored breathing.

"Oh, Cat. I'm sorry. I feel like I'm losing my mind. I can't remember you're not one of them."

"Not one of who? What's happening?"

"*It's* happening. The exchange. Right now, right outside the kitchen, right where you were headed. Drugs and money."

She jerked her head up. "Go! Make it stop!"

"Shh." He stroked her hair. "We're taking care of it. My partner's there. I saw you coming and— Oh, dear God, help. I can't think straight. How could I imagine . . . ?" He closed his eyes.

"Is everybody safe? Is everybody okay?"

"Shh, yes. Nothing's going down yet. We're just watching tonight. Please, please don't worry."

"But when—?" She leaned her forehead against his chest. "Why is all this happening?"

"That's an easy one." He clasped his hands behind her neck. "So I could meet you. *Mi gatita*," he whispered, his lips brushing her temple, "I keep hoping you're contagious."

"What?"

"Your goodness," he mumbled. "I need your goodness, Cat."

And then he was kissing her, and she was the one who couldn't think straight. It didn't matter who he was or where he had come from or where he was going. It only mattered that when the real Dominick breathed through the ice, he was the very essence of hope and safety.

"Mmm, I'm sorry," he murmured, his forehead against hers. "I wasn't going to do that. You are just so good, Catherine St. Clair, just so good and real and solid. Jill-of-all-trades. Wheaties box material—"

"Wheaties box?"

"Wholesome. Athletic."

She giggled. "You're so weird."

"At least you know that much."

She lifted her head to peer at him in the dim light. She touched his face. She loved his face with its cragginess and scars and angular nose, all untold tales of a life spent fighting evil. "I know more than that, Dominick. I don't know where you live or what you like for breakfast or who your favorite author is or where you went to school or what size shirt you wear or if you like boats, but I know you."

He kissed her forehead. "Just off Balboa Avenue, near the 5."

She heard the grin in his voice.

"Less than ten minutes from you when the traffic is right. One-bedroom apartment. University of Wisconsin. Frank Peretti. Extra-extra large. Speedboats yes, sailboats no. And Wheaties. Definitely Wheaties."

She smiled. "And I know you're very tired."

"Mm-hmm. I saw Carver with you today, out in the court-yard. It's easy to tell he's still crazy about you, huh?"

"So?" she teased.

He kissed her more intensely this time, totally scattering all traces of anger and castles and Trenton Carver.

"Cat?"

"Hmm?"

"Remember at the beach Monday morning, you said I was a stranger to you?"

"Mm-hmm."

"Now can we fix it?"

"Mmm." Words seemed to be slow in forming.

"Can we spend some time together?"

She swallowed. "Of course."

"We'll talk." He sounded weary.

"Okay. You should go home. Will you go home now?"

"Yes. I can take you home first."

"No, I'm okay." That was easy to say as she stood in the cir-cle of his arms. "What about tomorrow?"

"What about it?"

"Do we have to do this again?"

He combed his fingers through her hair. "I got the impression you liked kissing me."

She laughed softly. "You know what I mean. Are you coming here?"

"Yes, just like today. We have to do this again. It'll be over soon though. I promise."

"Okay." She took a step backwards. He gave her hand a squeeze and let it drop. "I—I guess I'll go. Aren't you coming?"

"Not with you. You go ahead first. Wait at the end of the drive if you want me to follow you home."

"Which way should I walk now?"

"Uh, any way. No, on second thought, go on the far side of the restaurant. I'm sure nothing is going on now, but that would be better, from that direction."

She walked a few steps, then turned back. "Dominick, promise me you'll sleep?"

"I promise. Soon."

~ *Nineteen* ~

LATE SUNDAY MORNING Cat drove by rote to her parents' home, her mind freed to ruminate over the last couple of days.

It had first been on Thursday that she awakened to a morning without the heavy nightmare fear. After that night's hushed conversation with Dominick at the edge of the property, she had slept well again, this time cocooned in the warm memory of his arms holding her, his voice whispering, his kisses. With the dawn, she again awakened to comfort.

Today she was greeted with her cool, practical nature racing in high gear. She was eager to get on with things. In spite of the ugly drug situation still looming, hope had replaced the fear. As if she had shed a jacket made of concrete and now her whole being felt light enough to fly.

It was an old and yet new outlook. Her relationship with God had been solidified. She was still herself, but with a new understanding of what it meant to be His. As far as the future was concerned, her calendar was empty, waiting for Him to fill it in whenever it was time, with whatever He thought best. As far as each day was concerned, she prayed she would know how to give Him the controls.

Then there was Dominick. Since that night she hadn't seen much of him, for which she was grateful because her obvious feeling of attraction to him was . . . unnerving. She had never felt this with Trent. Trent filled all the nuances she had in mind for a husband. He looked nice. He smelled nice. He played a nice game of tennis. His condo was nice. His family was an established part of nice society. He was predictable. He followed her lead, agreed with her decisions, wanted the same three children and lifestyle. He believed in God, attended church regularly.

Dominick, on the other hand, carried a gun.

And he talked to God with his eyes wide open in the middle of her office, grimacing with the pain of cracked ribs.

What he had done to her eight months ago at the mall was despicable. Under normal circumstances she should never speak to him again, except through lawyers while in the process of suing him. But she and Dominick weren't under normal circumstances. They were under God's shadow. It was possible to forgive him, even actually incredibly easy to forgive him, because she knew of two obvious life-changing results of his despicable behavior. First of all, he had been drawn to Christ. And second, she had been rescued from the major mistake of marrying for the wrong reasons.

The other matter of his not revealing his identity seemed a necessary part of his job. She couldn't hold it against him, but neither could she wholly trust him. An inner voice nagged that he lied, that she did not know him. It only quieted when he kissed her.

Which reminded her she truly was at a vulnerable time in her life. She had just defensively rebounded the ball, so to speak; she was still under the other team's basket. Dribbling down the court would take time. Setting things up for a shot would take time. She could hear the coach yelling to her to slow things up, while her heart was pumping and the irresistible urge was to plow ahead for the fast break. Falling for Dominick could happen in a minuscule amount of time.

But then again, maybe it would take a lot of time. Practically speaking, she did not have a clue as to what Dominick D'Angelo was all about. On top of that, how in the world could a DEA agent ever settle down into a regular relationship, let alone marriage?

Oops . . . Was that assumption stepping ahead of God?

But really, Lord! I mean, he works all hours of the day and night. It's extremely important work, horrifically dangerous work. He pretends to be someone he's not.

Cat shook her head, steered the car onto her parents' driveway, and parked. Figuring out this relationship was too difficult.

They would always have a special friendship because of what had happened. Perhaps that's all they would ever have in common. One thing was for certain—the kissing business would have to stop. She couldn't think straight otherwise.

At the Castillo yesterday he had met her in the parking lot when she pulled in. She had immediately jumped from her car.

"What's wrong?"

He frowned. "Calm down."

"This *is* calm."

"Cat . . ." He exhaled. "Listen, I'll do what I can to warn you before it goes down, okay? Please don't worry."

She noticed the dark circles around his eyes. He looked like she felt—exhausted and anxious. She bit her lip. "I'm sorry."

"I know this is tough for you. Can we take some time off tomorrow?"

"I plan to. It *is* Sunday."

"How about church?"

She hesitated. "Dominick, I'm still a little overwhelmed since last Sunday and—and everything. I need some time . . . And I have to tell my parents that I'm doing better. It is all right if I tell them that much, isn't it? That we went to the mall?"

"Of course. Cat, I'm not good at dancing."

"Huh?"

That corner of his mouth tucked inward. "Around the bush. The question is, *when* will you see me?"

He wasn't giving up. She liked that in a man. "Three o'clock tomorrow." She returned his smile.

"I'll pick you up at your place."

That was about three hours from now. She climbed from her car and walked toward the front door, eager to put her parents' minds at ease after all these months. Hopefully that wouldn't require too much dancing around the truth of why exactly it was that Dominick could erase the nightmare.

When Cat opened her apartment door to him, Dominick sensed the world was fading away behind him. That had been happening a lot lately, but it still caught him by surprise. Nothing mattered except that this gentle, honey-eyed woman shared this moment in time with him.

"Come in." Her low voice sounded distracted. The small smile on her mouth didn't crease the left cheek.

He resisted the urge to touch her face, to coax the dimple from its hiding place. If he didn't slow down, he might as well make it a good-bye kiss. In spite of all they'd been through, she was just this side of a rough eight months and probably still coming to terms with who he was.

She shut the door behind him.

"What?" he asked.

"What what?" She frowned at him. "Don't do that."

"Don't do what?"

"Tilt your head that way." She placed a hand on his cheek and pushed upward. "It's too *tender*."

He laughed. "What's wrong with tender? I thought women liked tender and sensitive."

"It's—it's unnerving." She strode over to an armchair and sat down.

He followed her and settled into the couch. *What's wrong with unnerving?* Evidently his suspicions about her emotional state were on target. "Want me to try macho?"

Her forehead was still furrowed.

"You've got five seconds to tell me what's bugging you, Catherine St. Clair, or I'm out of here! One, two—"

Tears welled in her eyes.

He jumped up.

"Sit down, Dominick!" She stuck out her arm and pointed. "Stay over there. I'm fine. I am fine." She sniffed.

"Guess macho doesn't work either."

A smile tugged at her mouth.

"How'd it go with your parents?"

"Okay. Fine. They're so happy. And they didn't ask anything about why you did it. I told them you let me go alone, and I talked to God, and then you hugged me. What did you have in mind for today?"

It took him a moment to catch up with her. "Uh, just hanging together. We could walk around Balboa Park, eat downtown . . ."

"I have Twenty Questions in mind."

"I see." This was it. This was what was bugging her. "All right. Here? Now?"

"What do you know about me?"

"Talk about not dancing around the bush!" He smiled, slipped his right ankle atop his left knee, and tapped his foot on the carpet. "You get straight to the point better than I can."

"Maybe I could interrogate suspects for you."

He stopped smiling. This one question could make them or break them. He doubted she was going to like his answer, and he wouldn't even consider sugarcoating it. Lying was totally out of bounds.

"Dominick, I've prayed about—" She took a long, deep breath and exhaled. "About us. I have to start here, at the beginning. Well, not counting the mall beginning."

Prayed about us? Dear Father, help us. Help her understand.

"I mean, before you came to the Castillo, what did you know about me? After all, I was one of your suspects, right?"

He uncrossed his legs, leaned forward to rest his elbows on his knees, and laced his fingers together. "Before I came I didn't know anything except that my immediate superior was the assistant manager who sounded like a feminine jack-of-all-trades. It was a last-minute assignment. I didn't have time to do much homework."

"Why did you come?"

"I can't tell you that just yet. When I met you, of course I recognized you right off the bat. That threw me for a major loop. I figured my cover was blown. Part of me wanted it to be, so I'd have to tell you everything. When you didn't recognize me, I had a choice. No, truthfully only one option—to presume you were a suspect."

She watched him, waiting, her face for once revealing nothing. "Don't you investigate your suspects?"

"Uh, yeah. The homework I mentioned. It's mostly public record kind of stuff." He swallowed.

"Like middle name?"

"Like middle name. Address. And previous address since you had moved within the past six months. Parents' name and occupations. Siblings. Date of birth." He smiled. "They missed the adoption record. Somebody got sloppy. Umm, education. High school and college attended. Just the basics. Rent. Salary."

"You know how much I make?"

He nodded slightly. "Income tax. School loan. Car loans. Of which you have none. Priors. Nothing there either, not even a speeding ticket. We're interested in the monetary side of your life, not what videos you rent."

"That makes me feel . . . violated."

"I know. I'm sorry."

"Do you know all that about everyone on the staff?"

Again he nodded slightly.

"So basically you knew things before I told you and then some."

"Except that you were adopted. Or engaged. Cissy told me you and Carver were engaged. Umm . . ." He hesitated. Better to lay it all out on the table right now. "I had you followed into Tecate. That night I sat outside your apartment for about an hour, until someone took over for me. So I knew where you lived before I gave you a ride home. The day I took your car to wash it, I had it searched." *Torn apart.* "Taken totally apart and searched because you brought something out of the orphanage and across the border."

"*Buñeulos?!*" Her face crumpled, and her breathing was shaky, but she didn't cry. "What about here? Did you search in here?"

"No. I went through your office, but no one came into your home." Dominick forced himself to sit very still while his heart pounded violently in his chest. She had to work through this on her own.

She hugged herself and shut her eyes tightly. "It's so *ugly*!"

"It is, Cat. I work in ugliness. I've been immersed in it for years. When I met you, it took me a long time to comprehend your genuine goodness. Can I hold you?"

"No," she whispered.

"I'm sorry," he repeated.

She leaned her head back against the stuffed chair and stared at the ceiling.

He waited.

It was a few minutes before her breathing steadied. She sat up, arms still crossed against her midsection, and met his eyes. "Have you—" She bit her lip. "Have you ever killed anyone?"

"No."

Her body noticeably relaxed.

"Not that I haven't tried, like when I was sixteen."

"The guy who sold the drugs to your friend?"

He smiled in surprise. "Now who knows things?"

She broke their eye contact and stared out the window, apparently mulling over what she had just learned.

He twiddled his thumbs, waiting, preparing his response for when she told him to get lost. Of course she wouldn't say it in so many words. She would not be offensive. She would be . . . gracious. That was the word. Gracious. He had never personally known a gracious woman before, let alone fallen for one.

"Dominick . . . ." Her hand covered his, halting the thumbs in mid-twiddle. "That's enough."

Here it comes. He looked up at her.

"Thank you." There was a hint of the dimple in her cheek. A trace of sunlight danced in her eyes. "Come on, let's go hang together. Can we start with your place?"

It was like a sunrise or sunset, another gift from his Father.

Cat had asked Dominick the unsettling questions, listened to his straightforward answers, and sifted through their details until they fell diffused and weakened, unable to shock anymore. As he drove her toward his apartment, she figured the worst was over.

And then he parked the truck on an unfamiliar street.

A new shock wave rolled through her. She knew the rock-solid feel of his arms around her. She knew the sweetness of his lips on hers. She knew he had awakened something deep within her that had caused her to turn again toward God.

But she didn't even know where the man lived!

"Cat?"

"Huh?"

He stood beside her open door. "Shall we go inside?"

She slid from the truck.

"Are you okay? Do these bother you?" He slipped off his sunglasses. "I should have asked sooner."

"No." She followed him from the street and then along a narrow sidewalk. She sensed the usual array of flowering bushes.

He smiled over his shoulder at her. "No, you're not okay, or no, they don't bother you?"

"They don't bother me." The nightmare of the stranger who wore those sunglasses had lost its power. She should leap for joy at that. Instead, she felt ill at ease.

Seldom in her life had she felt ill at ease. With everyone from teachers to coaches—even a few bully coaches—to obnoxious guests, she was secure in who she was, just Cat St. Clair, a take-charge, practical type. That was what had attracted Trent. It was what diminished after the mall incident.

Dominick stopped outside a door and selected a key from his

key ring. "Is there something else you want clarified? Something else to ask?" He looked at her. "It's totally understandable, Cat."

His gray eyes were warm. There was no hint of that familiar Secret Service hardness. Actually there was no hint of anything familiar about him whatsoever. She wasn't even sure what street they were on. "No, it's not that. It's . . ." She pressed her lips together and ran her fingers through her hair.

He grinned at her loss of words. "You are just so—just so incredibly *delightful.*" He leaned toward her.

Cat jumped back like a startled jackrabbit. "Oh, please! Don't kiss me."

"Okay, okay! I won't." He tilted his head, raised his eyebrows, and held out his arms. *Hug?*

"No." Her voice was almost a whimper.

"Hmm." His forehead creased in a look of puzzlement. "Guess you need a little space, huh?"

She wanted to fall into his embrace. "Oh, Dominick! It's just so weird. All of a sudden you're a whole different person. You're not my temp employee, this drifter guy who caught my attention on the rebound." She gestured with her arms. "You're not this Secret Service type, DEA whatever, a government goon who loves God and made sense out of my nightmare. You're— you're—I don't know! You kiss me, and I'm off in la-la land like we're smack-dab in the middle of a relationship that never even had a *beginning.*"

He scratched his head.

"It's like we've got to work backwards."

He crossed his arms and shifted his weight to the other foot. "Like this is our first date?"

Cat thought about that for a moment, then frowned. "I don't know if I'd go on a first date with you."

He blinked. "Now I'm lost."

"Wellll . . ." She shrugged. "When you first came, everyone thought you were, as they say, hot. Everyone, uh, else."

"Ahh. Except you." He lifted a shoulder and raised his eyebrows, not in the least offended. "Hmm. Not your type. I take it Carver is?"

She thought of Trent and his nice appearance, so unlike this solid presence before her who seemed oblivious to what others thought of him. "Was."

He smiled. "Would you consider a blind date with a not-so-hot government employee?"

"Depends who set it up."

"How about God?"

In spite of herself, Cat burst into laughter. "Okay, mister, you got me in the door."

— *Twenty* —

WHEN CAT SAW DOMINICK'S surfboard propped in the corner of his living room, her uneasiness began to lessen. This, at last, was familiar. It was what she had imagined of him.

His place reminded her more of a tiny, old-fashioned house than an apartment. It was at the end of an L-shaped row of connected bungalows, a simple square with one room across the front that served as living room and dining area, kitchen in the back left corner, hall space in the center, bathroom off of that, and bedroom in the back right. All four sides had windows, making it a bright home. Off the living room was a small, enclosed patio.

It was clean and organized. Given the sparse furnishings and bare walls, it wouldn't take much to keep it neat. The main area contained a couch, a recliner, a desk and computer, a television, a stereo, bookshelves, a table and chairs. And a surfboard.

It was nothing like Trent's elegant condominium. She liked it immensely.

As the hot late afternoon softened into summer evening, she delved into the private world of Dominick D'Angelo. The rough edges of their awkward situation softened.

He played his jazz CDs for her, music that was foreign to her ears. They discussed what she found on his bookshelves. He had all sorts of U.S. city maps, many books on the Christian faith, all of Frank Peretti's novels, two Bible translations, some spy novels, and drug reference books. He showed her a photo album full of pictures sent by his sister-in-law of his brother's family and his mother.

He was beginning to seem almost normal.

He offered to fix dinner for them. "I made bolognese this morning."

"Bolo what?"

He taught her how to say the word with the proper Italian accent.

"So are you fluent in that too?"

"Sort of."

Things like that crept into their conversation, little reminders that he had shaded the truth on earlier occasions. Their eyes would meet, he would tilt his head in that way of his, asking for understanding, and she would try to readjust her thinking. Sometimes when he moved she saw him wince, and she knew his ribs still hurt. It was a subtle reference to the dangers of his work, and it unsettled her.

Admitting they were both tired, they decided to stay in and eat his pasta. She followed him into the kitchen and teased him about the decidedly feminine shampoo she'd noticed in the bathroom.

His head was in the refrigerator, and he mumbled something about it being on sale.

It was then that Cat realized there was another side to Dominick she didn't know a thing about. "Maybe it's not yours?"

"What?" He set a large pot on a burner and flicked it on, glancing at her before turning his attention back to the stove. He stirred the ingredients with a wooden spoon. "Remember Cissy's somewhat forward question when we first met?"

Cat thought back to that day in her office. Cissy had entered and in her typically unabashed manner asked him if he was married, engaged, or otherwise involved. "Yes, I remember."

"I answered truthfully."

"You said no, no, and no."

He turned to her. "I haven't been with anyone for a long time."

"Okay." She decided to let it drop. "That smells great. What's in it?" She walked over to him and peered around his arm.

"Ground beef, ground pork, crushed tomatoes, a little olive

oil, and butter. The trick is letting it simmer for hours, which I already did. It'll be ready soon." He gently tapped the spoon on the edge of the pot, set it down, and stepped over to the refrigerator. "Why don't you go sit outside and read the newspaper or something."

"Let me help."

"No. Thanks." He pulled out a bottle of S. Pellegrino sparkling water. "It won't be long. I just have to cook the pasta and dump the salad out of a bag, stick garlic bread in the oven." He poured the water into a glass and added a twist of lemon. As he handed it to her, his fingers brushed hers. "And besides, I can't seem to concentrate when you stand this close."

"Oh." *Maybe we should have gone out*, she thought.

"Either that or I'm hungry." He grinned.

His humor took the edge off. Cat was still in the get-acquainted mode. Despite the fact that she was liking what she was seeing, she wasn't ready to enter into the tension of romance. She found the newspaper and wandered onto the patio with her water.

A while later she found that Dominick's simple meal was delicious. His plates didn't match and were chipped, but he lit candles and smiled across the table at her before thanking God for the food.

"Is this okay?" He pointed to his hair that he had pulled back into a ponytail.

"It's okay." She smiled. "No problem. Go ahead and put the bandanna on too."

He grinned. "I save that for the major grunge look. This is just my normal look. Not exactly the yuppie, executive type. What?"

She was studying his "normal" look, the strong features and tiny scars and the ever-present 5 o'clock shadow and the thick black lashes over gray eyes. She wondered again about his nose. "Uhh, nothing."

"Come on, Cat. We're trying not to avoid stuff tonight, right? Just say what you're thinking."

She tore apart a piece of garlic bread. "I was thinking that yuppie, executive looks don't have any character." She picked up her fork again. "This bolognese is absolutely great."

He corrected her pronunciation.

She laughed and repeated it. "Did you add Parmesan?"

He nodded. "Fresh. Not that canned stuff. What do you mean by character?"

"Oh, I guess it comes down to, why do you do what you do? I mean, your life is written all over your face."

He thought for a moment. "Like scars and a broken nose?"

"Yeah. And there's that look about your eyes."

"The Secret Service one?"

"I know it's more than that. It's an intensity for what you do. So why do you do what you do?"

"It goes back to what Adam and Meg told you about my friend. His name was Mike. We were a lot alike. Our dads were gone. Our moms worked hard, mended our clothes, kept food on the table. We drove them crazy, and they smacked us when we let them down. We knew they loved us, but it wasn't enough.

"We didn't fit in at school. It was just easier on the streets. Fighting, dealing, smoking a little weed, popping a few pills. I found I could con my way in and out of almost any situation. By the time we were sixteen, I had developed a major business, and Mike had developed a major habit. He was hooked on heroin. He OD'd on stuff I gave him.

"I went after the guy who sold it to me. He spent a long time in intensive care. The judge sent me to a reform school, and there the story gets better." He gave her a small smile. "I figured out I had ruined a lot of lives, not just Mike's and his family's. I had to make up for it somehow, so I went into law enforcement. It was perfect. A blank check to keep on fighting and conning, only with the purpose of bringing in the bad guys."

Cat pushed aside her empty plate and rested her elbows on the table. "It sounds noble and exhausting."

"I don't know about noble. I think I've done some good, made a small difference. But that ugliness we talked about ate

away at my soul. I hadn't realized how far gone I was until I met
Adam."

"How old are you?"

"Thirty-five."

"Are you tired of fighting?"

He nodded. "Some days. It might be time for a change. I just
can't see myself sitting behind a desk yet."

The phone rang. He reached for it on the desk behind him.
A few seconds after his hello, he said an address and stood. "On
my way." He hung up, found a pen and pad, and scribbled something. "Cat, I've got to leave for an hour. Two max. Somebody
needs backup. No big deal, but nobody else is available. I don't
have time to take you home."

"I'll do the dishes."

He handed her the pad. "If you don't want to wait for me,
call this number. A man named Toby will answer." He walked
toward the bedroom. "Just tell him you're at D'Angelo's and
need a ride. He'll take care of you. The Parkers are out of town."

"Elli can come get me—"

"No." He stopped and turned. "You'd have to explain why I
left you here. Not just yet, Cat. Do you understand?"

"All right. Yes." She began clearing the table. "I'll just clean
up and watch television."

A moment later he stepped into the kitchen where she
stood, running water into the sink. He had put on a denim
jacket and had a gun in his hand. "I'll be back as quick as I can."
He was doing something with the gun, not looking at her. There
was a clicking noise. A snap. "Lock the door behind me."

And then he was gone.

Cat stood still, her hands and wrists immersed in the warm
sudsy water. When the tears spilled over, she let them fall onto
the bubbles. When the sob burst from her chest into her throat,
she found a towel and held it to her face. When another sob
escaped, she went and sat on the couch.

It was the sight of the gun that exploded reality into the
kitchen. Their worlds were light-years apart. He had asked her

about the sunglasses and ponytail, asked if those fragments of her nightmare disturbed her. They were insignificant details on their own, simple mannerisms. He had not asked about the gun. And yet it was the gun that was his identity, what he had carried day in and day out for years like an extension of his arm.

Was it the same one he had pointed in her face?

Violent television shows and movies had always disturbed her. She took great care to avoid them, often staying at home even as a teenager rather than going with friends. She filtered news, shutting off her attention to much of it. She had wondered if events surrounding the first few months of her life could have subconsciously affected her. There had to have been violence in that place. The deaths were by overdose, but . . .

She looked around at the un-homey home that held such few traces of the man Dominick D'Angelo. What was she doing here? He had gotten up and left the table. What if they had still been eating? It wouldn't have mattered. It wasn't that he was just a night owl. Time meant nothing to him. His world was chasing criminals. His lifestyle was totally, completely beyond her comprehension.

She couldn't even call her sister because she couldn't confide in her who Dominick was. Come to think of it, she couldn't even call a taxi. She didn't know the address, she hadn't really paid attention to how they got here, and his number was unlisted, so he wouldn't be in the phone book. She wasn't about to wander out in the dark in search of a street name or knock on a neighbor's door. She wasn't about to call some stranger named Toby either. She'd just stay put, hopefully not all night. Hopefully he'd come home . . . and in one piece.

Cat felt just as confused as she had when this blind first date had gotten underway.

Dominick slipped his key into the door and was surprised to find it hadn't been locked.

He stepped inside. The lights and television were on. Cat was asleep on the couch, curled under a blanket. *She must be back* to her pre-nightmare, naive days to not lock a door, then fall asleep beside it.

He checked out the kitchen. Everything was put away. The room appeared brighter than he'd ever seen it. What'd she do? Maybe it was only her personality filling the place. No, the sink was a shiny white.

Back out in the living room he sat on the edge of the couch. "Cat," he called softly.

She didn't respond. Her breathing was deep and even.

He was pumped. He wanted to wake her and tell her about tonight. He couldn't, of course. The Castillo business should have been finished by now, but his partner Engstrom had stuck with the bread man and convinced them to hold off. The kid hung in there—like Dominick would have a few years ago—and found the bread delivery was clean, but the trash collection wasn't. Tonight they got the proof that this was a bigger piece of the action than he had thought.

The waste disposal service owned a warehouse that was a major collection point for cocaine carried across the border in small loads, in nondescript vehicles of all shapes and sizes. From there it was distributed to places like the Castillo, points from which dealers would be supplied. From there it hit the streets and found its way into the heart of America.

By Tuesday they could knock down the first domino and watch a long row of them fall one by one. They couldn't follow the trail back across the border and give Smitty everything he wanted, but they would effectively dry up one giant route. For a while anyway.

Dominick watched Cat sleep, wishing he could hold her like he had that night when she had the migraine. She was such a bundle of goodness. Who wouldn't want to wrap her in his arms and take her home? Even in his exhausted state just a few nights ago he had been serious when he kissed her and expressed the hope that she was contagious.

Tonight she had seemed almost shy with him, as if she were

in the apartment of some stranger. In truth, he was a stranger to her. He knew that, but he didn't want to admit it.

He had almost been glad for the phone call. It interrupted his difficulty in dealing with those compassionate eyes and gentle words as he told his story. He didn't know what to do with the emotions she set rumbling in him. The only expression he had for them was to hold her. And she had made it clear that physical contact was off-limits. She was at the beginning of a relationship, an unacceptable place for hugs and kisses and la-la land.

He brushed her hair from her cheek now. This was off-limits too, but— "Cat."

Her eyes opened partially. "Dominick?" She smiled and reached for his hand. She held it between hers, under her chin. "You're all right." She yawned. "I couldn't stay awake. What time is it?"

"Almost 2. I'm sorry. I'll take you home. Unless you just want to stay right where you are?" He would make her coffee in the morning. And an omelette. They'd sit on the patio in the morning sun—

"No, I'd better go." She squeezed his hand and closed her eyes for a moment, then sat up.

He noticed her rumpled, short-sleeved shirt. "Do you have a jacket?"

She shook her head and reached for her shoes beside the couch.

"I'll get something for you. It's cold outside." He went into his room and found a sweatshirt with a zipper for her. When he came out she was laying back down, half asleep. He pulled her to her feet and helped her into the sweatshirt. "Hey, thanks for cleaning up the kitchen."

"Mm-hmm."

It was a quiet, quick trip to her place. He walked her upstairs to her door. She mumbled good night and slipped inside.

He hadn't found the words to ask her if she would go out on a second, not-so-blind date. No, not words; rather nerve. He knew he would not be able to breathe if she said no.

~ Twenty-One ~

THE NEXT DAY CAT buried herself in life's everyday details. Laundry, cleaning, and grocery shopping filled the hours. It helped her not think about Dominick. By the time she headed to Elli's for dinner, the truth about him was buried in enough layers that she thought she could successfully avoid the emotional subject for one evening, even with her sister.

On Tuesday he didn't show up for work. Cissy informed her he had called to say he'd be in later. She lingered in the office doorway. "So, Cat, I hear he's crazy about you."

"Where'd you hear that?"

"From him." She studied her nails. "You know he's gone with me to a few parties. I invited him to a Sunday bash, and he said he had a date with you."

"That's it? That's crazy about me?" She chuckled. "Cissy, you have such a talent for filling in details."

"Well, it was his tone. I mean it's so *obvious*. And he said something along the lines of me being a wonderful *girl*, and he was a little on the old side. What'd you do on your date?"

"Oh, we, uhh, had dinner. We're just sort of friends."

"Nice restaurant?"

"His place. Ever been there?"

Cissy shook her head. "Nope. Didn't get to first base with the guy. He's sure a lot friendlier than Trent. You never know—maybe he'll change his drifter ways and stick around awhile. I better get back out front." Her heels clicked away.

Cat heard the hurt in the desk clerk's voice. The young woman knew Dominick was different. Despite his looks and his temporary role and seeming participation at her parties, she must know he had a depth about him. And he had chosen Cat over her.

Under the circumstances she didn't feel flattered. They weren't in a contest, though Cissy would see it as another put-down like she did when Trent had ignored her flirtations and chose Cat. Maybe when Dominick left, Cat could hire someone who fit Cissy's personality. Would the temp service think it discriminatory if she requested a certain age, physique, marital status, and future plans?

A feeling of anxiety for Dominick filled her. It was almost becoming familiar, this uncomfortable nagging at the fringes of her thoughts. The nightmare's stranglehold had been loosened, and she was praying more, trying to let God have more space in her life. However, at times it was impossible to fend off the anxiety concerning this man's safety. Not to mention the unsettled drug situation at the Castillo!

Isn't this what life would be like with him? She hugged herself.

Where was he now? Last week he had hinted that things at the Castillo were almost finished. What did *that* mean? Maybe he was off arresting people who used the motel. Maybe it was that man who delivered pool chemicals. His eyes were set close together. Maybe that new cook was involved. He hadn't warmed to her yet. Maybe—

The phone rang. "Hello?"

"Catherine!" It was her mother. "What's wrong?"

What was wrong? What *wasn't* wrong? "Huh?"

"You never answer 'hello.' It's always, 'This is Cat St. Clair,' your voice all confident and professional. What's wrong? Did you have an argument with Dominick?"

"Oh, Mother, there's just a lot going on. This weekend is the big end-of-summer celebration. I've still got a million things to do for that."

"Are you having the clowns again?"

"Yes, and all the competitions—golf and swimming and vol-leyball. And basketball."

"With prizes?"

"Mm-hmm."

"That sounds like so much fun. You know, I'm very proud of your work there. Well, did you have an argument with Dominick?"

"No!"

"We really liked him. Well, I guess you're just anxious then."

"I guess."

"You don't have to be."

"I know. 'Be anxious for nothing.'"

"'But in everything,'" her mother continued the verse, "'by prayer and supplication with thanksgiving let your requests be made known to God.'"

"I know!" Cat heard the screech and lowered her voice to a whine. "I'm sorry. I know. I really do."

"It's never easy. I'll pray for you. Now, there was a reason I called. What was it?"

She noticed the light for the other line on her phone was lit. "Mother, I think I have another call—"

"Oh, now I remember. Are you going to Tecate on Monday?"

"No, I'm running down Friday morning instead, to buy piñatas for the party. Why?" She kept her eye on the light. Was it Dominick? Cissy would talk to him until she was off. Would he call her if he was hurt? What if it were bad enough—

"We're doing a collection for you on Sunday. But it'll keep. I'll get it to you the next time."

"I have to go, Mother! Thank you." The light blinked off.

"You're welcome, sweetie. Good-bye!"

She called Cissy at the front desk. "Did I have another call?"

"No."

"Thanks." Confused but having too much on her mind to deal with it, Cat went back to her work.

To her relief, about 8 o'clock Dominick came into her office. "Take a walk?"

She followed him into the parking lot. She noticed he didn't wear a jacket. No gun then . . .

On the edge of the lot, behind his truck, he stopped. "You okay?" he asked, his voice barely above a whisper.

"Sort of."

In the lamplight she saw his grin. "Listen, I want you to know that it's almost over."

"You've said that."

"I know, but now I can tell you it'll be by the end of the week."

"Dominick! The festival is Saturday!"

He sighed loudly. "Get in the truck." He walked around it, yanked open the driver's door, jumped inside, and slammed it shut.

"Oh!" She followed suit on the passenger side.

"When things go down, it won't interfere." His voice was no longer just above a whisper. "I promise. You don't have to worry."

"I've seen you after an arrest, with broken ribs. You couldn't breathe—"

"That was different than this will be."

"I've seen you point a gun at me—"

"Cat, get a grip!" His exasperation was obvious, and his words ran together. "You won't even know it's happening. Just a few quiet arrests. Oh, why am I even telling you this?"

"It would be worse if I didn't know *anything*!"

"No, this is too much of a responsibility. Look, I'm sorry. I forget you can't understand this from my point of view. I was trying to make it easier for you. Can you just do your best to act normal for a couple more days?"

"Well, I've made it this far."

"Mandi and Kevin have things under control for the festival. Take some time off." He sounded angry.

"And I think you can't understand *my* job from *my* point of view! I'll probably put in ten hours tomorrow."

"Fine! Just keep busy. And don't worry."

"Will you tell me later exactly when it'll happen?"

"If I get a chance."

"Are you still our temp—"

"Cat!" His voice rose. "Nothing's changed as far as you're concerned, okay?"

She didn't reply.

"Please, just trust me?"

"I trust you, Dominick. But this situation—it's like my castle is falling apart, and I can't fix it no matter how hard I work. It's headed for disaster, and there's nothing I can do about it!"

It took him a fraction of a second to scoot across the bench seat and wrap his arms around her, cutting off her words.

She twisted, but he didn't let go.

"Sorry, Cat. You're overdue for a hug, and no one else seems to be available at the moment."

She closed her eyes.

"Now stop whining and listen to me," he soothed. "I will fix it for you, and it's not going to be a disaster."

He held her tightly for a few minutes until at last she felt her muscles relax. *How did he know this would work?*

"Hey," his voice was muffled in her hair, "maybe la-la land would help."

That broke the final tension. She giggled, remembering what she had told him about her feelings when he kissed her. "No, it would not!"

"All right. If you're sure?" She nodded as vehemently as she could manage against his shoulder. He laughed softly. "I'm teasing. You're much too good to get messed up with the likes of me. Well, we're both going to be busy for a while. I'll, umm . . . We'll, umm, touch base next week, okay? When it's all over."

She nodded again, wishing they could sit like this until it was all over.

Cat drummed her fingers on the steering wheel in time with music from the car radio. She sat in Tecate traffic, at least three blocks south of the border. The backed-up line stretched behind her around a corner, out of sight. It looked as if half of the city must be crossing into the States. The noon sun reflected in a glare from the car that sat just inches in front of hers. As usual, the top of her Tracker was off, but she turned on the air conditioning anyway. It might help alleviate the pungent exhaust fumes as well as the intense heat that beat through her sunglasses, straw hat, white oversized cotton shirt, and long, full skirt.

She groaned. Friday was whittling itself down to the bare minimum number of hours needed for festival preparations. It started at 6 A.M. with sleeping through what was supposed to be the jump-start alarm buzz. No, it had started last night, by not getting to bed until 2.

No, it really started before that, with Dominick D'Angelo complicating her life in so many ways. In the three days since he had hugged her in the parking lot she had wrestled with the facts that this man filled her heart and that every other aspect of her life was quickly fading into insignificant details. She didn't like his carrying a gun and dealing with violence and ugliness, but the fact was, they were a part of who he was. And who he was captivated her thoughts day and night.

That arrests had to be made at her Castillo would be undoubtedly the biggest difficulty she had ever tackled in her career. There was no getting around that, but it would not be catastrophic.

Dominick had kept an eye on her these past few days. He popped into the office, found her outside, smiled often, motioned thumbs-up signs at the oddest times, brought flowers from the garden or cookies from the kitchen, wrote down his pager number for her. She could call him anytime. There were no more hugs; evidently he respected her thoughts on that subject. Although those thoughts were changing . . .

Much of this had spilled out at the orphanage today, which was why she had stayed an hour beyond what she had planned, which of course put her even further behind schedule. But she reminded herself that emotionally unloading on Rosa was a relief. If she hadn't taken the time to do so and in return receive her *abuelita's* gift of showing her God's love, her fingers would be strangling the steering wheel instead of tapping out a tune.

While they had sat under the shade tree, each rocking a baby to sleep while the other children were inside cleaning up after lunch, Rosa studied her. "Catalina, I think you mourn your wedding day."

Cat could often sidestep her mother, but never her *abuelita*. Gently, she laid the baby on a nearby blanket in the grass, then did likewise with the one Rosa held. She sat on the ground and rested her head in her grandma's lap. The woman stroked her hair. Months ago Cat had shared with Rosa that there had been a police problem at the mall that frightened her, that Trent was unsupportive and subsequently they had canceled their wedding.

"Do you know for sure that the *señor* is no longer in your heart?" She had always referred to Trent as the *señor*. Somehow it fit his demeanor.

"*Sí.*"

"Still, it hurts." It was a statement.

Through the years her *abuelita's* statements had a way of shooing away clouds of confusion. There was understanding in them, acceptance, and often a nudge in the right direction.

Cat couldn't remember her grandparents and had no way of knowing her biological ones. When at the age of fifteen she met Rosa at the orphanage, she knew instantly that here was a grandma she would adopt in her heart. Cultural and language differences never interfered, and their friendship deepened.

"It is all right to mourn it, my child. Are you reading God's Word, to know how to mourn it?"

Cat nodded. "Now I am. Oh, *Abuelita*, I stayed away from Him for a long time. I was so angry, and now I'm so sorry."

"When you feel anger toward Him, you simply acknowledge that God is God. He could have prevented it, but He had to show you something. He wants you to see life as He sees it."

"But I'm not sure I want to trust Him again."

"Did you trust Him before?" Rosa laid her hand on Cat's fist. "I know you. You want Him to do things for you, but sometimes only the things you choose."

She nodded.

"Do you have someone better to trust than our heavenly Father?"

"No."

"No, of course not. So, you cry over the loss. It will ease. And what of the other man, the big one? The one who made you laugh?"

"Dominick." Cat smiled at the memory of him with the children. "Oh, he's—" She swallowed. "His job might move him away."

"Ahh. Then we will let God take care of it." She chuckled. "He knows I want to dance at your wedding. He can't wait too much longer, not at my age!"

The blast of a horn yanked Cat's attention back to the present. She inched her car forward and reminded herself that the weekend festival details really were falling into place. She had picked up three piñatas. One brightly colored donkey sat in the seat beside her; a fish and a rooster were in the back. She easily could have purchased them in San Diego, but these were made especially for her by an orphanage worker's cousin. It was important to her to offer support wherever she could, even in a small way like this.

Now she would drive straight to the Castillo, stuff the piñatas with candy, then ask Kevin to hang them in the courtyard. Mentally she reviewed the checklist of preparation details and prioritized them.

At last she approached the white overhang of the border station. There were two lanes, but as usual only one was open. Guards stood on the left, waving drivers through after momentary stops.

"Ma'am, please pull over to the side."

Cat smiled. The guard's face was familiar. He probably knew she often parked at the border as she proceeded to do now. Alberto, the Mexican guard on the other side checking traffic going into his country, was on duty today and was expecting his *buñuelo* treat that Rosa often sent with her for him.

Quickly she jumped from the car, brown paper bag in hand, and bounded across the single lane and onto the median strip.

"Alberto!" She checked for approaching traffic from her right. There was none, and she stepped into the lane, startled to see Alberto running toward her.

"*Parar!*" His gun was drawn.

Only then was she aware of the pounding footsteps behind her, shouting voices.

"Stop!"

"Freeze, lady!"

Safety catches clicked as they were released.

Guards surrounded her, a wall of blue shirts.

It was as if an invisible hand punched her chest, squeezing air from her lungs, pushing the heartbeat into her throat, gorging her with nausea. *No, God, no!* An image of another gun pointed at her flashed through her mind. That had been a mistake. That had just been Dominick. Just Dominick.

Air rushed back into her lungs, and she gasped.

"Hand over the bag." A guard grabbed it from her outstretched hand.

"It's for Alberto! It's just *buñuelos!*"

Someone pulled her arms behind her back.

She cried out.

"Right. And what do you call the stuff inside the piñatas? Extra sugar to sprinkle on the *buñuelos?*" Cold steel circled her wrists. The officer grasped her elbow at an awkward angle and guided her back across the street.

On her other side a female guard appeared. "Ma'am, you're under arrest for transporting a controlled substance across the international border. You have the right to remain silent—"

"What!"

A huge police dog on a leash was sniffing around her car. The piñatas lay on the ground, split open.

The concrete rose up to meet the bright blue sky, swirling before her in liquid waves of afternoon heat, flushing shame and panic through her.

Dear God, help me!

He finally had her undivided attention.

— Twenty-Two —

THEY LET HER MAKE A phone call from inside the border station.

She wanted to call Dominick, but she didn't even know his phone number. It was in a file, in her office—maybe. Besides, he wouldn't be home anyway.

The pager number! But no, she'd have to punch in the number here, and he'd have to call her back whenever he could.

When she hesitated, the woman suggested a lawyer would be a good idea. They left her alone in a small room at a table with a phone and telephone directory, handcuffs off. Dominick's home number was unlisted. Was the DEA listed? But she wasn't even supposed to know he did drug enforcement work.

Well, she knew one lawyer's number by heart.

She called Jacobs, Pemberly, Carver and Carver. When the youngest Carver finally got on the line, all she could say was "Trent" before she started crying. She blubbered through the story, ending with, "Tell them I didn't do it!"

For a few moments he said nothing.

"Trent!"

He let out his breath. "Tell me again—they found cocaine in your car?"

She heard the frustration in his voice. Again she felt cold steel, but this time it was an inner sensation clicking something shut, damming up the tears. "In the piñatas."

"For crying out loud, why don't you buy those things in town?"

There was a brief knock on the door, and the female officer appeared. "Ms. St. Clair, we're taking you to the DEA office in San Diego. You can tell your attorney to meet us there."

Cat stared at her. "DEA?"

The woman nodded. "Does he know where it is?"

Cat stared at her while Trent's voice bellowed in her ear, "DEA?"

"I can tell him," the officer volunteered.

She handed her the phone.

"Sir, do you know— Yes . . . No . . . It's the division office on Viewridge, just off 274, close to the 15. It's a large building, tan colors, not marked, across the street from Channel 9. Yes, sir . . . I'll put her back on." The officer raised her brows as if in bewilderment at the conversation. "Two minutes, Miss St. Clair." She left.

"Trent—"

"DEA!" he exclaimed again.

"Can you come? You have to help me. I have to have a lawyer fix—"

"Catherine, let me think. You're at the border now? That gives me about an hour. All right, I'll cancel my 3 o'clock."

"Will you call my dad?"

"Cat—"

"Please, Trent! He has to know immediately." The door opened again. "I have to go." She hung up the phone.

Ninety minutes later Cat again sat alone, at a rectangular wood table in a small, beige, windowless room. Hugging herself. Trying to take deep breaths in the airless atmosphere. Trying not to shake. Trying to sort her jumbled thoughts.

The ride had been a short, quick one in the back of a Border Patrol cruiser. Still, Daddy had had time to get here. He should have been here by now. Somebody always knew where he could be found. He was always available. Trent must not have called him right away. Had he called him at all?

Oh, Father! Help me!

Her prayers were simple, but they kept her from plunging over the edge. Absolutely none of this made sense. She wouldn't have knowingly bought drugs, transported cocaine. Anyone could see that about her, especially anyone who knew her. Then why did she feel guilty?

Because that poison was in her car.

And because Trent didn't believe her.

Oh, Lord.

Cold air began blowing from a wall register up near the ceiling. Her teeth chattered, and she scraped the chair along the floor, moving it from under the breezy path. She glanced around. Six chairs surrounded the table. The walls were bare except for one shelf that held a stack of Styrofoam cups. Where was the two-way mirror? An interrogation room would have a two-way mirror, wouldn't it? The door had been locked from the outside.

She shivered. At least the handcuffs were off again. Except for the fact that they put those on her, everyone had been polite enough. Even the mean-looking man named Smith had been gruffly polite. Not that they made small talk with her. Not that anything was normal—

Help me!

Dominick would come. This was his place. She couldn't tell anyone she knew that, but Dominick knew all about this stuff. He would come. He would believe her . . .

He had doubted once, though, that late night near the boulders.

But then he kissed her and called her good and wanted her goodness to be—what did he say? Contagious. That was it. Contagious.

The door opened, and she jumped. The man named Smith stepped aside to let Trent walk in, then shut and locked it again.

He stared at her across the table.

The look on his face was like a do-not-touch sign. His eyes were narrowed slits. His lips were undefined, they were so tightly pressed together. She didn't go to him.

"Cat, they're going to book you."

"Did you call my dad?"

His voice rose; there was an edge to it. "I left a message with his secretary. I said they're going to book you."

"What does that mean?"

"Fingerprints—"

"I mean, the message with his secretary. What did you say? Where was he?"

"I said you were being held at the DEA office, and it was urgent he come ASAP. She said he was on a site up in Rancho California, but she should be able to reach him." He pulled out a chair and sat down heavily, hands in his lap. "Do you understand, Cat, that there is enough evidence to arrest you and put you in jail?"

She blinked. "But I didn't buy any drugs!"

"Maybe not, but you transported twenty kilograms of cocaine across the border."

"Maybe not? Maybe—"

"In the piñatas."

"They were empty when I picked them up!"

"Under the seat."

"Trent, somebody put it there. I didn't do it. Why would I do it?"

"Who would put it there?"

"I don't know! That's your job!"

They stared at each other. Trent's mouth was white with tension, and she knew he was very angry. She also knew she was red-faced and angrier than he was.

"Catherine, you need a criminal attorney."

She flew to her feet, the chair flipped over, and she leaned across the table. "I need a friend who trusts me and knows the law."

He stood. "You know I only do corporate stuff, but I'll see what I can do about bail." He glanced at his watch. "Hopefully it'll all come together so you won't have to spend the night behind bars."

If there had been anything at all less cumbersome than the chair to pick up, Cat would have thrown it at him. Instead she screamed, "Get out! Get out!"

The door opened, and her father walked through. In the blink of an eye he was around the table, and his arms were around her.

Bear squeeze time.

"Nice set of lungs," Smitty remarked as he sat back down at his desk. "She should have used them at the mall. I guarantee, somebody would have tackled you."

The corner of Dominick's mouth lifted. He was in the SAC's office, down the hall and out of sight but close enough to have heard Cat's dismissal of Carver.

"D'Angelo, run this by me one more time. That was her ex-fiancé?"

"Yeah. Evidently her ex-lawyer too."

Smitty chewed his gum for a few moments, studying Dominick's face. "She was caught red-handed."

"Yes, I know." He met the other man's gaze.

"She's a good-looking chick. Exactly how involved are you?"

Dominick crossed his arms and leaned back, tilting the chair on its legs. "Not that way."

"Engstrom saw you kissing her at the motel."

"Yeah. But that's all. And that's only because I was too tired to think straight." He shook his head. "She's an honest-to-goodness angel, Smitty, way outa my league. When this is over, I seriously doubt I'll see her again."

He grunted. "If that spineless lawyer friend is in her league, I think you got your minors and majors confused."

"Whatever. Anyway, we can let her go, but not back to the Castillo just yet."

"I can hold her until you're finished there."

"No way." He stood and glanced at his watch. "I've put her through enough as it is. You saw her dad?"

"Big fella."

"Mm-hmm. He'll take care of her. I just hope he doesn't kill me in the process."

They went down the hall. Dominick knocked on the closed door while Smitty unlocked it. He heard a gruff "Yeah."

Cat and her father looked up at him from where they sat at the table, their hands clasped. Her eyes were dry, but puffy from crying, her wide mouth pinched, unsmiling. Her dark hair was disheveled, the white short-sleeved shirt wrinkled.

His heart melted at the pure, innocent sight of her.

He set her purse, straw hat, and sunglasses on the table.

With a cry, she ran to him.

"Umpf."

"Sorry."

"It's okay." His words were muffled in her hair as he held her tightly, ignoring the pain in his side. He glanced over at Stan St. Clair and gave him a little wave.

Cat looked up at him. "You believe me, don't you?"

"Of course." He ached at the nearness of her mouth, then thought of the nearness of her father.

She pulled his head toward her and kissed him soundly.

So much for his indecision.

"Oh, I knew it." She smiled. "I saw it in your eyes. Thank you, Dominick. I have to get to the Castillo right away."

"Uh, it's a little more complicated than that. First, sit down. Hello, Mr. St. Clair." He shook the burly hand and forced himself to make eye contact.

The older man looked like a bear awakened too early from a long winter's nap. "You have evidence to hold her." It was a statement. He understood the facts.

"Yes, sir, we do." He sat with them. "But I know it's a setup. Did Cat tell you who I am?"

"She did. And I have to say that if you weren't wearing that gun, I'd seriously consider carrying out my threat. That mall business was despicable."

"Yes. I—" Dominick cleared his throat. "I respect your

threat and can't tell you how sorry I am to have hurt your daughter."

"Apology accepted. Now her mother, on the other hand, probably *will* kill you. She kind of liked that fancy-schmantzy lawyer."

Silently Dominick gave thanks. "Would flowers help?"

"They might."

Cat clutched her arms across her waist, laid her head on the table. "Why did they stop me at the border?"

"They had a phone call, a tip describing you and your orange car, saying you would be carrying piñatas filled with coke. Who would be that angry with you? Is there some former employee maybe? Someone you fired?"

"I don't have a clue. And it's tangerine, not orange."

"Tell me what happened."

She straightened. "I went to Tecate this morning, stopped at a cousin of Maria's—she works at the orphanage—because she made piñatas for me. *Empty* piñatas. Then I visited the orphanage for about an hour and a half. Then I sat in traffic, drove across the border, parked like I always do so I could give *buñuelos* to Alberto, the Mexican guard, like I always do. And that's the last coherent thought I have."

He squeezed her hand on the table. "Monday's your usual day to visit Tecate, right?"

"Yes."

"Why today? Why Friday? For the piñatas for the festival?"

She nodded.

"Everyone knows your routine. Who knew you changed it?"

Her eyes widened. "I only told Ron and Trent last week. I mentioned it in our meeting."

He thought a moment, then shook his head. "Ron Hunter called us three months ago. He and Trent Carver suspected something was going on, something drug-related."

Now her jaw dropped. "They knew who you were?"

Dominick nodded. "Though I only met Hunter beforehand."

"Why didn't they tell me?"

"It was absolutely imperative no one else knew. Were there others at your meeting?"

"No."

"Your mother knew," St. Clair suggested. "You told her when she called to tell you she would have some things for you to take to the orphanage. She thought you were going next Monday."

"Cat, where were you when she called?"

"In my office."

"When?"

"Umm, Tuesday. Not late."

"Your mother and I were having dinner, around 6," her father added.

"Were you alone, Cat?" Dominick asked.

She nodded. "With the door shut."

"Someone could listen in on the line."

"From the front desk or Ron's office. But why—"

He squeezed her hand again. "Don't ask that just yet. It won't make sense. Who was out front that night?"

She hesitated. "The usual. Cissy. Amber. Paul."

"You're sure you told no one else?"

"I'm sure. I was so busy this week with the festival, I didn't make plans to see anyone. I saw Elli and Jim Monday night, but we just talked baby plans."

"All right." He placed his arm around the back of Cat's chair but made eye contact with her dad over her head. "You can go now, but I have to release you to your father's custody."

"Fine," she said.

"Cat, you're not allowed out of his sight." He saw St. Clair nod slightly. "I can't have you at the Castillo."

She clenched her jaw. "Well, that's exactly where I'm going."

"No, you're not. When Kevin unloads the cocaine stuffed in the turret above your desk and I arrest him, you'll go ballistic."

Her face crumpled. "Kevin?"

Anticipating her sobs, Dominick pressed her face against his chest as tightly as he could. "I'm sorry, I'm sorry. I promise it will be all right, but please stay away until tomorrow. Please." He kissed the top of her head and let go. "Stan . . ."

Her father took his place and held her. "Shh. It's okay, Kit-Cat."

"Please, sir, promise me you'll take her home with you, to Poway." His stomach was knotting.

"There's nowhere else she's going." His voice rose above Cat's cries. "You have my word, son. Now, do what you need to do to clean that place up." He stuck out his hand to shake Dominick's. "And take care of yourself. My wife will be expecting flowers. She's partial to anything chocolate too."

Cat felt like a little girl again.

By the time she and her dad reached the house, her mother was home. Unaware of what had transpired, she simply took one look at her daughter and hugged her. Without a word she drew a bubble bath, found sweats for her to change into, and left to make chicken noodle soup. While Cat soaked in the tub and let the tears flow, she knew Daddy would be explaining things. Not to have to do that was a relief.

They hovered, and she loved them for it. Snuggled against pillows on the couch in the family room, she ate the soup and tried not to think of anything except this comfort.

"Do you think I'll ever grow up and leave you two alone?" She bit her lip to hold back the tears that still bubbled just below the surface.

"Oh, sweetie." Mother laughed and hugged her. "You're grown-up. You just hit a bump in the road. Albeit a rather large bump. We'd make chicken soup for any family member who got arrested."

In spite of herself, Cat giggled.

Her dad chimed in, "I'm just glad we didn't have to put the business into hock to post bail."

"But, Stanley, dear, we would have."

"Well, sure, for Kit-Cat."

Her mother kissed her forehead and collected the empty dishes. "Do you want anything else?"

"Piñatas."

She smiled. "Will the Party Shop ones do?"

Cat nodded. "Three. Thanks."

Her dad settled into his recliner and reached for the television remote. "Want to see what's on ESPN?"

"Okay. What do you think is happening at the Castillo?"

"Well, my guess is that things are pretty normal. While you were in the ladies' room at Dominick's office, he told me that Ron would be there to cover for you. He guessed about six people would be arrested. They'll have unmarked cars pick them up in the back parking lot, without a lot of fuss." He paused. "I like him, Kit-Cat."

"You're just saying that because he drives a pickup."

"Yep. That says a lot for him. But the important thing is he cares about you."

"I don't know him, Daddy."

"Hmm," he grunted. "A mystery man. Reminds me of our mystery baby."

Cat rearranged the pillows and squiggled deeper into the soft cushions, pulling an afghan up around her shoulders. She hadn't heard a mystery baby story in a long time. They seldom varied, but she always listened, enraptured. It was only about five years ago that she realized she was searching for clues to her real identity. Who was her mother? Who was her father? Were they Los Angeles natives? Or maybe from another state? Maybe another country. Maybe her mother had been a budding movie actress who fell in love with a visiting prince who left before he knew a baby was on the way, and he couldn't be contacted afterward.

The stories, of course, never offered any more clues, but each time she did find what she was looking for. In her dad's twinkling blue eyes she saw an unconditional love that had plucked her from a cesspool and given her the life of a princess in a castle. Their home was simply comfortable, not a mansion full of rich furnishings, but she knew the emotional wealth was priceless and a thing to be cherished.

"You know, Kit-Cat, we didn't know anything about you. How old were you? Were you addicted to cocaine? Would your hair ever grow? Were you allergic to milk? For a long time we didn't know if you would even smile. But what we did know was that you needed somebody to love you. We knew we could love you and that God would give us enough love to love you through anything. Do you understand what I'm saying?"

"I think so." Dominick was an unknown in the details, but he needed somebody to love him. And her family might be the ones to do that.

"There's something I never told you." He stopped, his lips pressed together.

Fear tightened her throat. Her dad never ever hesitated, even if he was wrong about something. What was this? She could only raise her eyebrows in question.

"I prayed that God would break you and Trent up."

She stared at him. "You didn't."

"I stayed up all Christmas night." He studied the remote in his hand. "He wasn't right for you, Kit-Cat. I couldn't trust him to take care of you. He wasn't big enough on the outside or the inside. When that mall business happened and Trent turned goosey, I thanked God for whoever that man was."

"I remember you prayed for that man." That man . . . Dominick D'Angelo . . . her angel in disguise.

"Yeah, I did that too. I couldn't endure how he hurt you. I had to forgive him."

She hadn't told him everything yet, just that Dominick was that man and what he was doing at the Castillo. "Daddy . . ." He looked at her. "That's when Dominick became a Christian. Right after. He felt so terrible about what he had done. His friend Adam had been telling him about Jesus. All of a sudden it made sense to him."

"Well." He grinned. "Hallelujah. Pickup truck and a believer. And he's kind of macho too, like me."

She burst into laughter.

"Seriously, Kit-Cat, I could trust him to take care of you. If that guy makes a vow, you know he'll die before breaking it."

She thought of the vow he'd made as a teen, to avenge his friend's death, how he had spent his life fighting drug crime. "You got that right."

"So bring him to Sunday dinner again."

"Daddy, I have to get to know him better first. I mean, what if he bites his toenails?"

"Yeah, you wanna check that out. Or what if he never watches baseball?"

"Or leaves wet towels all over?"

"You should talk."

"Hey, I cleaned my place three weeks ago. What if he leaves the cap off the toothpaste?"

"Or belches at the table?"

In between their jokes and her dad's channel surfing for a baseball game, Cat drifted to sleep, still smiling, praying in her heart for Dominick and her castle.

— Twenty-Three —

THE CHAOS STARTED FIRST thing the next morning.

Cat was thankful that she had slept so long—all evening on the couch, then in her old bedroom through the night. She awoke at 6 A.M. rested and alert. The mathematical side of her brain snapped immediately to attention. The twenty kilos of cocaine found in her car had to be worth an unbelievable amount of money. What was the point in forfeiting that? Just to have her arrested? And why didn't it work? How did they let her go when, technically speaking, she *was* guilty?

She swung her feet to the floor and reached for the telephone. This line of thinking would go nowhere, and she had work to do. She dialed the Castillo and, as she guessed, reached Ron there.

"Cat! Thank goodness. Where are you? How soon can you get here?"

"An hour. Is everything okay?"

"Well, the place is still standing, and only two guests checked out. So far. Cissy'll be here by 9. I need you to work with the temp agency as soon as they open. We're going to need help in the restaurant and kitchen and— Never mind. I'll fill you in when you get here. Maintenance is covered because I knew Dom— Oh, don't say anything yet about—you know. Hurry." The line went dead.

Cat stared at the phone in her hand. Restaurant. Kitchen. Who in those areas would . . . ?

This was going to be difficult. Insanely difficult. They were all her friends. Weren't they?

She sighed and got ready. Her mom had anticipated her wardrobe needs so she wouldn't have to go home first this morning. Last night Mother had gone to her sister's. Although shorter, Annie was similar in size and had sent two outfits that would be long enough. Cat chose the casual red dress over the black business suit. She wanted to look more festive today to counteract the somber events that had taken place yesterday.

In the meantime, her dad made phone calls. He learned that her car had been impounded.

"I don't want it anyway," she announced. "I couldn't drive it again, not after—" She shuddered. "Between that stuff and Trenton Carver— Oh! I'll buy one myself."

Mother offered to drive her. Daddy offered to car shop and bring her one to try out for a few days.

Forty-five minutes later they sped down the freeway with three new piñatas in the backseat, already stuffed with candy by her elementary school teacher mom who loved this sort of thing. By 8 o'clock Cat had slipped into her Jill-of-all-trades mode, doing everything except festival coordinating. She hired her mother on the spot as she stood in the courtyard directing a gardener in the hanging of the piñatas.

"Catherine, don't be silly." She attached a walkie-talkie to her belt, then accepted the clipboard with its list of activities. Her short blonde hair shone in the early morning sunlight, and her eyes crinkled as she smiled. "I could pay *you* for letting me do this. Oh, it's going to be a gorgeous, wonderful day. Now, where do I start?"

Back at her desk, telephone tucked between ear and shoulder, Cat studied another list while on hold with the temp agency. Ron had briefly filled her in on what happened yesterday. Twelve people had been arrested, most from her shift, along with the night security guard. Ron had written their names. She wished he had just written their jobs, not their names.

Kevin . . .

Terry . . .

Jacey . . .

Pedro . . .

Deanne . . .

Reed . . .

"Cat!"

She looked up to see Ron walk in.

"Don't analyze it." His eyes were dark sockets in his somber face. "Just fill the vacancies."

"But . . . why?" She pulled another tissue from the box in front of her. "And how?"

"I don't know." He propped his hands on his hips and shook his head. "I don't know. I do know they're not all hard-core. They just found an easy way to make more than minimum wage."

"You look awful, Ron. Have you been here all night?"

"No, just until they hauled off our trusted security guard about 1 A.M. With him gone and a few DEA guys still hanging around, I figured it was safe. Are you on hold with the agency?"

She nodded. "She's going through some files. I think we can get the kitchen and security covered. And I have Mandi rounding up her dorm friends to wait tables. Miguel's coming in early."

He leaned over her desk and squeezed her shoulder. "That's my girl. We'll get through this. Just keep your guests in mind. We'll sort out the other later."

She gave him a small smile, then shifted her attention as the woman on the other end of the line began discussing business.

A short time later Cissy walked past her open door, then doubled back. "Hey, you're here! I didn't see your tangerine gumdrop in the parking lot."

"It got stuck at the border yesterday."

She laughed loudly. "You get a flat tire or were you running drugs?"

Cat winced at her choice of words. "Oh, it's a long story. I'll tell you later. Did you get along all right last night?"

"Yeah, but it was one weird shift. Kevin disappeared. Then

Deanne left Housekeeping without a word to Ginger. We figured Kevin and Deanne are seeing each other and couldn't wait until quitting time. Two families checked out, said they didn't like the looks of a cop car in the back lot even though I explained they sometimes cruise by. Now today Ron calls me before 6 A.M., says he needs me because first shift is short and he'd pay me double time since it's my day off."

Cat thought things must have gone smoothly last night if the front desk clerk didn't know any more than this. "We appreciate you, Cissy. All your extra efforts. Well, we've got a couple of temps coming in for kitchen duty. With the festival we need—"

"Good morning, ladies." Dominick stood in the doorway.

Cissy grinned. "Hey, handsome. You're kind of dressed up for maintenance, aren't you?"

Cat barely noticed his sportcoat. What held her attention was the grim line of his mouth, the icy look in his eyes. *Oh, dear Lord.* Things weren't finished yet.

"I'm just stopping by. Actually, to talk to you, Cissy, privately. Why don't we go outside? Excuse us, Cat."

She watched them go through her door, then out the other door that led to the employee parking lot. Disbelief rooted her to the chair.

No! This had to be a mistake. Another major mistake.

She rushed around her desk and into the hallway, then shot through the exterior door, crashing it against the outside wall as she went. In the far corner of the lot, Dominick held Cissy's arm. His other hand was atop her head, guiding it as she slid into the back of a police car.

Before he shut the door, Cat was beside him, clutching his arm, speechless.

"Cat, this doesn't concern you."

"Yes, it does! She's my friend! Cissy!"

The twisted face turned toward her was almost unrecognizable. Cissy's hands were in her lap, the handcuffs shiny bracelets on her wrists.

Dominick started to close the door, but Cat stepped in front of it. "What is going on?"

"Get out of the way."

"Dominick!"

"Tell her," Cissy snarled. "Go ahead and burst her bubble. It'll do her good. She's just a spoiled brat!"

As if the words were physical blows, Cat backed away.

Cissy's eyes narrowed. "St. Clair, you've always had everything handed to you on a silver platter. You don't have a clue. You're just a stupid—"

Dominick slammed the door shut, then brushed past Cat. Through the glass she saw Cissy turn her head toward the wire mesh divider that separated her from the front. A uniformed policeman in the driver's seat started the engine. Across the top of the car, she met Dominick's gaze.

"Just go back to work," he ordered.

"Tell me. I'm okay. Just tell me." She bit her lower lip.

For a moment the ice melted. "Cat," he said softly, "she called the Border Patrol yesterday."

Cat blinked. She tasted blood from her lip. Cissy had set her up.

"*Mi gatita*, there are 200 guests who need your special touch. Right now." He opened his door and quickly climbed in. Before he shut it, the car had sped halfway across the lot.

Cat stood alone on the pavement under a brilliant blue sky, wearing her sister's red dress, listening to the wail of a distant siren, staring at her mother's station wagon parked in her spot, hoping ten strangers would show up to help run her castle. Cissy, her right-hand coworker, was gone. Trent, still her backup until his unsupportive response yesterday, was gone. Dominick, the mystery man who had tenderly breathed life into her dead emotions, was gone.

It was an upside-down world.

Dear Father, please be my right hand, my backup, my healer.

After the police car whisked away Dominick and Cissy, and Cat flung her desperate prayer heavenward, she stumbled back to her office as if in a state of shock. The urgency of hotel management details soon swamped her. A kind of numbing fog crept in, swallowing all other thoughts and feelings, enabling her to function.

She pitched in at the front desk, in Housekeeping, in the kitchen. Later, as temporary employees sporadically arrived, she helped train them in each area. In between she checked on her mother and the staff who were running the special swimming, miniature golf, basketball, and volleyball contests. She smoothed guests' ruffled feathers and answered their questions. She waited on tables at lunchtime. She accepted unfamiliar car keys from her dad and sent her mother with him; they had evening plans. She smiled.

Until 4:30. "Ron," she yelled, "I am *not* going home!"

He walked around the desk and shut his office door, then returned to his chair. "Sit down. Did you eat yet?"

"No. Did you?"

He ignored the question and rubbed his bloodshot eyes. "Sit down. We can't both keep this up—"

"Then *you* go home! This is my festival, and you look awful. I'm fifteen years younger, and I slept last night."

"Sit down and talk to me."

Cat took a deep breath and sat down. "We're in good shape. At least okay shape anyway." She counted on her fingers as she talked. "The caterers have the hog roast under control, so the restaurant tonight is not a problem. Mandi's filling in at the front desk; she's helped there before. No problem. I'll handle the new security guard; he's coming at 9. No problem. So go home, Ron. I am not going to miss the breaking of the piñatas or the fencing demonstration."

In the end he agreed.

She stayed until after midnight, then drove to her apartment in the nondescript white car her dad said would be an excellent buy. In the dark she shook her head at his choice, too tired to know if she was amused or put out that he thought she would like it.

As her head sank into the pillow, thoughts of Dominick came to mind. Within a few moments, though, exhaustion took over, and it was easy to push him aside, letting the internal fog engulf him once again. She knew it was a self-defense mechanism, one she planned on clinging to for a long time.

Sunday and Monday were sixteen-hour days for her and Ron, filled with one crisis after another. Cat felt as if she were treading water. It wasn't until Tuesday afternoon that her feet touched bottom and she breathed easily. The last of the temps and applicants had either left or had been interviewed and hired. All the vacancies were filled. Tentatively anyway. She and Ron were in the process of setting up their own police record checks and drug testing.

"It seems a crummy thing to have to learn," she observed as she tore open a bag of spicy tortilla chips. Wedging toe against heel, she pushed off her flats, scrunched down in a chair opposite the manager's desk, propped her stocking feet on another chair, and bit into a chip.

"What's crummy to learn?" Ron pulled a candy bar from his drawer.

"To be wary. To not take people at face value. To open all their closets looking for a skeleton."

"Welcome to the real world, Cinderella." He bit into his chocolate.

"Why didn't we do all this before?"

"All right, so I had one foot in fairy-tale land too." He shrugged. "I thought we had it covered. At least we'll be more efficient now."

"You never told me. What made you suspicious?" She crunched into another chip.

"It was just an undercurrent, really. Whispered conversations that stopped when I came by. Things like that. A couple

of fancy cars that didn't jive with income or family. I heard
Deanne lock your door once when she went in to clean. When
she came out, the trash bag appeared too heavy for your junk,
even if it would have been combined with the whole building's."

Cat thought a moment. A question needed to be asked. The
numbing fog that had kept emotions at arm's length these past
few days now propelled her ahead. Since feelings didn't matter
at this point, it didn't matter what she might learn. "Ron, did
you ever suspect me?"

"Of course not!" he barked out of the corner of his mouth.
He finished chewing the candy, then swallowed. "Cat, you're a
thoroughbred. I know one when I see her. You've proven yourself over the years. Trent Carver's an idiot, but we won't go down
that road. I didn't want you getting hurt if I could help it. It
seemed best you didn't know. For the record, I didn't even tell
my wife."

Not sure what to say, she simply stared at him.

There was a loud rap on the door, and Ron called out,
"Come in!"

Dominick opened the door.

Before the hello was out of his mouth, Cat's numbing fog
had dissipated, leaving an onslaught of emotions in its wake.

"Hey . . ." Ron dropped his candy bar and stepped around
his desk to clasp Dominick's hand. "There's my man." He
slapped him on the shoulder, grinning. "I haven't thanked you
properly yet. We've been a little preoccupied."

"Same here." He lowered his large frame into the chair from
which Cat had just removed her feet. "I see you're both enjoying a nutritious late lunch." He eyed the chips in her lap.

She lifted a shoulder, her throat too dry for words, then bent
forward to guide her feet into the shoes. The plastic tortilla chip
bag crackled loudly.

Ron answered, "Lunch, dinner, and breakfast, I think.
Dominick, I can't tell you how much we appreciate you keeping
the Castillo out of the newspaper."

"No problem. How are you doing?"

"Hanging in there. We're devising new hiring policies. Can you tell us what was going on, give us an idea of where we were so dense?"

"Oh, it's not that you were dense. You did notice some things, which is why you called us. As far as not catching on, I think it has to do with not looking at life in a particular way. It's not wired into your everyday world to suspect that drugs are being sold right under your nose."

Cat watched his profile as he explained things to them. He wore a white shirt, unbuttoned at the neck, black slacks, and a gray tweed sport coat. She wondered if he also wore the gun shoulder holster. His thick black hair was brushed back. His 3 o'clock shadow jaw was relaxed, the smile genuine with its right corner tucking itself upward. And yet in his deep voice she heard . . . what?

"The thing is," he continued, "it's important to notice things. If you hadn't called and we'd learned about the trafficking through another source, you could have been held responsible. It's called 'tacit consent,' and we could have shut you down. I'm glad that didn't happen." He smiled. "I'm kind of partial to this place. Particularly the paint job."

Ron laughed.

"Anyway, we're grateful. Your phone call set in motion an investigation that ultimately led to a trafficker we didn't know about."

She thought his tone was professional. It lacked that unemotional ice he was capable of, but . . . it also lacked the essence of the man who had held her hand in church, who had kissed her while whispering about her goodness being contagious.

That was it. Dominick D'Angelo was a different man, one she didn't know, hadn't even *met*. If he cared for her, cared to continue the relationship, he would have called by now. He would have, at the least, greeted her as he used to—warmly. There was an obvious standoffish air about him.

Intuitively she avoided eye contact. Whatever had happened between the two of them had not happened between herself and this guy. She knew if she looked at him now, it would somehow erase everything they had shared. When he glanced in her direction, she averted her gaze.

"Cat," Ron was addressing her, "add that to our list. New waste disposal service." He shook his head in disbelief. "So you're saying they delivered the cocaine on Saturday mornings?"

Dominick nodded. "Around 3 A.M., usually once a month. They had a key to the kitchen. While one of them collected garbage, the other collected money and stashed twenty to thirty kilos behind the stockpots. Cat, do you want to hear this? You look a little pale."

"I—" She sighed. "I'd better hear it."

He took a deep breath. "You know the trash bag you sometimes found left in the kitchen and then would carry out to the dumpster?"

She remembered, of course. She had had to reprimand the busboy about leaving garbage in the kitchen. She also remembered that night Dominick frightened her; he said he saw her placing the trash in the bin when he was coming from the maintenance garage. She had wondered how he could have seen her from there with the fence in the way. He couldn't have! Obviously he had been watching her.

"Well," he said, "there was probably about half a million dollars in it. I guess they were changing their routine. You okay?"

"What?"

"Are you okay?"

"Oh, I'm just great!" She tossed the chip bag onto the desk. "Not only do I transport drugs, I move the money around too. And half the people I manage know more about what goes on around here than I do. Talk about dense!" She frowned.

Ron gave her a small smile. "Formerly managed. And for the record, it wasn't quite half your staff. Finished?"

She nodded.

He turned back to the agent. "Okay, Dominick, what happened after the stuff was delivered?"

"Westin, the night guard, would take over. He stashed most of the coke in the two turrets—in the restaurant and above Cat's desk. The biggest chunk he sold to middle-of-the-night visitors. Over the next few days Kevin and Deanne distributed the remainder of it and—"

Cat winced.

"And collected money. They kept the money in the turrets too. It was all just another part of a route that starts in Colombia. We were able to stop these small-time peddlers and trace the system back to your waste disposal service. That was a big break. It turns out they're a good-sized front for money laundering. By the way, someone will be contacting you. We'll need to look at your invoices from them."

"But where did they get the cocaine?" Ron asked.

"We traced only one small shipment to their site from the border. The trail goes cold beyond that. More than likely the Arellano-Felix Organization is behind it, also referred to as the Tijuana Cartel. They organize every aspect of the drug trade, even into our country. We're not allowed to work in Mexico. It's too dangerous because of widespread corruption; too many officials are on their payroll. The best we can do is what we did here—stop as much trafficking as we can. By shutting down the waste disposal business, we effectively shut down, for a while anyway, everyone who delivered to them."

"And," Ron added, "all the little guys like our employees who sold on the streets for them. I take it the Castillo wasn't the only drop-off point?"

"Exactly. It's mind-boggling to think of all the lives affected. Just imagine one scenario, like your busboy, and multiply that by hundreds. He takes his weekly eight-ounce bag, gets nine grand on the street for—"

"Nine grand!" Ron exclaimed. "Exactly how much money are we talking?"

"Well, that's street value. Twenty kilos are worth almost 900,000 dollars."

Cat swallowed. Hadn't Trent said there were twenty kilos in

her car? Worth how much? "Why would anyone throw away almost a million dollars to set me up?"

"Good question," Dominick replied. "It turns out only the donkey piñata had the real stuff, and not very good stuff at that. So she probably forked over only five to six grand for you."

"She? Cissy paid for it?" Had she hurt Cissy that much?

"She could afford it. She ran things from the inside here and, umm, kept a close eye on you, Cat. She always knew where you were so she could tell the others when the coast was clear. And she was smart. She had bank accounts that took us a long time to uncover. When she called the Border Patrol, she described you and your *tangerine* car in about ten seconds flat. They couldn't trace the call. We suspected her and got her home phone records. So we also know who she called in Tecate to plant the stuff in your car, but that's in the hands of the Mexican authorities." He shrugged.

"Is that why they let me go, because it was such a small amount?"

"No. We just learned that tidbit yesterday. You still could have faced ten years in prison and a huge fine. It was because none of us work alone. When Border Patrol punched in your name, the computer red-flagged it. They knew the DEA was investigating you. So they called. My boss knew I was . . ." His voice trailed off, and he cleared his throat. "Uhh, well, that I knew your name in connection with what we were doing here. He had them bring you to the office, then called me in. From the information we'd gathered, it was almost a foregone conclusion that it was a setup."

"What if she had done it two months ago?" she wondered aloud.

They sat silently for a few moments. There was no simple answer. If she had been "caught" before Dominick knew her—

Cat shuddered, overcome with the magnitude of the sadness and all the confused lives enmeshed in the situation. "Why did she do it?"

"I think," Ron offered, "she wanted your job. Once in a

while she'd come in early, flirt with me, point out your mistakes. She really got her hopes up when you were going through that time of migraines and so on and so forth. I mean, she had legitimate complaints then."

"She was jealous of you," Dominick added. "It's not your fault. You grew up in a nice house with a loving family, and she didn't. If she didn't know the circumstances of your adoption—"

"You're adopted?" Ron asked. The phone rang at his elbow, and he turned to answer it.

Cat laced her fingers together. She could have shared more of herself with Cissy. She could have taken her under her wing, not been so preoccupied with being a manager, so engrossed with Trent—

"Cat, it's your mother."

She stood and took the phone. "Mother?"

"Catherine! The baby's coming! Elli's at the hospital. Jim's flying in from San Francisco. He can't get here until 6."

"I'm on my way. Bye." She handed the phone to Ron and hurried to the door. "I gotta go. Elli's in labor. Her husband's out of town. I'm her stand-in breathing coach. Oh, man, this is three weeks early."

"Go! I'll cover for you. Call me."

"Thanks, Ron." Her hand on the doorknob, she looked over her shoulder at Ron, then finally at Dominick.

His eyes held hers for a long moment. Without another word, she left.

Less than ten minutes later she eased her car into freeway traffic, glad she hadn't been stopped for going sixty on her way to the on-ramp . . . thinking this little nondescript white car wasn't so bad . . . hoping the baby wouldn't come until her brother-in-law got here . . . ignoring the fact that Dominick D'Angelo had just told her good-bye.

— *Twenty-Four* —

THE TIGHT-FITTING, dolphin-like skin of the wet suit supported Dominick's rib cage, making the sharp pain bearable as he paddled facedown on his board toward the horizon. His exposed forearms, legs, and face tingled from the cold, salty water. The early morning sun, still too low in the sky to offer any warmth, beat on the back of his wet hair. The ever-present wind and the rhythmic whoosh of distant waves crushing against the shore filled his ears.

Adam had warned him that surfing could aggravate his injuries, even push the crack into a full-fledged break that could puncture something. If he fell, as he always did, hard enough, just right— But Dominick had tuned him out. He needed the shock of cold water drenching him inside and out, cleansing him in a way, reminding him he was still alive despite that feeling of deadness he couldn't shake.

The board lifted slightly as a wave rolled beneath him. The Pacific was more calm than wild this morning, a glassy surface that he skimmed easily, racing alongside a low-flying seagull. Only a handful of surfers lingered in the distance, in that promised land where the "big ones" ascended from the ocean's depths, offering to those crazy enough to trust, the chance to walk on water.

A wall of water began to build there now. He didn't have time to reach it and so lay prone, watching its ominous approach until it towered over him. He saw the first curl of its snarling descent and for a split second he wondered what he was doing here, then dove toward the murky tranquillity beneath the crashing beast. A moment later he emerged into the foamy white aftermath, spitting out the salt that coated his throat and mouth.

At last he made it to the waiting area and straddled the sticky fiberglass, his legs dangling in the water. He gazed at the navy-blue horizon. Waiting. Watching. A dull pain shot through his right side, but not enough. He had hoped for continuous, violent waves, for the chance to push himself to the limit, to see how much physical pain he could endure.

He didn't know how else to endure the other pain.

Maybe this leave of absence wasn't such a good idea. He should be working. Not that his opinion counted. Smitty and Adam didn't know each other, but between the two of them he had a SAC-ordered and a doctor-ordered vacation. There wasn't any getting around that.

In reality there wasn't any getting around his exhaustion either. He knew he couldn't function in any realm, except maybe the spiritual. It wasn't like last December when he had hit bottom. That bottom was flat line. There was no way to survive without accepting a new life in Christ. This bottom was different. In a sense it was more terrible though. Now he had a beating heart, and it was breaking in two.

Cat was precious in every way. Her athletic, healthy good looks attracted him. Seared in his memory were the honey-colored eyes shedding tears over him, the taste of her mouth. Her practical, easygoing mannerisms always made him feel welcome, even when he was deceiving her. If she were spoiled, it was only because her needs had been met by a loving family. She knew what she had come from and appreciated the gift given to her. She cared for the less fortunate in a Tecate orphanage, worked hard creating castles for others. She was imperfect but real. And she was precious.

He had pointed a gun in her face and brought her world tumbling down. She called him an angel in disguise, landed with her feet on the ground pointed away from Carver, accepted the friendship he offered. Then again he had pulled the rug out from under her when he told her what he really did for a living. While she attempted to get to know him, he was chasing down deal-ers, not fulfilling his maintenance responsibilities at her Castillo, grabbing her in the dark, and suspecting her once again of deal-ing. When they finally got together and began in earnest a totally honest dialogue, he had raced off, leaving her alone to clean up his kitchen and reach her own conclusions.

To top it off, he had known all along that Cissy despised her and could easily betray her. True, he hadn't realized the weapons available to the young woman, but he could have warned Cat not to trust in that friendship.

And yet, what right did he have to talk about not trusting? He had encouraged Cissy just enough to keep her talking to him. On that last Thursday night she invited him out, he turned her down and foolishly let her know that he cared for Cat. That, of course, had been Cissy's last straw. The next day she set about removing Cat from the scene.

Even without being aware of all the details, it was no won-der Cat was leery of him in Hunter's office. He carried with him all the world's ugliness, and he spread it wherever he went. There was no place for it in her life. He would protect her from it. As he had told Smitty, she was out of his league.

Water lapped gently under his longboard. No hint of a real wave. The ocean was flat.

He had two weeks to begin working Cat out of his system, let scar tissue grow around that wound that felt like death. At least he knew he was not alone, knew that God loved him, knew He had a path for him and was available to show him.

He needed to get to know Him better.

Adam had given him a standing invitation to attend a men's Bible study downtown on Saturday mornings. He had balked at the thought of mingling with politically correct busi-nessmen. Adam agreed some of the group were that but said the leaders were different. One guy worked part-time as a government consultant, coached Little League, and hung out with disabled vets. The other one was a rock-climbing high school teacher. And then, he thought, there was Adam himself, who chose to do middle-of-the-night surgeries on the dregs of society so he could pray for them.

Maybe he should give the group a try.

The sun was warming his back now. On the horizon the sky separated from the blue-black ocean into a brilliant aquamarine.

Maybe it was a good day to be alive after all.

A bell jangled above the door as Cat opened it and stepped inside. She clutched a shopping bag at her side and looked around.

It was a big, old house. The small entryway was bright with morning sunshine pouring through a tall, yellow-paned window alongside the front door. The worn linoleum floor was clean. Dark wood framed an opening that led to what looked like a hall.

"Cat?" Megan Parker's voice called. "Is that you?" She appeared then, smiling as usual, brown curls bobbing every which way.

"Hi, Megan." She returned her new friend's hug and glanced down at her own clay-splattered jeans and sweatshirt. "Excuse my appearance. How are you?"

"Fine, fine. Welcome to my home away from home! Come on in."

She followed her into the hall. Voices and clanging dishes could be heard from the back of the house. The scent of cooking food wafted through. It was a welcoming first impression, an obvious haven for homeless women and children.

They entered a tiny office where a woman stood beside the desk, stuffing crayons and coloring books into an attaché case. Two small children sat on folding chairs, suckers in their mouths, legs swinging.

"Cat, meet Tori Steed. She's been interviewing me about the shelter, for a weekly newspaper."

"Hello." Tori smiled and offered her hand. She was attractive with sparkling eyes and short black hair tucked behind her ears.

Cat shook her hand. "And who is this?" She smiled toward the identically dark-haired, round-cheeked twosome who had the biggest blue eyes she'd ever seen. "They must be twins?"

"Hard to tell, huh?" the reporter teased. "This is Sara and Philip, and they're three and ready to skedaddle, aren't you, kiddos? I'm sorry, I didn't catch your name."

"Cat St. Clair."

"She's originally from your neck of the woods," Megan added.

"North County?" Tori asked.

Cat nodded.

"St. Clair. That sounds— You're not related to Betty and Stan, are you?"

"They're my parents. Do you know them?"

"We're acquainted from church. Oh, and your mother teaches with a friend of mine who goes there too—Kendall Zukowski."

"Adam," Megan explained, "is in a Bible study with their husbands, which is how I happened to get to be interviewed, for which I'm very grateful."

"It's been delightful." Tori hugged her, then hoisted the bag onto her shoulder and held her hands toward the children. "Let's go. It's time to pick up Daddy. Megan, the article should be in next week's issue. I'm sure it will draw attention to your work here."

"And funds, I hope."

"We'll pray that way. It's a good work." The twins chattered and pulled on her arms. "Good-bye. Nice meeting you, Cat." They made their noisy way out the door.

Megan sat behind the cluttered desk. "Have a seat, Cat. I'm so glad you called. How are you?"

"Well, okay. It's been a full week. Just when all that business was taken care of at the Castillo, my sister had a baby. This was my first morning to get to the pot shop in a long time. And I thought since you were close by, I'd bring this bowl . . ." She pointed to the bag she had placed on the floor. ". . . to you so you could pass it on to . . ." Her voice trailed away.

Megan's face softened.

Cat imagined what a saint she must appear to the homeless women and children who made their way here. "I don't know his phone number or his address." She hoped they wouldn't be offered. She hoped just to get this bowl, this reminder of a special moment between them, out of her sight. "Anyway, I don't think we'll see each other again, so . . ." She shrugged.

"I think he's at that Bible study right now with Adam and those other guys."

"Oh, that's nice."

"Adam made him take some time off. I guess his boss did too." She smiled. "His other boss."

"That's good. I'm sure he could use a break. Well, I should go. I have to stop and see my new nephew before work."

"Why won't you be seeing each other again?" Megan clapped a hand over her mouth. "I'm sorry—it's not my business."

"No, that's okay." She stared at the desktop for a moment without seeing it. "I think we had a relationship for a particular situation, and that situation is over now. I mean, I never got to know him really. And what he does for a living, well, it's just a different lifestyle than what I'm accustomed to. And vice versa, I'm sure. So it's for the best that we, uhh— You know, he probably doesn't want this bowl either. Just use it here." She stood. "Well, I'm glad I met you, Megan."

"Same here, Cat. Will you promise to keep in touch?" She came around the desk.

"Sure." They hugged each other. "Good-bye!"

Cat made her way quickly out the door before the tears in Megan's eyes spilled over. The woman really was too emotional.

During the next few weeks Cat devoted much of her spare time
to cuddling her new nephew while studying the apartment-to-
rent classifieds. She avoided working overtime and made a con-
scious effort to get reacquainted with old friends. Many of those
friends lived nearer the neighborhood she had moved from. She
met them now in familiar cafes and in the church that was
within walking distance of her old home.

Strolling through the familiar blocks, she recalled how
frightening the area had become right after the mall incident.
What she had referred to as intriguing turned threatening. The
eclectic array of peoples and stores wreaked of potential for
crime. The church that opened its doors all week long to the
homeless then left her feeling insecure. The late-night busy sidewalks had made her frantic for a quiet castle in the desert, one
with high walls, a moat, and Trent. When it became clear he
wasn't of the same mind-set, she moved to a bland, safety-con-
scious place with double bolts on three sets of doors.

Now, with Trent long gone and castles too distant to imagine, she began to pray for an apartment to become available in
the old neighborhood.

When the new front desk manager fell in love with the new
second shift maintenance man, Cat drove to Cissy's apartment
near the beach. She wasn't sure why she was doing this or if
Cissy would be there, though she assumed she was probably out
on bail. She had never been there before but found it easily with
a street guide map. As she had both hoped and feared, Cissy
opened the door.

"Hi," Cat said.

The young woman stared at her. She didn't look well. Her
skin was blotchy, her long blonde hair uncombed. A loose sweatshirt hung over her shorts.

"Can we talk?"

Cissy twisted her mouth, then shrugged. "This place is too
crowded. Let's go down to the boardwalk." She shut the door
behind herself and led the way down the rickety wooden, out-

door stairway. She was barefoot, a common sight so near the beach.

"Want some breakfast?" Cat asked.

Cissy lifted her hands, palms up.

"My treat."

"Sure."

They walked silently the few blocks to a cafe that offered outside seating. Cissy did not bother with small talk, nor did Cat. She had a purpose in mind for this visit. There was no reason to smother it with fluffy chitchat. They spoke first to the waiter and gave their orders.

"So, Cat, how's Dominick? Or is that even his real name?"

"It's his real name. I don't know how he is. I haven't seen him in a few weeks. He's a DEA agent, and I work at a motel, and I want a husband at home every night with me and the kids." She smiled.

"Like I've said before, you are one naive girl."

"I know. And I know that's why it was so easy for you to run your side business and put the Castillo in danger and set me up. But I forgive you. Is there anything I can do for you? Do you need a job?"

Cissy almost dropped her coffee cup. "Ouch!" She grabbed a napkin to wipe away the hot liquid that had spilled on her hand. "You can't be serious."

"I am. We worked well together. But you don't know me, Cissy." And then she began to tell the former employee all about herself, all the vulnerable details she had never bothered to share before. She began with her birth and finished with Dominick's gun in her face at the mall. Somewhere in the middle the waiter served the food.

She concluded, "I apologize for coming off like a snob to you. I'm no different, no better than you. I'm just a few years older and have parents who can more or less give me whatever I need. But if I didn't trust that God loves me, I'd hate you and I'd hate Dominick and I'd hate Trent. I'd be a basket case and angry and one lousy assistant manager."

"You hate me," Cissy scoffed. "You're just classy enough to hide it."

"I don't hate you. I'm offering you a job."

"How can you not hate me?"

"Jesus."

"You're crazy."

"No, it's supernatural but real."

"I don't want to hear it."

"Yeah, well, He loves you. Now tell me if you need a job." Cissy stared at her.

"Are you addicted to any drugs?"

She shook her head. "I was in it for the big bucks. You can't deal if you're addicted."

"Are you going to jail?"

She shrugged. "It might work out I'll just get probation and one humongous fine that'll put me in debt for the rest of my life."

"Then you need a job. I'll give you one."

Cissy bit her lip and looked away.

"There's a catch though."

"Figured there would be."

"You have to go to a Bible study. Once a week."

She blinked. "That's it?"

"For now. We might have to throw in church too. You obviously need a new set of friends. What do you say?"

"I'll think about it." She stood. "Hey, thanks for breakfast."

"Wait." Cat reached into her purse for a pen and paper. She wrote her phone number and handed it to her. "I'm moving in two weeks. Call me."

"I'll think about it."

"All right. I'll call you. Bye, Cissy. Take care of yourself."

— Twenty-Five —

IT WAS A SATURDAY, the last one in September. A Santa Ana wind had been blowing for a few days, its fine desert dust irritating throats and tempers.

It would have been a horrible day for an outdoor wedding reception.

Tucked away in the low-lying dry creek bed, in the shade of the footbridge, Cat hid from the wind. She also hid from the hustle and bustle in her parents' house. It was one of those, as her mother called it, bustling in-and-out days. Every family member stopped by for one reason or another at least once during the day. Food was fixed, spontaneous plans made, projects shared. And of course today everyone tended to hang out longer because Elli and the baby were camped in the cool family room for the afternoon.

She hid, too, from work. Ron was the one who insisted she take the day off, but she didn't argue. He blamed her cheerless attitude on recent events, exhaustion, and the Santa Ana. Had he realized it, he would have also blamed it on this being her canceled wedding day.

Cat didn't know what to blame her attitude on. All she knew was that the magic had gone out of the Castillo. Why? She had moved into another apartment in her old neighborhood. Fears and migraines were long gone. Trent never stopped in during her shift. Business was good. What more could she ask for?

While she hid for a while this afternoon from family, work,

251

and wind, she recognized that she wasn't hiding from God any-more. That was a significant development during the past month. She had gone twice now to the church she found years ago when she first moved out on her own but had not set foot in since the nightmare. She redeveloped the habit of reading the Bible and praying. Her thoughts were often a monologue with God, as now.

Father, please help me figure this out. My life is full. You put me at the Castillo, and it's everything I ever wanted in a job. You've given me a wonderful family and good friends who don't fuss at me for ignor-ing them for months . . . quiet times making pottery . . . an outlet for giving at the orphanage. Why is it all so empty now? Why is it—

All right, she would say it, say the words she had been hid-ing from for four weeks.

Why is it I can't stop thinking about Dominick?

She leaned back against the earthen bank and gazed up at the iridescent blue sky. A hawk, its wings spread, soared grace-fully overhead, silent. Just like God.

In frustration she kicked a grouping of small rocks, scatter-ing them in every direction, smashing what had been one of her imaginary castles. She had arranged this one just before the nightmare. It represented not only a floor plan but the future husband and children who would occupy it with her, enjoying a lifestyle she was convinced best suited her.

She stared at the disarray.

You want that too?

In the silence she understood the answer, covered her eyes with her hands, and took a deep breath.

Okay. The castle dreams are Yours. No more opinionated, cast-in-concrete plans for marriage, a big North County house, three or four kids, the Castillo work forever. You decide. I'll let You decide.

She opened her eyes.

Help me let You decide.

She fiddled with the stones, stacking them, rearranging them.

And what about Dominick? It's pointless to think about him!

There is no future in that relationship. Not that there is a relationship. He hasn't even bothered to call. Even an acquaintance would call after such an ordeal. His lack of interest is rather obvious.

Besides, he told me I was too good to get messed up with him. Not to mention there's no way on earth I could live with his lifestyle. Besides, he's probably been transferred from the area. Or will be soon, and that one really is not negotiable, Lord. I won't leave here.

She took a deep breath.

I'm sorry. I know that You don't negotiate. I know You know what's best.

But will You just take him from my thoughts? I'm tired of seeing him at every turn, his strong face, his laughing with the Tecate kids, his playing basketball with me, his Italian at the restaurant . . . that red tie and black suit with his black hair.

She sighed.

His saving me from getting arrested. He is not what I want in a man! He just is not. He doesn't fit my mold. He's unpredictable, mysterious, and too . . . too intensely alive with his muscular arms and shoulders and focused eyes and unwavering commitment to fight drug dealers, figuratively and literally. He's—

There was a noise on the dry hillside above her. Someone was slipping and sliding, out of sight behind scrub trees, boulders, and sagebrush. Probably a niece or nephew come to fetch her. With the heel of her hand, she wiped away a stray tear. A long jeans-covered leg came into sight.

A very long jeans-covered leg.

It was Dominick.

He wore loafers, jeans, a pale yellow polo shirt. His sunglasses were pushed atop his head. His black hair glistened in the sunlight. He jumped down into the creek bed and sat on the ground facing her. "I want to give it another shot." Just like that. No preamble, no hello, no how-have-you-been?

She stared at him.

The corner of his mouth tucked inward. His gray eyes were soft and warm. "I did all my dancing around the bush getting down here."

Her thoughts tried to leap from his disinterest at their last meeting to her convoluted reasoning that she wasn't interested to his impact right now on her ability to breathe. "I don't get it."

"The point is, I haven't been able to stop thinking about you. Can we just start over and get to know each other?" He held out his right hand and smiled. "Hi. I'm Dominick D'Angelo."

His genuine smile cleared her head. She took a breath and accepted his handshake. "Hello. I'm Cat St. Clair."

"We've met once. I'm a special agent for the Drug Enforcement Administration, and I mistakenly tried to arrest you in a shopping mall."

"Oh! *You're* my angel in disguise!"

He grinned. "And I've been trying to find you for about nine months now, to apologize, to ask your forgiveness."

"I forgive you. As a matter of fact, I *thank* you. You changed my life. Really."

"For the better, I hope?"

She hesitated. "I—I don't know yet."

"Cat." He took both of her hands in his. "You are so beautiful, so precious. And I love you. I don't have much else to offer. My faith is new, but it's strong. I've done a lot of despicable things in my life, things too horrible to tell you about. There are scars, wounds that may never heal. Do you understand what I'm saying?"

She nodded.

"I don't fit into nice society. I don't know how to be a husband or a dad. I'm not the least bit interested in a house and all the American dream frills. May I keep going?"

She tilted her head in a sort of half nod. This was hard. He was laying it all on the line and in the process was crushing those dreams she had just been trying to gently let go of. He was also leaving himself totally vulnerable.

"I'm getting out of the DEA."

"What! Why?"

"It's time. When my friend died, I promised I'd go after all of them, all the dealers. I'm not done, but I want to do it in a different way now. There's a new task force being organized, working with the kids on the street." He lifted a shoulder. "Besides, if the DEA transferred me to Timbuktu, how would you get to know me?"

"Dominick—"

"Wait, please." He gently squeezed her hands. "I'm not done yet. I've been going to a men's Bible study. Now besides Adam hounding me to grow, I've got these two other guys, Jade and Erik. And I need a date for tomorrow night. They're all taking their wives to dinner and they think— Well, will you go with me? That would be a good way to start, wouldn't it, to get to know each other? Did I say too much?"

She bit her lip. She had never heard him say so much, and it was almost too much to process.

"They think I didn't give us a chance. Cat, I promise to go slow. I won't say I love you until and unless you're ready. I won't even kiss you. I'll give you all the time and space you need. And by the way, I've already cleared this with your dad. No way was I going around his back. And I gave your mother flowers and chocolate." He squeezed her hands once more, then released them. "Now I'm done. If you say it's a no go, I understand and I'm out of here."

"Oh, Dominick." No other words would take shape. She became aware of her heart beating in her throat, in her head. An emotional tumult broke loose. A part of her laughed, a part cried, a part shook with fear. Sitting there on the ground, he filled her vision, and she knew intuitively that he could fill every nook and cranny of her heart, castle or no castle. "Dominick . . ." She breathed his name, her voice tentative.

He stood. "That's okay. I just thought I'd—"

"Sit down!" she squealed.

He did so.

"Dominick . . ." Her voice faltered. "Five minutes ago I was praying that God would take you out of my thoughts."

"I was in your thoughts?"

"Well, yeah, and I was tired of you being there!"

"Hmm." His eyes widened as the significance of the answered prayer sank in. He grinned. "Guess He told you no, huh?"

Loud and clear! She took a deep breath. "I feel like I'm on a roller coaster ride."

"I do too. Isn't it great?"

The only choice seemed to be to either struggle against that ride . . . or to fly with it. She groaned. "Will you wear your black suit? With the red tie?"

His laughter echoed through the valley.

She lowered her eyes to the rocks—her future—scattered under the footbridge. "I, umm, was just throwing out some American dream frills here. I think it's time to rearrange my castle floor plan. Want to help?"

In reply he picked up a stone and moved it aside.

She knew he felt as she did. It was time to let God move aside old visions and replace them with His own. It was time for them both to dream again.